Praise for *The Island*

"One of the author's best plots, layered with that dour Scandinavian atmosphere we love."

—*The New York Times Book Review*

"[Will] snatch you up by surprise and carry you along in unrelenting suspense . . . If you relish seeing how ordinary people of good heart and intentions can get twisted off the right path, and sink deeper into serious trouble while they wrestle with their consciences, then *The Island* will satisfy your desire to think, feel, and shudder to its logical and somewhat surprising resolution."

—*New York Journal of Books*

"Masterly . . . Jónasson delivers a mind-bending look into human darkness that earns its twists."

—*Publishers Weekly* (starred review)

"Jónasson, who could give lessons on how to sustain a chilly atmosphere, sprinkles just enough hints of ghostly agents to make you wonder if he's going to fall back on a paranormal resolution to the mystery. Don't worry: The solution is both uncanny and all-too-human."

—*Kirkus Reviews*

"Brilliantly plotted."

—*Dayton Daily News*

"*The Island* was short-listed for the Crime Novel of the Year Award in Iceland. Read it, and you will see why."

—*BookPage* (Top Pick for June)

"Dark, chilling, and utterly gripping, *The Island* is Nordic noir at its best, and is destined to become a classic of the genre. I couldn't put it down. I can't wait to read the rest of the Hulda series!" —Shari Lapena, *New York Times* bestselling author of *An Unwanted Guest*

"Ragnar Jónasson writes fire-and-ice novels: white-hot suspense stories set in the magnificent, forbidding terrain of his native Iceland. Few writers at work today conjure atmosphere with such power, or plot their mysteries with such craft. And *The Island* is his best book yet, an unflinching thriller that braids past and present, good and evil, love and loss. I can't wait for Hulda Hermannsdóttir's next case." —A. J. Finn, #1 *New York Times* bestselling author of *The Woman in the Window*

Praise for *The Darkness*

"Jónasson pulls no punches as this grim tale builds to its stunning conclusion, one of the more remarkable in recent crime fiction. Fans of uncompromising plotting will be satisfied."
—*Publishers Weekly* (starred review and Book of the Week)

"*The Darkness* melds an insightful character study with a solid plot for an outstanding novel." —*The Washington Post*

"A complex, fascinating mix of Icelandic community and alienation, atmospheric tension, and timely issues (immigrant exploitation and vigilante justice), Jónasson's latest series is another must-read for crime fans who follow the work of Arnaldur Indridason and Yrsa Sigurdardóttir."

—*Booklist* (starred review)

"As an older female detective, Hulda is a refreshing addition to the genre. This intricate and timely work explores the dehumanization of refugees, sexism in the police force, aging, and more without overwhelming the core mystery. Verdict: This heart-pounding tale will appeal to fans of Camilla Läckberg and those looking for a darker, more modern Agatha Christie–type mystery."

—*Library Journal*

"If you think you know how frigid Iceland can be, this blistering standalone from Jónasson has news for you: It's much, much colder than you've ever imagined. Warmly recommended for hot summer nights." —*Kirkus Reviews*

"*The Darkness* is a bullet train of a novel, at once blazingly contemporary and Agatha Christie old-fashioned. With prose as pure and crisp as Reykjavík snow crust, Ragnar Jónasson navigates the treacherous narrative with a veteran's hand. I reached the end with adrenalized anticipation, the final twist hitting me in the face. I dare you not to be shocked."

—Gregg Hurwitz, *New York Times* bestselling author

The Island

RAGNAR JÓNASSON

Translated from the Icelandic
by Victoria Cribb

MINOTAUR BOOKS

NEW YORK

Published in the United States by Minotaur Books,
an imprint of St. Martin's Publishing Group

www.minotaurbooks.com

The Library of Congress has cataloged the hardcover edition as follows:

Names: Ragnar Jonasson, 1976– author. | Cribb, Victoria, translator.
Title: The island : a thriller / Ragnar Jonasson ; translated from the Icelandic
   by Victoria Cribb.
Other titles: Drungi. English
Description: First U.S. edition. | New York : Minotaur Books, 2019.
Identifiers: LCCN 2019002772 | ISBN 9781250193377 (hardcover) |
   ISBN 9781250193384 (ebook)
Classification: LCC PT7511.R285 D7813 2019 | DDC 839/.6934—dc23
LC record available at https://lccn.loc.gov/2019002772

ISBN 978-1-250-62185-6 (trade paperback)

Our books may be purchased in bulk for promotional, educational, or business use. Please contact your local bookseller or the Macmillan Corporate and Premium Sales Department at 1-800-221-7945, extension 5442, or by email at MacmillanSpecialMarkets@macmillan.com.

First published in Iceland under the title *Drungi* by Veröld Publishing

Previously published in Great Britain by Michael Joseph, an imprint of Penguin Books, a Penguin Random House company

First Minotaur Books Paperback Edition: 2020

10 9 8 7 6 5 4 3 2

To María

Special thanks are due to my guides, Sigurður Kristján Sigurðsson from the Westman Islands and Sara Dögg Ásgeirsdóttir, for showing me around and providing me with information about Elliðaey.

I would also like to thank prosecutor Hulda María Stefánsdóttir for her assistance with police procedure.

Last but not least, grateful thanks to my parents, Jónas Ragnarsson and Katrín Guðjónsdóttir, for reading the manuscript.

'A mind can be turned by a single cruel word.
Care should be taken in the presence of a soul.'

— *Einar Benediktsson,*
from 'Starkaður's Soliloquies'

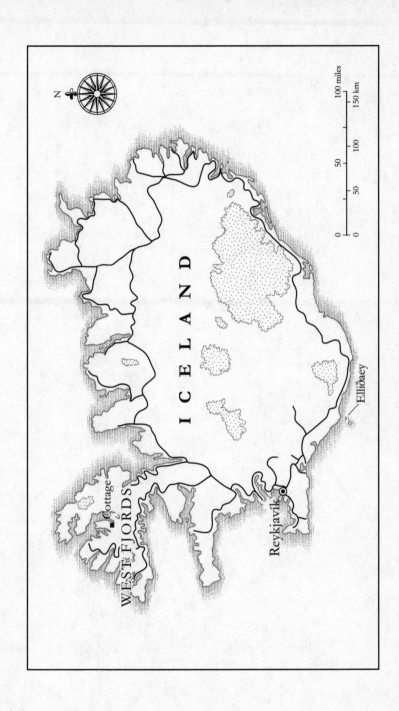

Prologue

Kópavogur, 1988

The babysitter was late.

The couple hardly ever went out in the evening, so they had been careful to check she was free well in advance. She had babysat for them a few times before and lived in the next street, but apart from that they didn't know much about her, or her family either, though they knew her mother to speak to when they ran into her in the neighbourhood. But their seven-year-old daughter looked up to the girl, who was twenty-one and seemed very grown-up and glamorous to her. She was always talking about how much fun they had together, what pretty clothes she wore and what exciting bedtime stories she told. Their daughter's eagerness to have her round to babysit made the couple feel less guilty about accepting the invitation; they felt reassured that their little girl would not only be in good hands but would enjoy herself too. They had arranged for the girl to babysit from six until midnight, but it was already past six, getting on for half past, in fact, and the dinner was due to start at seven. The husband wanted to ring and ask what had happened to her, but his wife was reluctant to make a fuss: she'd turn up.

It was a Saturday evening in March and the atmosphere had been one of happy anticipation until the babysitter failed to turn up. The couple were looking forward to an entertaining evening with the wife's colleagues from the ministry and their daughter was excited about spending the evening watching films with the babysitter. They didn't own a VCR but, as it was a special occasion, father and daughter had gone down to the local video shop and rented a machine and three tapes, and the little girl had permission to stay up as late as she liked, until she ran out of steam.

It was just after half past six when the doorbell finally rang. The family lived on the second floor of a small block of flats in Kópavogur, the town immediately to the south of Reykjavík. It was a sleepy sort of place, stuck between Reykjavík and other towns in the metropolitan area, with most of its inhabitants commuting to work in the capital.

The mother picked up the entryphone. It was the babysitter at last. She appeared at their door a few moments later, soaked to the skin, and explained that she'd walked over. It was raining so hard it looked like she'd had a bucket of water emptied over her head. She apologized, embarrassed, for being so late.

The couple waved away her apologies, thanked her for standing in for them, reminded her of the main house rules and asked if she knew how to work a video recorder, at which point their daughter broke in to say she didn't need any help. Clearly, she could hardly wait to bundle her parents out of the door so the video-fest could begin.

In spite of the taxi waiting outside, the mother couldn't tear herself away. Although they went out from time to time, she wasn't very used to leaving her daughter. 'Don't worry,' the babysitter said at last. 'I'll take good care of her.' She looked comfortingly reliable as she said this and she'd always done a good job of looking after their daughter in the past. So they finally headed out into the downpour towards the taxi.

As the evening wore on, the mother began to feel increasingly anxious about their daughter.

'Don't be silly,' said her husband. 'I bet she's having a whale of a time.' Glancing at his watch, he added: 'She'll be on her second or third film by now, and they'll have polished off all the ice cream.'

'Do you think they'd let me use the phone at the front desk?' asked his wife.

'It's a bit late to ring them now, isn't it? I expect they're asleep in front of the TV.'

In the end, they set off home a little earlier than planned, just after eleven. The three-course dinner was over by then, and, to be honest, it had been a bit underwhelming. The main course, which was lamb, had been bland at best and, after dinner, people had piled on to the crowded dance floor. To begin with, the DJ had played popular oldies, but then he moved on to more recent chart hits, which weren't really the couple's sort of thing, although they still liked to think of themselves as young. After all, they weren't middle-aged yet.

They rode home in silence, the rain streaming down the taxi's windows. The truth was they weren't really party people; they were too fond of their creature comforts at home, and the evening had tired them out, though they hadn't drunk much, just a glass of red wine with dinner.

As they got out of the taxi, the wife remarked that she hoped their daughter was asleep so they could both crawl straight into bed.

They climbed the stairs without hurrying and opened the door instead of ringing the bell, for fear of disturbing their child.

But she wasn't asleep, as it turned out. She came running to greet them, threw her arms around them and hugged them unusually tightly. To their surprise, she was wide awake.

'You're full of beans,' said her father, smiling at her.

'I'm so glad you're home,' said the little girl. There was an odd look in her eye: something was wrong.

The babysitter emerged from the sitting room and smiled sweetly at them.

'How did it go?' asked the mother.

'Really well,' the babysitter replied. 'Your daughter is such a good girl. We watched two videos; a couple of comedies. She really enjoyed them. And she ate the meatballs you'd prepared – most of them – and a lot of popcorn too.'

'Thanks so much for coming; I don't know what we'd have done without you.'

The father took his wallet from his jacket, counted out some notes and handed them to her. 'Is that right?'

She counted the money herself, then nodded. 'Yes, perfect.'

After she'd left, the father turned to their daughter.

'Aren't you tired, sweetheart?'

'Yes, maybe a little. But could we watch just a bit more?'

Her father shook his head, saying kindly: 'Sorry, it's awfully late.'

'Oh, please. I don't want to go to bed yet,' said the little girl, sounding on the verge of tears.

'OK, OK.' He ushered her into the sitting room. The TV schedule was over for the evening but he turned on the video machine and inserted a new cassette.

Then he joined her on the sofa and they waited for the film to begin.

'It was a nice evening, wasn't it?'

'Yes . . . yes, it was fine,' she said, not very convincingly.

'She was . . . kind to you, wasn't she?'

'Yes,' answered the child. 'Yes, they were both kind.'

Her father was puzzled. 'What do you mean, *both*?' he asked.

'There were two of them.'

Turning round to look at her, he asked again, gently: 'What do you mean by *them*?'

'There were two of them.'

'Did one of her friends come round?'

There was a brief pause before the girl answered. Seeing the fear in her eyes, he gave an involuntary shiver.

'No. But it was kind of weird, Daddy . . .'

PART ONE

1987

I

The weekend break in the remote north-west had been a sudden whim, a way of defying the autumn darkness. Having flung their things into Benedikt's old Toyota, they had set out from Reykjavík in a high pitch of excitement. But the long drive, often on rough gravel roads, had taken hours, and night was closing in by the time they reached the West Fjords peninsula. They were still some way from the remote valley that was their goal and Benedikt was growing increasingly anxious.

They had driven over high moors, the treeless landscape stretching out bleak and ominously empty in the gathering dusk, and descended to the coast in the innermost arm of the great fjord known as Ísafjardardjúp. Benedikt relaxed his grip on the wheel as the road hugged the low shoreline for a while before rising to climb over another pass. His knuckles whitened again as the road began to descend, winding its way in hairpin bends back down to the sea. The mountains loomed long and low on either side, dimly visible in the gloom. There wasn't so much as a pinprick of light to be seen. The fjord was uninhabited, its farms long deserted, the population having fled the hard living on the land, some for the small town of Ísafjördur, 140 kilometres away up the fjord-indented coast, others for the bright lights of Reykjavík in the far south-west of the country.

'Haven't we left it too late?' Benedikt asked. 'We'll never be able to find the hut now it's dark, will we?' He had insisted on driving, despite never having visited this part of the country before.

'Relax,' she said. 'I know the way. I've been up here loads of times during the summer.'

'During the *summer*, right,' Benedikt replied, focusing grimly on following the thin ribbon of road through its unpredictable twists and turns.

'Now, now,' she said, her voice light, laughter rippling just below the surface.

He'd been waiting so long for this moment, admiring this slight, high-spirited girl from afar and sensing that maybe, just maybe, she felt the same. But neither of them had made a move until a couple of weeks ago when something had finally shifted in their relationship and the spark had ignited a blaze.

'Not far now to the Heydalur turn-off,' she said.

'Did you ever live up here?'

'Me? No. But Dad's from the West Fjords. He grew up in Ísafjördur. The summer house belonged to his family. We always used to come up here in the holidays. It's like a sort of paradise.'

'I believe you, though I don't suppose I'll be able to see

much tonight. I can't wait to get out of the dark.' He paused, then added, doubtfully: 'It does have electricity, doesn't it?'

'Cold water and candlelight,' she replied.

'Seriously?' Benedikt groaned.

'No, I'm kidding. There's hot water – plenty of hot water – and electricity too.'

'Did you tell . . . er, did you tell your parents we were coming up here?'

'No. It's none of their business. Mum's not home and, anyway, I do what I like. All I told Dad was that I wouldn't be around this weekend. My brother's away too, so he doesn't know either.'

'OK. All I meant was . . . it's their summer house, isn't it?' What he'd really wanted to know was whether her parents were aware that they were going away together, since it would send a pretty clear signal that they were starting a relationship. Up to now the whole thing had been a secret.

'Yes, of course. It's Dad's house, but I know he's not planning to use it. And I've got a key. It'll be great, Benni. Just imagine the stars tonight: the sky's supposed to be almost perfectly clear.'

He nodded, but his doubts about the wisdom of the undertaking wouldn't go away.

'Here, turn here,' she said abruptly. He slammed on the brakes, almost losing control of the car and only just managing to make the turn. Finding himself on an even narrower road, hardly more than a track, he slowed to a crawl.

'You'll have to go faster than that or we won't be there till morning. Don't worry, you'll be fine.'

'It's just that I can't see anything. And I don't want to write off the car.'

She laughed, that bewitching sound, and he felt better at once. It was her voice and the guileless quality of her laugh that had originally drawn him to her. And now, at last, all the obstacles had been cleared from their path. He had an overpowering sense that it was meant to be; that this was only the beginning, a taste of the future.

'Didn't you say something about a hot tub?' he asked. 'It would be great to have a soak after bumping over these roads all day. I swear every bone in my body's aching.'

'Er, yes, right,' she said.

'*Right?* What do you mean? Is there a hot tub or not?'

'You'll see . . .' This tantalizing sense of uncertainty was never far away with her. It was part of her charm; she had a gift for making even the mundane seem mysterious.

'Well, anyway, I can't wait.'

At last they entered the valley where the summer house was supposed to be. Benedikt still couldn't make out any buildings in the gloom but she told him to stop the car and they both got out into the cold, fresh air.

'Follow me. You need to learn to be more trusting.' Laughing, she took his hand, with a feather-light touch, and he followed. He felt as if he were taking part in some beautiful black-and-white dream.

She stopped without warning. 'Can you hear the sea?'

He shook his head. 'No.'

'Shh. Wait. Keep still and don't talk. Just listen.'

He concentrated on listening and then heard the faint sighing of the waves. The whole thing seemed unreal, magical.

'The shore isn't far away. We can walk down there tomorrow, if you like?'

'Great, I'd love that.'

A little further on they got their first glimpse of the summer house. In spite of the darkness he could see that it wasn't particularly large or modern. It looked like one of those seventies A-shaped huts with the roof sloping almost to the ground on either side and windows at the front and back. She found the keys after searching in the pockets of her padded jacket, opened the door and flicked on the light, instantly dispelling the gloom. They entered a cosy living area, full of old furniture that lent the place a rustic charm. Benedikt sensed at once that it had a good atmosphere.

He was going to enjoy their stay, this weekend adventure in the middle of nowhere. The sense of isolation was enhanced by the thought that nobody knew they were there; they had a whole valley to themselves. It really was like a dream.

Most of the hut was taken up with the living area, but there were also a small kitchen and bathroom opening off it, and a stair ladder at the back of the room.

'What's up there?' he asked. 'A sleeping loft?'

'Yes. Come on, quick.' She swung up the ladder in a few agile movements.

Benedikt climbed up after her. It was indeed a sleeping

loft under a sloping ceiling, furnished with mattresses, duvets and pillows.

'Come here,' she said, lying down on one of the mattresses. 'Come here.' And when she smiled at him like that, he was powerless to resist.

II

Benedikt was standing outside under a star-studded sky, grilling hamburgers on an old coal barbecue in the chilly autumn breeze. The trip had got off to a good start and he was filled with optimism at the thought of what was to come. Although he was essentially a city boy and had always regarded the West Fjords as cold and inaccessible, he was surprised to find that he was enjoying himself. Of course, he couldn't have wished for better company, but there was something about the place itself, the solitude. He filled his lungs with the cool, clean air and tried closing his eyes and listening out for the sea again. The scent of autumnal leaves mingled with the appetizing aroma rising from the barbecue. He opened his eyes. He was standing behind the hut, and only now did it occur to him that the hot tub was nowhere to be seen.

After they had finished their supper in the living room, he asked, 'So where's this hot tub you promised me? I've walked right round the hut several times and I can't see any sign of it.'

She laughed mischievously. 'That can't have taken you long.'

'You're just trying to dodge the question.'

'Not at all. Come with me.'

She was on her feet and out of the door before he knew what was happening. He hurried after her into the October night.

'Are you going to conjure up a hot tub?'

'Just come with me. Are you cold?'

He hesitated for a second, because he was rather chilly in his thin jumper, but he didn't want to admit it. Reading his mind, she went back inside and emerged with a thick woollen *lopapeysa*. It was grey, with a traditional pattern in black and white. 'Do you want to borrow this? It's Dad's. I pinched it to bring along. It's far too big for me, but so warm.'

'I'm not wearing your dad's jumper. That would be weird.'

'Up to you.' She chucked the jumper back inside, where it landed on the living-room floor, and closed the door behind them.

'It's about a five-, ten-minute walk further up the valley,' she said, pointing.

'What is?'

'The hot pool,' she threw over her shoulder as she set off. 'There's a fantastic natural hot spring, perfect for two people.'

A full moon had risen while they were having supper, flooding the whole valley with its cold radiance. Benedikt thought privately that he wouldn't want to walk that way on a dark night, since there were no other lights to be seen. No sign of human habitation apart from the summer house, now out of sight behind them. Still, it was an adventure, and he was so head over heels in love with this girl that he was determined to make the best of it.

But there was no hot pool anywhere near, as far as he could tell.

'Is it much further?' he asked uncertainly. 'You're not having me on, are you?'

She laughed. 'No, of course not. Look.' She pointed up the narrow valley and there, at the very roots of the mountain, he glimpsed a small building and next to it a wisp of steam rising white in the moonlight. 'Yes, there. Can you see the shelter? It's by the pool. It's an old hut which people use as a changing room.'

They picked their way towards the pool but, as they drew closer, Benedikt realized that their way was blocked by a mountain torrent. He could see the moonlight glittering on the rush and swirl of the water.

'Where's the bridge?' he asked, stopping short. 'Or do we have to go round?'

'Trust me. I know this place like the back of my hand.'

When they reached the riverbank, she said, 'There is no bridge, but this is the best place to cross. Can you see the stones?'

Benedikt nodded. He could see some rocks poking up through the surface and he didn't like the look of them one bit now he realized what they meant.

'There's nothing to it. Just one stone at a time, then you're across.' Taking off her shoes and socks, she picked her way over as if she'd been doing it all her life. As nimble as a cat, Benedikt thought.

Oh well, there was no getting out of it. He was too ashamed to let her see his apprehension, so, following her example, he removed his shoes, stuffed his socks into them and carried them in his hands. Bracing himself, he stepped into the water, only to flinch and retreat, swearing under his breath, when he discovered how bone-numbingly icy it was.

'Come on, just get it over with,' she called, seeming impossibly far away on the other side.

He waded into the river again, stepped on to the first stone, then jumped on to the next. As he made the leap to the third, he stumbled, only just managing to find a toehold and avoid disaster. Finally, he was across, heaving a sigh of relief and trembling slightly.

When he looked up, he saw that she had stripped off her clothes and was standing stark naked on the bank of the pool. 'Come on,' she said again, picking her way into the hot water.

He didn't wait to be told twice but took off his clothes and climbed in to join her, almost falling flat on his face, so slippery were the stones on the bottom.

'This is absolutely . . . incredible,' he said, gazing up at the sky, at the moon and stars and the surrounding darkness, feeling cocooned by the steaming hot water. He moved closer to his girl.

III

Benedikt's teeth wouldn't stop chattering when he got back to the hut after the trip to the pool. He hadn't a clue what time it was; his watch was somewhere in the car and the only clock in the summer house, a small one on the living-room wall, had stopped. It seemed appropriate that here, in the empty region between mountains and sea, time should stand still.

'Let's go straight to bed,' he said. 'Get under the covers. I'm freezing.'

'OK,' she said. 'Hurry up. You head up the ladder first,' and the caress in her voice warmed him a little.

Benedikt was going to wait for her but, when she showed no signs of moving, he started up the ladder. It was dim in the sleeping loft and he fumbled in vain for a light switch.

'Isn't there a light up here?' he called down.

'No, idiot,' she said affectionately. 'This is a summer house, not a luxury villa.'

He groped his way around in the faint illumination from

the moon outside the tiny window. They'd left their bedding in the car but Benedikt was too cold to go back downstairs, let alone venture outside. He rearranged the mattresses, pushing two of them together, then got under the duvet. A shiver spread through his body, but in spite of that he was filled with happy anticipation. At the bottom of the ladder was his dream girl, about to come up and join him, and they were so utterly alone, miles from the nearest settlement. They might have been the only two people in the world.

Soon he heard light footsteps. She was on her way up the ladder, accompanied, quite literally, by a glow. She was holding an old candlestick cupped in both hands, the flame lighting up her face, lending it a mysterious, enchanted quality. The situation was so unreal that Benedikt shivered again.

She placed the candlestick carefully on the floor. If there was an accident with a flame in this old wooden hut, he thought nervously, the consequences would be a foregone conclusion. But in that moment his attention was distracted by the realization that she was half naked.

'Wow,' he blurted out involuntarily. She was so bloody gorgeous. But then, glancing at the candlestick, he felt compelled to ask, 'Isn't it dangerous having a candle up here?'

'How do you think people manage in the countryside, Benni? Honestly, you're such a townie.'

He laughed. 'Aren't you going to get under the duvet? Aren't you cold?'

'Do you know, I never feel the cold. I don't really

understand why.' He could see her smile in the glow of the candle. Then she turned and descended the ladder again, without explanation.

'Are you going back down?'

She didn't answer. He shifted a little closer to the candle, as if he could use its warmth to drive the chill from his bones. The same word – 'unreal' – popped into his mind again. Or 'otherworldly', yes, perhaps that was it. And at the same time, it felt a little forbidden, which made it all the more exciting.

She reappeared almost immediately, this time with a bottle of red wine and two glasses.

'This is f–fantastic,' he shivered.

She wriggled under the duvet, close beside him. 'There. Cosier now, Benni?'

The feeling was indescribable, hearing her say his name here, like that.

'Yes,' he replied, inadequately.

'You know, one of my ancestors used to live near here,' she said, and from her tone it was clear that there was a tale attached. She was always telling stories; it was one of the things he loved about her. It had been so easy to fall in love with her, far too easy, but he didn't regret a thing. Not any more.

'People say . . .' She left a little pause for dramatic effect, then added playfully: 'I don't know if you'll want to hear . . .'

'Of course I do.'

'People say his ghost haunts the valley.'

'Yeah, right.'

'It's up to you whether you believe me, Benni, but that's what they say. That's why I'd never, ever want to spend the night alone here.' She snuggled closer.

'Have you seen him?' he asked, waiting for her to stop messing about, but at the same time deriving a sneaking enjoyment from the story. He loved to hear her talk, though he knew he couldn't always take what she said seriously.

'No . . .' she replied, but there was something about the ensuing silence that filled Benedikt with unease. 'No, but I've sensed him . . . heard . . . heard things I can't explain.'

She sounded so serious that Benedikt was thrown.

'Once, when I was up here with Dad – I was only a little girl at the time and it was just the two of us – he popped out somewhere after I'd gone to bed. Anyway, I woke up to find myself alone. It was an evening in early spring so the nights were still dark. I tried to light the candle but the wick refused to catch . . . and then I heard these noises and – do you know, Benni? – I've never been so scared in my life.'

Benedikt didn't say anything; he was beginning to regret having agreed to listen to her tale.

He turned his head to look at her and for a moment thought he saw genuine fear in her eyes. He closed his own, trying to shrug off the spooked feeling. Fancy falling for this kind of rubbish.

'I don't believe in . . .' He didn't finish.

'That's because you don't know the whole story, Benni,' she said softly, her tone hinting at something chilling left unsaid.

'The whole story?' he repeated helplessly.

'He was burned at the stake. Imagine that: burned at the stake.'

'Bullshit. Are you having me on?'

'Do you think I'd do that? Haven't you ever read about the witch burnings in Iceland?'

'The witch burnings? You mean in the seventeenth century, when they burned old women for doing black magic?'

'Old women? There were hardly any women burned here; it was mostly men. And my ancestor was one of them. Think about it, Benni, try for a moment to imagine what it would feel like to be burned on a bonfire.' She made a sudden gesture to emphasize her words and knocked over the old candlestick. Benedikt gasped.

The candle fell out on to the wooden floor.

IV

Reacting fast, she grabbed the candle and put it back into its holder.

Then she grinned. 'That could have gone badly.'

'Yes. For Christ's sake, be careful,' he said, momentarily breathless with fright.

'And do you know what?' she continued, in the same soft, beguiling voice, as if nothing had happened: 'I reckon he was guilty.'

'Guilty?'

'Yes, of witchcraft. Don't get me wrong, I don't mean he deserved to be burned to death, but he'd obviously been dabbling in black magic. I've been looking into it, you know, into magic symbols and that kind of thing. It's really fascinating.'

'Fascinating? Messing about with the occult?'

'No, seriously, I believe it's hereditary, it's in my genes.'

'What? Black magic?' he asked, hardly able to believe his ears.

'Yes, magic.'

'You've got to be kidding.'

'Benni, I don't joke about things like that. I've been experimenting a bit. It's exciting.' She gave him a little nudge as he lay next to her.

'Experimenting?'

'Yes, casting spells.' She added archly: 'How do you think I managed to trap you in my net?'

'Oh, come on.'

'It's up to you what you believe.'

'I can hardly believe I'm here with you.'

She laughed. 'Aren't we going to have a drink?' The bottle of wine and glasses were standing forgotten by the candle.

'I'm not getting out from under the duvet, I'm still too cold.'

'Cold?' She added teasingly: 'You're not scared, are you?'

He didn't answer.

'Seriously, are you scared?'

'Of course not.' He moved closer to her again, feeling the warmth radiating from her naked body.

'Nothing'll happen as long as the candle's lit; he won't make a sound. Only when it's dark, Benni, only when it's dark . . .'

She reached for the candle, snuffed out the flame with her fingers and, turning back to Benedikt, kissed him with infinite tenderness on his mouth.

V

Much to his own surprise, Benedikt woke up early. He'd been expecting to sleep like a log and wake up late out here, far from the noise of traffic and alarm clocks.

He hadn't slept that well either. Perhaps the bedtime story about black magic and witch burnings was to blame. Or maybe it was just the excitement of finally getting to spend the night with her.

Seeing that she was still fast asleep, he crept down the ladder, pulled on his jumper, trousers and shoes and poked his head out of the door. It looked as if it was going to be a beautiful day, the air a little chilly but perfectly still. He wandered away from the hut, down towards the sea, getting his first proper look at the surroundings in the pale morning light. He had thought of the north-west as characterized by great blocky mountains looming over fjords so deep that they didn't see the sun for months in winter, but here, in the innermost part of Ísafjardardjúp, the landscape was gentler, the grassy valley surrounded on three sides by long, low fells. What the scenery lacked in drama it made up for in its all-encompassing tranquillity, its sense of space and emptiness. The only accents of colour in the treeless landscape were provided by patches of bilberry and crowberry plants and the calm blue waters of the fjord below.

It took him longer than expected to reach the shore. Once there, he sat down on a rock for a rest and gazed out over the water. Beyond the mouth of the fjord the eternal snows gleamed white on the north coast of the Djúp, a reminder of how close he was here to the Arctic Circle. She had told him that almost the entire northern peninsula, from Hornstrandir to Snæfjallaströnd, was uninhabited now, apart from a tiny handful of farms that were still clinging on. The thought made him feel a little desolate.

Keen not to be away too long in case she woke up in his absence and wondered where he was, he strode back up the slope at a brisk pace; it had been good to stretch his legs but he was looking forward to getting back into the warmth.

But when he got to the hut and climbed up the steps to peer into the sleeping loft, she was still out for the count. He was surprised at how long she could sleep.

Well, this was his first-ever chance to make breakfast in bed for his girl; nothing too fancy, just bread, cheese and some orange juice. He took this simple meal up to the loft.

She looked so beautiful when she was asleep. He gave her a gentle nudge but she didn't react, only stirring when he bent down and whispered in her ear that breakfast was ready.

'Breakfast?' she said, half opening her eyes and yawning.

'Yes, I went out to the shop.'

'To the shop?'

'Only joking. I've made you a sandwich.'

She smiled and whispered: 'Thanks, but I'm still rather sleepy. Is it OK if I have it later?'

'Yes, of course. Do you want to rest a bit longer?'

'That would be great.'

Benedikt thought about the scenery outside – the deserted valley had won him over, in spite of his initial reservations. 'OK, no problem. Maybe I'll go for a walk, then have a dip in the hot pool.'

'Yeah, great idea. You do that,' she said, rolling over. 'Take your time.'

Benedikt set off with no real idea where he was heading, and the thought appealed to him. For the first time in ages he was properly alone. No one could get hold of him. Being surrounded by nature was having an unexpectedly exhilarating effect on his mood. There was still a definite nip in the air but he had pulled on his down jacket this time and soon warmed up as he walked. His ultimate goal was to relax in the hot pool, but when he reached the river he decided to keep going and explore further up the valley. It would be hard to get lost in broad daylight, especially with the mountains to give him his bearings.

Sometimes it was good to have time to yourself, time to think. There was no doubt in his mind now that he had found the right woman, however difficult it had been getting to this point. They were so well suited, he felt; they really got along and yet they were different enough to make things exciting. He didn't even mind her lurid ghost stories; they had their own charm, although he still couldn't decide whether to believe everything she'd told him last night. An ancestor burned for witchcraft ... well, it was possible. His spine prickled at the thought. It had been a nasty shock when she'd knocked over the candle, and he had a suspicion that it hadn't been an accident, that she'd done it deliberately for – well – for effect. She was unpredictable – you never knew what she was going to do next – but the only thing that mattered now was that he was in love with her, flaws and all; that she was his at last.

What he needed more than anything was peace and quiet to think about the future. His long-cherished dream of studying art had recently received a boost when a friend of his from college had decided to apply to one of the top art schools in the Netherlands. Encouraged by his example, Benedikt had sent off for the application forms, which were now lying on his desk as a reminder of the decision he had to take. He still had a little time left before the deadline.

There were several reasons why he hadn't yet taken the plunge. Firstly, of course, he was in love, which made it hard to concentrate on anything else. But the course didn't begin for nearly a year, and by that time a temporary separation wouldn't necessarily doom their relationship. In fact, maybe he could mention, at some point, the possibility of her moving to the Netherlands with him. After all, she was adventurous, like him. Secondly, there was the question of money. His family weren't very well off so he didn't have any private funds to fall back on. Although, if he was careful, he should be able to survive on a student loan. Then there were his parents. He was their only child and, since they'd had him fairly late in life, they were both getting on for sixty now. Perhaps he was influenced by a subconscious sense of guilt about abandoning them. But, if he were honest, the real reason for his dithering was fear of making a decision, pure and simple. He'd always taken the path of least resistance in life, going to the college his parents chose for him, taking part in the social activities and sports that were expected of him, and this autumn he had embarked on an engineering degree because he was good at maths, like his parents. But just because the subject came easily to him, that didn't mean he could summon up the slightest enthusiasm for his lectures.

This weekend, while the other freshers were buried in their books, stressed about keeping up with the course, Benedikt intended to forget about his studies for a while. He couldn't see himself lasting in engineering anyway and he could sense a rebellion brewing. The pure country air had an oddly galvanizing effect on him; it was as though he could see everything properly at last and knew, with sudden clarity, that he couldn't face turning up to one more bloody lecture. Best leave all that sort of thing – numbers and equations – to other people, people who were really interested in them. All he needed was to find the courage to confront not just his parents but his own cowardice and take what he knew to be the right decision. Of course, it would be a blow for his mum and dad if he told them he was dropping out of university and heading to the Netherlands instead to study art . . . The thought was almost funny; he could just picture the look on their faces when he told them. But they knew he was never happier than when he was shut away in the garage, pottering about with his brushes, paints and canvas. That's how it had been for years and they'd been supportive in their way, even encouraged him, while never budging from their conviction that he should study something practical instead. Art could never be more than a hobby.

He remembered so well the time his art teacher had spoken to them after he'd finished his course and tried to explain how promising their son was. Yes, they'd said, they were well aware of that. But when his teacher had gone on to say that a boy with Benedikt's potential should take up painting professionally, they had been rather taken aback, though they'd mouthed a polite response. Ever since then, Benedikt had known that it was up to him to choose his own path in life, and he had known what that path was to be; all he lacked was the guts to make his dream come true.

Yes, maybe it would all be easier now, with her beside him . . . He raised his eyes to the mountains, buoyed up with optimism, and discovered to his surprise that he had walked much further than he had intended. He felt happy, his mind was made up, the air was bracingly fresh, and he had an intuition that this morning would later turn out to have been significant, a turning point of some kind; that it would shape his future in some fundamental way. We're all masters of our own fate, he told himself, and believed it implicitly. All he had to do now was follow his heart when he got home.

He sat down at the foot of the mountain for a breather after his strenuous hike, but the cold soon started to creep into his bones, striking up from the ground, piercing his clothes. He'd better keep moving.

He wasn't in any great hurry, though; he'd let her have a proper lie-in. On the way back he paused frequently to take in the scenery. He was looking forward to having a good long soak in the hot pool. It would be a shame to miss out on that. And he needed practice in crossing the river too; it wouldn't do to clamber across like an idiot in front of her next time they went for a dip, exposing himself as a hopeless townie again.

As he walked he indulged himself in fantasies about the future, wondering if they could move to the Netherlands together and, if so, where they would live. He pictured a small flat, a cosy student bedsit in one of those impossibly tall, narrow Dutch houses by a canal. And after his course they could perhaps move back to Iceland, preferably to Reykjavík's old city centre, where he would feel at home.

His heart was set on art, and now on her as well.

After a vigorous walk he found himself back at the hot spring. This time he managed to keep his balance on the stepping stones across the river, though they were as slippery and treacherous as they had been the night before, and it was only when he'd reached the other side that it occurred to him to wonder what might have happened if he'd slipped, even broken an ankle. His shouts for help were unlikely to have carried as far as the summer house, and the pool couldn't be seen from there.

Dismissing the thought, he stripped off his clothes and picked his way into the steaming water, a wonderful contrast to the keen autumn air. Yes, he would sit here for a while, letting the geothermal water lap his body in warmth. The pool was edged with flat slabs of rock and a thin stream of hot water poured in from a pipe at one end. Lying back, he gazed around at the treeless mountainsides with their long, horizontal rock strata scored with gullies, at the autumnal vegetation glowing rust-red and yellow in the low sun. He was used to the geothermal swimming pools in Reykjavík but this was the real thing: out in the middle of nature, birds piping overhead, the sound of running water. It really was idyllic. He hoped that visits up here would become a regular feature of their lives.

Benedikt had lost all sense of time. How long had he been away? Too long, he feared. He hoped she wasn't awake and getting impatient with him. He ought to get out, but the water seemed to be pulling at his limbs, making it impossible to drag himself away from the warmth. He told himself he deserved a bit more of a rest after his hike. She would hardly have started to wonder where he was yet.

At long last he got up, warily, taking care not to slip on the slimy bottom or cut himself on the sharp stones.

Since he hadn't had the presence of mind to bring a

towel with him, he had to dry himself as best he could with his clothes. Then he pulled on the damp garments, shivering, a little afraid he'd ruin the trip by catching a cold. After that he faced the challenge of the stepping stones again, nervously, but driven on by the excitement of getting back to the hut and to her, his true love.

VI

Hulda Hermannsdóttir looked up from her desk at a knock on the door. At this time of the day, when most of her colleagues had gone home, she was, as usual, immersed in writing reports. She always stayed late, although, having agreed to fixed overtime, she had nothing to gain financially from her diligence. But it mattered to her to perform her duties to the best of her ability; she was competitive, felt driven to perform better than other people, and never took anything for granted. Being a detective was a good job, she knew, but the pay was lousy and she was impatient to progress to the next level in CID, aware that this would open up new opportunities.

She couldn't forget what a struggle life had been, not only for her and her mother but for her grandparents, who they lived with, as well. They'd had to watch every penny when she was growing up and the necessity of scrimping and saving had impinged on all their lives in one way or another. Her mother and grandfather had worked in a series of poorly paid labouring jobs, while her grandmother had been a housewife, but from a young age Hulda had nursed a secret ambition to escape the poverty trap when she grew up. And for that, getting an education was essential. Defying all the pressure put on her to go straight out to work and start paying her way at home, she had stayed on at school and passed her leaving exams with flying colours, one of only a handful of girls in her year. By then she was the most educated person in her family. For a while she had toyed with the idea of going to university, but nothing had come of it because her grandparents had put their foot down, telling Hulda it was high time she left home and started supporting herself. Her mother had objected on her behalf, but feebly. Perhaps she had been satisfied with what her daughter had already achieved: after all, passing her school-leaving exams was nothing to be sniffed at. Partly by chance, partly due to pig-headedness, Hulda's path had quickly led to the police force. She'd been looking at job adverts with a friend from school when they'd spotted a summer temping position for a 'policeman'. Hulda's friend had remarked that they could forget about that as it was obviously no job for a woman, provoking Hulda to disagree and argue that she had as good a chance of getting the job as any. To prove her point, she had applied and got in. The temping job had led to a permanent position – several vacancies had opened up while she was there, which had made it difficult for them to disregard her application – and she had finished her training at the police commissioner's office in Reykjavík, before moving into criminal investigations and ending up as a detective in CID. Her boss, Snorri, was an old-school detective, quiet yet firm, with an aversion to modern technology, and it was he who was standing in the doorway now.

'Hulda, could I possibly have a word?' he asked politely. He was always a little stiff, not exactly friendly by nature, but on the other hand he never raised his voice to her, as he did to some of his other junior officers. She thought she knew why: it was because he saw her as a woman, not as a colleague, and simply didn't take her seriously enough.

'Yes, of course. Come in. I was just about to leave, actually.' She glanced around, surveying her desk and wishing she'd left hours ago. It was buried in piles of papers, reports and documents, information that Hulda spent far too much time analysing. There were only two personal items, a photo of Dimma and one of Jón. The former had been taken quite recently, the latter years ago, when she and Jón were first getting to know each other. It showed him with long hair, dressed in hopelessly outmoded seventies clothes in garish colours. That was Jón as he used to be in the old days, very different from the preoccupied businessman of 1987. Both pictures faced her rather than being on display to visitors.

Instead of sitting down, Snorri remained standing, allowing a silence to develop before he resumed, as if giving her a chance to finish what she was working on.

'I just wanted to check that you – and your husband, of course – were definitely coming round to my place before the do on Friday?' As was customary, Snorri had invited his team to pre-dinner drinks at his house before the annual police party. Although Hulda found this event excruciatingly dull, she turned up dutifully every year, dragging Jón along with her, but he always stood in a corner, not even trying to be sociable. She wished he would be a bit more positive about her job and make more of an effort to get to know her colleagues.

'Yes, of course,' Hulda said. 'Didn't I RSVP? Sorry, I must have forgotten.' It occurred to her that this might be a good chance to talk to Snorri about something that was on her mind. 'By the way . . .'

'Yes, Hulda?'

'I hear Emil's retiring soon . . .'

'Yes, that's right. After all, he's getting on. He'll leave a big hole, though.'

She hesitated, casting around for the right words. 'I'm thinking of putting myself forward for his job.'

Snorri seemed disconcerted. Clearly, he hadn't been expecting this.

'Oh, are you?' he muttered at last. 'Are you indeed, Hulda?'

'I think I've got plenty to offer – I know the job, I'm experienced.'

'Of course, of course. Though you're still quite young. But yes, you're certainly experienced and reliable, there's no denying that.'

'I'm nearly forty, actually.'

'Ah, right. Well, that's still young in my eyes, Hulda, and . . . well, quite apart from which . . .'

'I'm planning to apply when the position comes up. Isn't it ultimately your decision who gets the job?'

'Well, that is, yes, I suppose . . . technically.'

'I can rely on your support, can't I? None of the other officers serving under you have been working for you as long as I have . . .' She'd wanted to say: *are as good as me.*

'Quite right, absolutely right, Hulda.' After a short, awkward pause, he added: 'But I gather Lýdur's intending to put his name forward as well.'

'Lýdur?' Although their paths hadn't crossed that often, Hulda didn't think much of the man. He had a brusque manner and could be rude, though admittedly he got results. Still, Hulda had considerably more experience, so surely he couldn't pose too much of a threat.

'Yes, he's very keen,' Snorri said. 'He's already spoken to me about the job and . . . shared his views on what could be done better and how he'd tackle the responsibilities.'

'But he's only just joined the department.'

'That's not quite true. And length of service isn't everything.'

'What are you saying? That I shouldn't apply?'

'Of course you can apply, Hulda,' Snorri said, looking uncomfortable. 'But, between you and me, I have a feeling Lýdur will get the job.' He smiled briefly and took his leave. And that, Hulda knew, was that.

VII

'What a total waste of time, having to slog all the way out here on account of some silly girl,' Inspector Andrés of the Ísafjördur police remarked to the young man beside him, a rookie officer in his first year on the force.

Andrés had lost count of the years he'd been doing this job. These days, everything seemed to get on his nerves, and the phone call from the woman in Reykjavík had been no exception. She was looking for her daughter – her grown-up daughter, mind you; the girl was twenty, for crying out loud. Andrés had given the woman short shrift, telling her bluntly that he didn't understand how it was possible to lose an adult. She had remained polite in the face of his rudeness, he'd give her that, patiently explaining that she hadn't heard from her daughter for several days and that it was unlike her. The family owned a summer house at a place called Heydalur in Mjóifjör-dur, an hour or two's drive from Ísafjördur, and the girl had a key to it. She was wondering, if someone from the Ísafjördur police happened to be passing, whether they could possibly drive up to the valley and check for signs of life at the house.

Andrés had replied curtly that it wasn't the job of the police to run errands for people, then added grudgingly that he supposed he could swing by himself later since he would be going in that direction anyway. This wasn't true, but it was a slow day and he thought he might as well take a drive with the new recruit, rather than sitting around and twiddling his thumbs at the station. But he made sure to grumble the entire way. The foul weather merely gave him a further excuse to complain.

'A total waste of time,' Andrés repeated.

The rookie mumbled some reply. He didn't speak much. After all, whenever he did open his mouth, Andrés had a habit of jumping down his throat and sneering at his inexperience.

Andrés was the one with the power and the years of policing under his belt and no one was allowed to forget it. He was forever talking himself up. What the new recruit didn't know was that Andrés had lost his life savings and more in a mink-farming business venture with a local partner and had been forced to throw himself on the mercy of a loan shark. These days, far too large a proportion of his police salary went on paying the bastard back.

When, after following the tortuous coast road in and out of six fjords, they finally reached the valley, Andrés drove along it until the road ran out, but there was still no sign of any building. Grousing and bitching, he got out of the car, ordering the rookie to stay where he was, and continued on foot, battered by the wind and rain, until the summer house finally appeared.

'This has got to be it,' he muttered under his breath.

He was sick and tired of the Icelandic climate and the drab monotony of life up here in the harsh north-west. The summer had been all too brief and cold and now autumn had set in already. An old schoolfriend of his had taken to spending the worst of the winter months in Spain, but that was a luxury Andrés could only dream of. Instead, his days were spent driving endlessly back and forth along the countless fjords on his patch, dealing with pointless callouts like the present one. If the girl wanted to get away from it all and spend a few days in a secluded valley in the West Fjords, who could blame her?

The hut was one of those old-fashioned A-shaped structures, with no windows in the side walls, only on either side of the front door and, presumably, round the back as well. Andrés strode over to the building, stolidly ignoring the lashing wind and rain; he was used to worse. He knocked at the door and waited, but there was no answer. Come to think of it, he hadn't seen a car parked anywhere in the valley, so there was almost certainly no one here. He knocked again.

When there was still no response, he peered through the window, unwilling to give up straight away. The glass was old and cloudy, which made it hard to see anything, but Andrés had already made up his mind that there was no one inside. He'd decided early on that this was a wild-goose chase, but he'd dragged himself out here anyway, perhaps purely so he'd have something to moan about for the next few weeks, telling stories about what a pain in the neck city folk were. But then he saw, or thought he saw, a shape.

Was he seeing things, or could that be a body lying on the floor?

He could hardly believe it, but there was nothing wrong with his eyesight.

Christ.

He would have to enter the property to take a closer look. He pondered his options. Break the glass or force the door? He'd be capable of the former; the latter would take some doing. Then it occurred to him to try the door handle, and – would you know it? – it opened, releasing a stench that sent him reeling backwards.

What the hell?

He sprinted back in the direction of the police car and waved at the new recruit to get out and come over.

'You need to wait outside,' he told him. 'I'm going in.'

'What . . . what's that smell?' asked the boy in a shocked voice when they reached the hut.

'That, my lad – that's the smell of death.'

VIII

Even an old hand like Andrés was badly shaken by the scene that greeted them. But then you never got used to something like this.

On the floor lay the body of a girl, her eyes horrifyingly wide open, a dark pool of dried blood under her head.

Andrés's immediate assumption was that she must have either fallen over backwards or been pushed. He shuddered at the thought and only hoped that her end had been quick and painless. From the description the mother had given him, he took it that this, sadly, was her missing daughter. He hoped to God that someone else would be given the task of breaking the news to her.

His attention was distracted by a sudden noise outside. Glancing round, he saw that the new recruit was puking his guts up. He bit back the urge to tear a strip off him; this wasn't the moment. Besides, it couldn't be helped now. The girl was obviously dead, but Andrés bent down anyway to check her pulse and in doing so discovered that her body felt cold to the touch. The poor thing must have been lying here for days.

What the hell had happened?

Was it an accident? He was puzzled by the lack of a car. How could she have got here without one? Logically, there must have been somebody else with her. But if so, why hadn't they reported her death? His mind presented him with another possibility – murder. On his patch? Surely that was unthinkable.

He knew he would have little say in the investigation. On reflection, though, this was probably for the best, given that he had no experience of murder inquiries. There hadn't been a murder in his part of the country for years and, to be honest, he could hardly think of many in Iceland as a whole in the last decade. But he did at least know that he must be careful not to destroy any evidence.

Then again, perhaps it had been an accident. But Andrés had an uncomfortable foreboding that a terrible crime had been committed here.

IX

Veturlidi had woken up far too early after a restless night. It was only 6 a.m. and the house was quiet. The boundary between sleep and waking was blurred these days; there seemed to be a haze over everything, turning day to night and night to day. October was passing and it was almost perpetually dark outside, or that's what it felt like, though the weather had been unusually good for the time of year.

Veturlidi and his wife, Vera, lived in a maisonette in Kópavogur, a commuter town just to the south of Reykjavík. It was a sort of ill-defined cross between a terraced house and a block of flats. 'An ideal place,' had been Vera's verdict when they bought it, 'with plenty of room for the family.' It certainly was spacious, consisting of two storeys, a basement and a good south-facing balcony, with a communal garden and play area round the back.

Veturlidi worked for a small accountancy firm but, because he was currently on leave, he wasn't immediately sure what day of the week it was when he woke up. Either Wednesday or Thursday, he thought. They hadn't bothered to set their alarm clocks as Vera, a cashier at the local bank, was on leave too.

He could have done with sleeping longer, at least until their son had to get up to go to college. The boy had been offered more time off but, determined to stay strong, he had gone back after only a week. His parents had tried to dissuade him, but it was futile; the boy had always gone his own way. He was self-reliant and single-minded, and extremely bright too. He'd make something of himself one day, they were both agreed on that.

Veturlidi closed his eyes, wanting to go back to sleep but afraid of the dreams that might be lying in wait for him. He felt permanently exhausted at the moment. Dreamless sleep was the greatest luxury he could imagine. He lay there for a while, but it was no good, he was wide awake. He needed to occupy himself with something or his thoughts would start to spiral, taking him to places he didn't want to go, not now.

He sat up, as warily as he could, and got out of bed, doing his best not to wake Vera. Mercifully, she seemed to be sound asleep for once. The mattress creaked slightly as he stood up and she stirred but, to his relief, didn't wake up. It was a good thing that at least one of them could sleep.

It occurred to him to go down to the kitchen and make himself a coffee, but on second thoughts he was worried about making too much noise. Tiptoeing out into the hall, he went to look in on his son. The boy's door was shut, as usual.

Veturlidi opened it with infinite care and put his head round, just to reassure himself that everything was all right. Yes, there he lay, fast asleep. Smiling, Veturlidi pulled the door to again. Of course his worries had been unnecessary, but that's what their life was like now; they were permanently anxious.

God, he needed some caffeine to get himself into gear. More than anything, though, he craved a drop of something stronger. It was astonishing that he hadn't yet succumbed to the temptation. It must be a sign of some core of inner strength he hadn't known he possessed. Alcohol had first become part of his life at school, but he'd always managed to control his drinking, or so he'd believed. Then he'd met Vera. Although she didn't touch alcohol herself, she hadn't objected to his having the odd glass, but over the years those drinks had multiplied. In the end his habit had begun to have a detrimental impact on his work and he had come close to losing his job more than once. He had tried to keep the fact from Vera but, of course, she saw through the deception. Instead of getting a proper grip on the problem, though, and giving up altogether, he had merely cut down his intake.

It was inevitable that sooner or later he would bring the problem home with him. He had got into the habit of drinking in secret at the house, whenever he had a chance. It was a dangerous game that could only end badly. Within a few months alcohol had become such an important part of Veturlidi's life that his family had been pushed into second place, and this caused all sorts of upsets at home, even threatened his marriage. He would drink openly, in front of his wife and kids, and sometimes lost his temper, though he was never violent; he drew the line there. But by then he had crossed all sorts of other lines with his behaviour, and in the end Vera had presented him with an ultimatum: either go into rehab or move out. The choice had been straightforward yet painful: there was never any question of allowing alcohol to destroy his marriage, so of course he had chosen to get help, but eliminating the alcohol from his bloodstream and the longing from his soul was the toughest challenge he had ever undertaken. To make matters worse, Vera had been desperately ashamed of the situation. She wouldn't hear of telling their friends that he'd been at a treatment centre; appearances had to be kept up at all costs. But their neighbours couldn't have failed to hear all the screaming and shouting, and sometimes when Veturlidi came home late at night after a binge he used to feel as if curious eyes were watching from the darkened windows. In his paranoia he imagined the whispering behind the twitching curtains as the neighbours talked about the drunk who lived next door and how terrible it must be for his family.

Actually, it wasn't simply paranoia; he knew for certain there had been rumours doing the rounds while he was at the drying-out clinic. Some people had correctly guessed the reason for his absence and the gossip had eventually got back to him and Vera. Fed up with all the subterfuge, Veturlidi had asked his wife if they couldn't just tell the truth. She had looked at him as if he'd lost his mind. What mattered, more than anything, was to present a flawless façade to the outside world.

The day he finally came home sober was a huge relief. His family gave him a heart-warming welcome. Vera was like a completely different person, as though a great burden

had been lifted from her shoulders. And Veturlidi discovered, as time wore on, that he could remain sober. So
successfully, in fact, that he began to wonder if it might
be all right to allow himself the odd tipple – in moder-
ation, of course, when no one was there to see. He mulled
over the idea for a while, before putting it into action one
weekend when he had the house to himself.

He still hadn't been found out. He was careful, only
drinking when he had a weekend alone. Either at home,
when the rest of the family were out, or somewhere else, if
he could get away for a whole weekend without rousing
suspicion. Sometimes these trips could be at least partly
explained as connected to his job, but at other times he
had to make up white lies to provide himself with an
excuse to leave town. This wasn't something he could get
away with often, though, as it was vital that Vera didn't
suspect anything. On these occasions he usually headed
for the West Fjords, to their summer house in the middle
of nowhere, with only a bottle for company. Or bottles,
rather. He had hidden several with great ingenuity around
the property, in case of emergency.

He justified the deception to himself, though he was
perfectly aware of the contradiction, by rationalizing
that its very success was proof that he had his drinking
well under control and so it was fine to carry on. He
couldn't be a serious alcoholic if he was capable of this
level of restraint.

But right now his need for a stiff drink had never
been greater. He had to hold out, though. Had to wait for
the right opportunity. He couldn't even make himself a

coffee this early in the morning without the risk of waking his wife and son. Damn it all.

Veturlidi went downstairs to the sitting room, almost on tiptoe. The room was neat and tidy, and curiously peaceful, as if nothing had happened, as if their whole world had not been blown apart.

It promised to be a beautiful autumn day. Veturlidi opened the balcony door and peered outside, in his pyjamas, breathing in the fresh morning air. Everything was quiet in their neighbourhood at this early hour. Not a soul about. Hardly even a car, except perhaps a faint drone of traffic in the distance. He stood there for a while, oblivious to the cold, and experienced a sort of peace, a long-desired serenity, simply from listening to the silence and looking out into the darkness, alone in the world.

Afterwards, he went upstairs, intending to lie down again and see if he could get back to sleep. He'd just entered the bedroom and got into bed when, without warning, the silence was broken.

Veturlidi started, his heart pounding, and jumped out of bed again.

Was that the doorbell? This early in the morning?

He stood frozen into immobility for a moment, fervently hoping that he had been hearing things.

The bell rang again, for longer this time. There was no mistaking it; someone was at the door. Veturlidi hurried downstairs, but the action seemed to take a strangely long time, as if he were moving in slow motion. And now someone was banging on the door, quite literally. Veturlidi felt his heart begin to race. What the hell was going on?

He had reached the door and was just about to open it when he heard a noise behind him. Looking round, he saw Vera standing on the landing in her nightie, half asleep.

'What's going on, Veturlidi?' she asked anxiously. 'Is that someone knocking? It's so early. What . . . has something else happened?' Her voice was trembling. 'Is everything OK with . . . with . . . ?'

Veturlidi answered quickly: 'Yes, love. He's fine. He's fast asleep in bed. I don't know who's making this racket but I'm just going to find out.'

There was another round of knocking, even louder than before.

Veturlidi opened the door.

X

Outside, Veturlidi saw two men in plainclothes who he immediately recognized as the detectives investigating his daughter's death. He felt an overwhelming sense of dread: they would hardly have come at this hour of the day to bring good news.

He felt like an idiot as he stood there in his pyjamas, unable to speak for a moment, then he cleared his throat and croaked out a greeting.

When he glanced over his shoulder, Vera was still standing rooted to the spot, as if reluctant to come any closer.

'Good morning, Veturlidi,' said the older of the two men, who could only have been in his early thirties. Lýdur – that was his name. 'Could we come in for a minute?'

Veturlidi stepped aside and the detectives entered the hall but seemed disinclined to go any further.

'Would you like to . . . come into the sitting room?' Veturlidi asked diffidently. 'We could . . . make some coffee . . .'

'No, thanks all the same,' Lýdur said, then added, address-ing Vera rather than him: 'We apologize for bothering you so early. And we're sorry to . . . er . . .'

This time he was the one groping for words.

At that moment Veturlidi heard another sound upstairs and looked up to see his son appear beside his mother on the landing, sleepy and tousled, in nothing but his underpants.

'What's going on?' the boy asked Vera. 'Mum? What are they doing here?' She didn't answer. 'Dad?' He turned to Veturlidi, his face full of apprehension.

'We'll have to ask you to come with us,' Lýdur said, after an awkward silence.

It took Veturlidi, who was still watching his wife and son, a moment to realize that the words had been directed at him.

He turned round.

'Who?' he asked.

'You. I'm talking to you, Veturlidi.'

'Me? You want me to come with you? Now? Do you know what time it is?' He tried to stay calm.

'Yes, you need to come with us. We're well aware that it's early, but this is urgent.'

'What do you mean? Why?'

'I'm afraid I can't discuss that here.'

The younger detective hung back slightly, saying nothing.

'I . . . I . . .' Veturlidi floundered, unsure how to react. He couldn't work out what was going on.

'Come on, let's not drag this out,' said Lýdur in a per-emptory tone.

'I . . . Just give me a minute. Just give us time to wake up properly and see our son off to school.'

'I'm sorry, but you'll have to come with us now.'

'But I must . . . surely that's up to me?'

'I'm afraid not. We're here to arrest you.'

'Arrest me? Are you mad?' He raised his voice, surprising himself. 'Arrest me?' he repeated, shouting now, his words echoing in the quiet morning.

He could hear Vera crying. Turning his head, he saw the look of horror on her face, the tears pouring down her cheeks. 'Veturlidi!' she gasped. 'Veturlidi . . . ?'

'You're not arresting my dad?' the boy broke in loudly.

'Well . . .' The detective hesitated, apparently unsure how to explain this to the son. 'Your father needs to come with us so we can take a statement. That's all.' Yet it was glaringly obvious that there was more to it.

'It'll be all right,' Veturlidi said, his gaze swinging between his son and his wife as he spoke. 'It'll be all right.' He didn't really believe it himself, but he had to try, for their sake.

'No, you can't take him!' shouted the boy, though he still hung back uncertainly, visibly tired and confused.

'It's all right, son, it's all right,' Veturlidi reassured him, then looked back at the policemen. Appealing to the younger officer, he said, 'Surely I'm allowed to get dressed? You can't expect me to go in my pyjamas.'

The detective glanced at his older colleague, who answered for him, laying a heavy hand on Veturlidi's shoulder as he did so. 'No, I'm afraid not. You're coming with us right now. We'll have your clothes brought along later.

There are officers outside, waiting to search the house while you're at the station.'

'Search . . . search our house?' For a horrible moment Veturlidi thought he was going to faint. Closing his eyes, he took a deep breath and tried to calm down. He had to stay on his feet, had to remain strong in front of his wife and son.

'You're not taking him anywhere!' Vera yelled, belatedly emerging from her frozen state and storming downstairs. When the younger officer blocked her path, she tried to push him aside.

'Calm down, darling,' said Veturlidi. 'It'll only make things worse.'

His son followed her downstairs and shoved at the young detective. 'Leave him alone! Leave my dad alone!'

The front door was still open. Escorted by Lýdur, Veturlidi walked outside on to the steps, into the dark morning, and saw now that there were two police cars parked in front of the house. He descended the steps with Lýdur gripping his arm unnecessarily tightly. Did he really expect a family man in his pyjamas to make a run for it? Veturlidi's humiliation was complete.

'Dad!' he heard his son screaming. As he reached the police car, he glanced round to see the boy racing down the steps in nothing but his underpants, despite the cold. 'Let him go! Dad!' He was making such a racket Veturlidi could imagine all the curtains in their street twitching. The peace had been shattered, both in the neighbourhood and in his family. No one who witnessed it would ever forget the sight of Veturlidi being dragged out of his house by the police at the crack of dawn, wearing nothing but his pyjamas while his son screamed at the top of his voice.

People would be bound to ask: what exactly had the man done?

And he knew that most would be quick to draw their own conclusions.

XI

Veturlidi's mood fluctuated between hope and despair. He sat in the cramped cell with his eyes closed, unable to comprehend the mess he was in. The last few weeks must have been some kind of nightmare; surely it was only a matter of time before he woke up, drenched in sweat, to find himself safe at home in bed next to Vera. And everything would go back to how it had been before.

He let his mind wander through the realms of impossibility, partly to create an illusion of better times to come, partly to torment himself about what could never be undone.

He spent a lot of time worrying about Vera. The police had forcibly arrested her husband in front of her and their son. What in God's name must she be thinking? That it was a mistake – that it must be a mistake – because the alternative would be unbearable; it simply couldn't be true. Or had she come to a different, darker conclusion? Veturlidi couldn't let his mind go there.

He had no idea how long it was since they'd locked him in here. They had confiscated his watch and he had completely lost track of time. The morning must be fairly advanced. All normal people would be at work by now . . . Again, his thoughts strayed to their neighbours. For God's sake, as if what they thought mattered now, and yet . . . and yet he felt it did matter. They'd lived in the area for ten years; their reputation, the impression other people had of them, was important. Other people's opinions – in this case the neighbours', though he hardly knew any of them by name – were like a mirror, and when he looked in that mirror he wanted to like what he saw. Wanted to be able to hold his head high. But after this he wouldn't be able to do that ever again, and nor would his wife. The whole family would bear the burden of his shame.

He tried not to let the confinement get to him, knowing that if he did the game was up, he might as well throw in the towel. He wasn't naturally prone to claustrophobia and had no problem with narrow spaces, which was lucky, because his present predicament could hardly have been worse from that perspective. Four walls, no windows, a locked door. Thrown on the mercy of the justice system. No, he had to keep his head and cling to the hope that, sooner or later, he'd be released.

They had asked if he wanted a lawyer. His immediate response had been to tell them he didn't know any lawyers and never had; he hadn't a clue who he was supposed to call. They told him that didn't matter: they could appoint a solicitor for him; he needn't worry about who to choose. He considered their offer for a while before realizing that it was bound to look like an admission of guilt. It might even be a trap; if he decided he needed a lawyer, it might be interpreted as tantamount to a confession.

XII

To be honest, Andrés was both surprised and flattered when he got an invitation to meet his Reykjavík colleague for coffee.

His visit to the capital was connected to that terrible day when he had found the girl's body in the summer house in his district. The scene was etched in his memory, though he'd assumed he was hardened to that sort of thing after all these years of dealing with the fallout from suicides, accidents and cases of neglect, where old people had died and sometimes not been discovered for days or even weeks. Murder, though, was outside his experience.

He had already spoken on the phone to Lýdur, the detective in question, who was running the investigation. A young man who sounded like he was in his early thirties and came across as quite a go-getter.

They'd agreed to meet at Mokka Kaffi, a Reykjavík institution that Andrés knew only by reputation.

He got there in good time, ordered a black coffee and took a seat by the window. He was the only customer in the place. Shortly afterwards a young man walked in, with the uncompromising air of someone who likes to be in charge. What he lacked in height he made up for in muscle. He came straight over.

'Hello. I take it you're Andrés?' he said, extending a hand and taking Andrés's in a wince-makingly firm grip.

'Yes, hello.'

'I see you've already got a coffee.' The young man went over to the counter and returned with a cup of his own.

'Good that you could come,' he said, sounding matey now.

'Least I could do.' Andrés was a little uneasy all of a sudden. Now he stopped to think about it, this was an odd setting for a work-related chat. Why hadn't Lýdur invited him along to his office? Was CID headquarters too fancy for a country cop like him? He tried to shrug off his suspicion; wasn't it more likely the man was just being friendly to an out-of-towner?

'This is a nasty case,' Lýdur said. 'Deeply shocking.'

'You can say that again.'

'And you were first on the scene. It can't have been a pretty sight.'

'Well, I've experienced a thing or two in my time.'

'Thanks for agreeing to come to Reykjavík. I'm aware it must disrupt your work.'

'Oh, that's not a problem,' Andrés said.

'Yes, I'm afraid it was unavoidable. You see, you're in a better position than anyone to describe the scene.' Lýdur added, rather perfunctorily: 'Poor girl.'

Andrés nodded. He couldn't work out where this conversation was going.

'At any rate, we're confident we have the right man in custody,' Lýdur continued. 'Our inquiry's gone pretty smoothly. All the evidence points to him.'

'Mm, yes,' Andrés muttered into his coffee cup.

'We need a quick solve. The public don't like it when young girls are murdered. It's not what we're used to. Murders are such a rare event here that people are impatient to see results.'

'Yes, you've done well.'

'Good thing he forgot his jumper,' Lýdur remarked.

'His jumper?'

'Yes, the *lopapeysa* they found by the body. Grey, with a black-and-white pattern round the yoke. Hasn't anyone filled you in? We've been trying to keep the details out of the press.'

'What? No, no one's been in touch with me.'

'He left his jumper at the scene. He's admitted it was his. And we've got a witness who saw him wearing it in Reykjavík a few days before, so it stands to reason he must have been at the summer house that weekend, although he claims otherwise. Do you really not remember seeing it?'

'No, but then all I really noticed was the body and all the blood. It was hard to take in the rest. It was such a shocking sight.'

'Right, right, I can believe it,' Lýdur said, unmoved. 'The jumper's key because there was blood on it. So it would be great if you *could* remember it, you know, seeing as you were first on the scene. Our forensics team found it, but we wouldn't want there to be any doubt that it was there when she died.'

'Great if I could remember it?' Andrés repeated, disconcerted. 'But . . . the fact is I don't.'

'I hear you, of course. But it would be better.'

'Better?'

'Naturally, we've got a variety of other evidence. The whole thing's a dead cert – he's bound to confess before the trial . . . but we want to make absolutely sure of that, don't we? Do you happen to remember whether she was holding the jumper or lying on top of it?'

'Look . . . I really don't . . .'

'She was holding the jumper – that's what points so strongly to his guilt. It's either evidence of a struggle, or perhaps she was trying to send us a message.'

'I'm afraid I just don't know . . .' Andrés could feel his breathing becoming quick and shallow, as sometimes happened when he was under pressure. The excess kilos taking their toll, no doubt. He broke out in a sweat. 'But I—'

'We'll be asking you about it. It would be great to have it established beyond a doubt.'

'Well, I don't know what I can do. The fact remains, I don't remember it.' Despite his advantage of age and experience, Andrés found himself on the back foot when confronted by this pushy Reykjavík detective. The man's determination was making him nervous.

Lýdur sipped his coffee, waiting. Finally, he remarked, 'The coffee's not bad here, is it?'

Andrés nodded.

'There's a guy we've been investigating recently,' Lýdur

said, apparently changing the subject. 'Seems he's a loan shark. Do you get many of his type up your way?'

Andrés gasped as the implications of this hit him, or at least of where he thought Lýdur was going with this, though he fervently hoped he was wrong. He couldn't get out a word in reply.

'It's a disgrace, of course. The man's taking, what, a hundred per cent interest, two hundred per cent, even. I pity the poor sods who get mixed up with him.'

Andrés didn't speak. He tried to control every muscle, to give nothing away.

'You get the most unlikely people cropping up in this kind of investigation – you know how it is. He's been lending money for all kinds of dodgy business, but it turns out ordinary members of the public have been borrowing from him as well. After all, people who get into a financial hole have to dig themselves out somehow. Of course, we'd rather keep their names out of the inquiry. Or out of the papers, anyway, since the case is bound to generate interest.'

'I don't see what this has got to do with anything,' Andrés said at last, with an effort.

'Oh, right. It's just that I hear your name came up.' Lýdur let this hang in the air for a moment. 'Know anything about that?'

Andrés didn't answer.

'I thought maybe you'd prefer it if word didn't get out. It was quite a substantial sum you borrowed, wasn't it?'

'There's nothing shady ab— about having money trouble,' Andrés stammered.

'Yeah, well, if you say so.' Lýdur rose to his feet. 'Think it over. I don't suppose they've got wind of it yet in Ísafjördur, and maybe it won't affect your standing there. I wouldn't know. Anyhow, I hope you'll be clear when you give your testimony. We can't afford to let this bastard get off.'

XIII

Andrés was taking his time getting home after his trip to Reykjavík to give a formal witness statement. He had a lot on his mind. The road conditions were reasonable, as good as could be expected in winter, even when he reached the beginning of the West Fjords peninsula and turned on to the high road leading up over the moors. All day the world had formed a monochrome backdrop to his thoughts – white snow, black rocks, grey sea, grey sky – but he scarcely took in the view, preoccupied as he was by what he had just done.

His meeting a couple of months ago with that young detective Lýdur had turned his life upside down. Although Andrés knew he hadn't precisely broken any laws by borrowing heavily from a loan shark, the last thing he wanted was for news of it to get out. He knew he had been making a pact with the devil when he took out that loan. The man who'd lent him the money was an extremely dodgy character, with a dubious past and links to the criminal underworld. A respected police inspector like Andrés should have had nothing to do with a crook like that, certainly not put himself in the vulnerable position of being financially dependent on him, yet there was no getting away from it, that's exactly what he had done.

A respected police inspector . . . yes, that was the problem. Andrés had spent his entire career building up a reputation as unimpeachably honest and trustworthy, as a man who upheld law and order, a pillar of his small community, member of all kinds of clubs and associations like the Lions Club and the Freemasons. An upstanding citizen. It would be gut-wrenching to see that image destroyed. He wasn't thinking only of himself but of his family too. Of his wife, waiting for him at home, who would ask how his journey had gone and whether he'd helped put the guilty man behind bars. Of his grown-up son and daughter, who looked up to their father and always had done. And his grandchild, hopefully the first of many, who worshipped him. It wouldn't be fair to drag them into this scandal.

Lýdur had contacted him again, just before he was due to testify in court, to tell him that there were photos showing the *lopapeysa* on the floor near the body but shoddy police work meant that there were no images of the deceased actually holding her father's jumper. He repeated that it was vital Andrés confirm that she'd been clutching it, as proof of a struggle and perhaps a last-gasp attempt by the girl to hint at her killer's identity. Lýdur promised that, if he did make a statement, he would do a deal with the loan shark, who was now in custody, to cancel Andrés's debt and keep his name out of the inquiry.

Andrés couldn't believe he was hearing this, but there was no denying that the offer was tempting. And it wasn't as if they were asking him to lie, at least not directly. It was true that Andrés couldn't remember the detail about the jumper, but that was no reason to suspect Lýdur of falsifying the evidence. Surely the young detective was simply determined to see justice done and the guilty man punished for his heinous crime against a young girl – against his own daughter, for God's sake. Andrés kept trying to convince himself that this was what had motivated him to change his testimony in line with Lýdur's request; that all he'd wanted was to see justice done. But deep down he knew that this hadn't been the real reason, and he couldn't stop brooding on the fact. His testimony had been more or less dictated to him by Lýdur. All he could hope was that the suspect would confess as a result. Because Andrés was becoming increasingly prey to doubts: what if the police had arrested the wrong man?

Obeying a powerful urge to revisit the spot, he took the turning to the valley where the summer house was located. He wanted to think back over what he'd seen, try to convince himself that he hadn't done anything wrong, only smoothed the path of justice.

Having parked the car, he trudged along the snowy path to the hut, wishing with all his heart that the poor girl hadn't died there, that this case had never come up. Scraping at the frost on the glass, he peered through the window by the front door as he had done the day he discovered the body, but this time he could see nothing. The building was dark, forlorn, deserted. It went without saying that it wouldn't be used again, not by the family. Perhaps one day, when the incident had faded from people's memories, it would be sold to some unsuspecting city type who would be blissfully ignorant of what had happened there.

The case was closed, thank God. That must be the end of it. The police had arrested the murderer: Reykjavík CID wouldn't make a mistake, not in a major case like this. That was unthinkable. Andrés wouldn't have been capable of conducting the investigation himself, but then his role had been a very minor one, an insignificant cog in the wheels of justice. A brief witness statement, nothing more, though perhaps it had made a difference.

The defendant was currently awaiting the verdict and most of the officers Andrés had spoken to seemed confident that he would be found guilty; that there was no real doubt. Sickening as the case was, people seemed to derive a ghoulish pleasure from discussing the grisly details. The story, as presented by the police and the public prosecutor, featured unusual, even sensational, elements, which were a gift to malicious tongues. Andrés couldn't help feeling a twinge of pity for the suspect, though there shouldn't be any reason to. Not if the police were to be believed. Yet he did pity him. Andrés's greatest sympathy was reserved for the man's family, though; for his wife and son. The boy was almost an adult, admittedly, but he had looked so lost, so bowed and beaten, during the trial.

Andrés snapped out of his reverie to find himself still standing outside the summer house in the freezing cold. He didn't know what he was doing there or why he was rooted to the spot like this, as if his legs were made of lead. He couldn't move. Closing his eyes, he relived the horrifying sight that had confronted him back in the autumn.

The more he thought about it, the more his certainty grew. He hadn't seen the poor girl holding the jumper; no, he'd have remembered that.

Shit.

He had lied in court. And, what was worse, he had known it all along – in his heart of hearts – though he tried to kid himself that it was only now, revisiting the scene of the crime, that the details had started to come back to him.

The question was whether his lie mattered. Whether his statement had in fact been the deciding factor.

If the father was found guilty, how large a part would Andrés have played in condemning him?

And if he were to turn round now, head all the way back to town and withdraw his statement, what impact would that have? Would the judge conclude that the prosecution's entire case had been built on sand and find the suspect innocent? A man who might be guilty of an appalling crime . . .

No wonder his legs felt leaden. He had to come to a decision before he continued his journey. Should he leave matters as they were, or drive all those hundreds of kilometres back to Reykjavík and make a clean breast of things?

Could he live with the lie, or should he tell the truth and risk being sacked and disgraced? What would happen to his family?

He wasn't moving an inch from this spot until he'd made up his mind, one way or another.

XIV

The turmoil raging in Veturlidi's head as he sat in his cell waiting for the verdict was such that it was all he could do to hang on to the shreds of his sanity.

The trial was over and he had read in the defence counsel's eyes that he wasn't optimistic, though he had tried to put a good face on things. 'Justice always prevails in the end,' he'd said. 'Try not to worry,' he'd added, but Veturlidi couldn't help worrying. His lawyer made a show of being sorry for him but always seemed in a great hurry to leave. He had a life outside the walls of the prison and other things to think about apart from Veturlidi's fate.

Veturlidi could hardly let his thoughts stray to his family without breaking down. The confinement had broken his spirit; he wasn't half the man he used to be. Scarcely a shadow of himself. The sense of claustrophobia was so suffocating that for the first few nights he had woken up screaming and banged on the walls until his fists bled. He couldn't sleep; felt as if he couldn't breathe. Things had improved slightly since then, but you never really got used to it. Being in solitary confinement had been worst, but the cell he was in now was little better, a cramped space with no escape.

Officially, he could receive visits from his family, but he had refused to consider it. He couldn't meet their eyes. His shame was so complete, so crushing; being arrested, accused of such a heinous crime . . . He kept wondering how Vera and his son must be feeling. Of course, the boy was nineteen years old, almost a man, but when he'd stood on the steps that morning, screaming with terror, his father had felt an agonizing stab in his heart.

Regardless of the verdict, Veturlidi wondered if his life could ever return to normal. He sincerely doubted it. His relationship with his family had been permanently damaged. They would always feel a sneaking doubt, even if he was found innocent. And what about other people? Could he ever go back to work, for example? Ever hold his head high in his street? Look his neighbours in the eye?

These worries weighed even more heavily on him than his fear of the judge's decision and the possibility of a prison sentence. Taken together, it was almost more than he could bear. No living man would be able to carry such a burden. Sometimes all he wanted was to sleep and never wake up again.

XV

Hulda was exhausted by the time Friday came round, but at least she had the enticing prospect of a rare weekend off. Her job took it out of her; the cases she dealt with were demanding, sometimes downright gruelling. There was no such thing as a routine day in the police; she had to be prepared for anything when she went to work in the morning – or evening – every imaginable type of callout and problem, including violent incidents, even deaths. Over the years she had learned how vital it was to keep her home life separate from work.

In the early days she hadn't been very good at this, and even now there was a sense in which she was always on the job, always on call, constantly preoccupied with those cases that couldn't be neatly wrapped up by the end of the day. But she did draw the line at discussing her work at the kitchen table or in the sitting room – in fact, any-where within the four walls of home – because home was her refuge from the rigours of her job.

The traffic moved slowly at first, the usual Friday-afternoon congestion, but things began to flow more easily as she approached the turn-off to Álftanes and she could give her new Skoda its head. She'd bought it at the beginning of the year and was quite pleased with her purchase. It was the first time she'd had a car of her own. Until recently, she and Jón had made do with sharing one, an arrangement that had required a considerable amount of organization and patience, especially since they'd taken the decision to live so far out of town. But Jón's business had done well last year and they'd decided to invest in a second vehicle. She'd been given a free hand in choosing it, within limits, of course. In the event, she'd fallen for this green, two-door Skoda.

Hulda had prepared in advance for this evening: the hamburgers she was planning to fry were already in the fridge, along with the Coke. This meal had the twofold advantage of being popular with her husband and her daughter and requiring little effort to prepare on a Friday evening. Afterwards, the three of them usually sat down in front of the TV. Hulda didn't watch much television herself; she only did it to keep her daughter company. Personally, she'd rather spend her free time outside, either in the garden, gazing out to sea, or hiking in the mountains, if she got the chance. Jón wasn't really the outdoorsy type but he did his best and obligingly let her drag him on trips into the highlands.

Naturally, there hadn't been as many of those trips after Dimma came along; they didn't fancy the thought of carrying a young child around the treacherous highlands. However, it wouldn't have been particularly hard to find a babysitter. Hulda's mother had begged to look after the little girl from day one and, whenever they let her, she put her heart and soul into the task. In fact, Hulda sometimes had the impression that her mother got on better with Dimma than she did with her; that their relationship was inexplicably closer and more affectionate than that between Hulda and her mother. The girl was about to turn thirteen, which had its good and bad sides. On the one hand she was more independent, but on the other the onset of adolescence had brought problems. Dimma was moody, even temperamental on occasion, less keen than she used to be on spending time with her parents. These days, it wasn't unusual for her to go straight to her room when she got home and even to lock herself in. What was worse, Hulda was afraid that Dimma was shutting herself off from her friends as well. If she carried on like this, it could lead to her dropping out of the group she'd gone around with for so long. From time to time, Hulda tried to sit down and talk to her about it, but their conversations tended either to end in silence or to erupt into blazing rows. Yet Hulda clung to the hope that this was just a phase her daughter was going through, an inevitable part of growing up.

It probably didn't help that she and Jón spent little time at home on account of their work. Hulda had to take the odd evening or night shift, and Jón was a bit of a workaholic, on the go from morning to night, despite his doctor's warning that his heart wasn't in great shape. Although Jón was conscientious about taking the pills the doctor had prescribed for the problem – pills that the doctor had told him in no uncertain terms were a matter of life or death – he completely ignored the additional advice, or rather orders, to take it easy at work. Hulda supposed she should be stricter with him but, on some level, she was conscious that their comfortable lifestyle was almost entirely down to Jón, as her police salary didn't contribute much to the household. She had only the vaguest idea what Jón's business involved: all she knew was that he had made a handsome profit on imports and that he made this money 'work for itself', as he put it, by investing in other people's companies. As far as she could tell, he spent his days in meetings or in talks with banks. She had remarked more than once that he should slow down a bit – surely he didn't need to watch over every investment day and night. He had retorted that this was exactly what he had to do. If he took his eye off the ball, he might as well chuck in the towel and give all his money away. Hulda left the subject alone after that.

As she drove out on to the green Álftanes peninsula, leaving the built-up area behind, passing the white buildings of the president's residence at Bessastadir and seeing the sea stretching wide and blue to the horizon, Hulda found herself looking forward to the evening ahead, hoping it would be like the old days. She needed to distract herself from the week's cases, from the harrowing images that sometimes felt as if they had been branded on her consciousness after the terrible tragedies she was forced to witness in the line of duty.

Jón and Dimma were her sanctuary; seeing them, hugging them, gave her the strength to carry on.

Hulda's mother had rung her at work that morning. As usual, her conversation had included a well-intentioned reminder that they didn't see enough of each other, in addition to a request that they have a coffee together that weekend. Hulda had pretended she had to work. The truth was that she wasn't in the mood to see her. She was fond of her mother, in a way, but their relationship wasn't all it might have been. She wished it was better, but wished even more that she'd had a chance to get to know her father. However, since she was the result of a one-night stand with an American soldier, this was unlikely ever to happen. Her mother hadn't had the guts to tell him she was pregnant, or made any attempt to trace him after Hulda was born.

Still, it was Friday evening at last and Hulda was looking forward to forgetting her troubles over a trashy film on TV.

An odd silence greeted her when she entered their lovely house on Álftanes.

'Dimma?'

No answer.

'Jón?'

Her husband called out: 'Here, in the office.'

She went and stuck her head round the door. He was sitting at his desk with his back to her.

'Jón, love, can't you leave that now? Where's Dimma?'

'Yes, in a minute,' he said, without looking round.

'Are you working?'

'Yes. Yes, darling, there's something I've got to clear up this evening. It's rather urgent. You two start without me. Have you got us something for supper?'

'Burgers.'

'Fine. Just leave mine till later.'

'Where's Dimma? Isn't she home yet?'

'She's . . . er, she's in her room. She's locked the door, I think. Some bother at school.' He still had his back to Hulda.

'Again? We can't have her locking herself away all evening, day after day . . .'

'It's just a phase she's going through, love,' Jón told her firmly. 'It'll blow over.'

PART TWO

Ten Years Later, 1997

I

Dagur

Outside, it was summer, real summer for once, the thermometer rising to almost twenty degrees and not a breath of wind. The laburnums were in flower, their yellow blossoms hanging in thick clusters in the gardens on Dagur's route through town. Once, he paused to take a deep breath, inhaling the heady scent of a true Reykjavík summer. As he did so, he remembered hearing somewhere that laburnum flowers were poisonous. It wouldn't surprise him: he knew from bitter experience that the world was a treacherous place. That it could be toxic.

Entering the nursing home was like stepping into perpetual autumn. The muted decor, which seemed more faded every time he visited, and the frosted windows that filtered out the sunlight, always had a depressing effect on him. He visited because he cared, but also from a sense of duty, and was always relieved when he emerged into the fresh air again. No matter what the weather was like outside, it was infinitely preferable to the stale, heavy atmosphere in the home.

At sixty-three, his mother was unusually young to be living there, but it had been the only alternative. She was exhausted, both mentally and physically. It had taken her ten years of slow but steady decline to reach this point. There was no real medical explanation for what was wrong with her; it was as if she'd simply abandoned the struggle.

Dagur walked briskly up the stairs and along the dingy corridor to her room, which was small and impersonal, but at least she had it to herself. As usual, she was sitting by the window, staring out, though there was nothing special about the view. Dagur always got the impression that her gaze was directed inwards rather than out, dwelling on the good old days, on memories of the past.

It had been three years since he was forced to put his mother in a home. It wasn't only that he couldn't cope with caring for her any longer; he'd needed to get on with his own life too, break out of the vicious circle that kept him trapped in the past. The silence in their house had become so overpowering that things simply couldn't go on that way.

In spite of the difficult circumstances, he had managed, goodness knows how, to pass his school-leaving exams. After that, he had taken a year off, though he hadn't gone travelling, like some of his friends. No, he had stayed in Iceland, got himself a job and helped his mother find the strength to carry on. She had still been working as a bank cashier then, though she had cut down her hours. At first she had coped fairly well emotionally; rather, the shock and strain had found an outlet in physical symptoms ranging from fatigue to a plethora of aches and pains. It was extraordinary that she'd managed to go on working even part time. In the end, she'd been forced to give up her job and live on disability benefits. Dagur, realizing the way things were going, decided to enrol in a vocational course at university, foreseeing a time in the near future when he'd have to stand on his own two feet and support his mother financially as well. With this in mind, he had opted for business studies, shelving his dreams of a different sort of career. For the time being, at least.

He had derived no particular enjoyment from his studies, but the subject had come easily to him. A good head for figures and the ability to think on the spot had led him, after graduating, to take a job in finance, a world he'd now been working in for seven years. A banker at twenty-nine: the nineteen-year-old Dagur would never have believed it.

He'd had several relationships – if you could dignify them with that name – but hadn't been in love with any of his girlfriends. He supposed he would have to take the plunge sooner or later, though: find himself a good woman, start a family, make a home of his own. For now, he was still living in the house where he'd grown up, rattling around in a place far too large for one person, surrounded by too many memories. But for some reason he had always balked at the idea of moving, perhaps out of consideration for his mother, though, admittedly, these days she only came home for major holidays like Christmas and Easter.

Yes, it was time to move on, to come to terms with the past. He and his mother hadn't been offered any trauma counselling at the time, though it might have been different now, a decade later; back then, they had been left to cope on their own.

Recently, a restlessness had taken hold of him. He felt a real desire to make something of himself, build more of a future for himself. If he didn't, he knew he'd remain trapped for ever in his dreary existence. And that was out of the question – that wasn't who he was. Perhaps he would give up his job on the trading floor and try something else instead.

'Hello, Mum. It's me,' he said gently. He was still wearing his suit, having come straight from the office, but his mother never commented on how he was dressed; she probably didn't even notice.

She looked round, her gaze still disconcertingly remote, yet her eyes were at least resting on him, and he thought he saw a glimpse of the person she used to be, the mother who used to keep their household going.

'Dagur, dear, how are you?' she asked after a little delay. Some days she was on the ball, other days she seemed to reject the present and retreat into the past. The doctors were unable to provide any concrete explanation for this, usually blaming it on the trauma – or, rather, traumas – she'd experienced. Even when she was having one of her good days, there was still some indefinable distance between them that Dagur couldn't bridge. He sensed that she cared, that she still felt a mother's love for him; she just found it hard to break out of the protective shell she had developed over the last few years. Perhaps she felt happier in there. Dagur was sure that this was how things would go on until, in the end, she simply gave up the fight.

'OK, thanks, Mum.'

'Good, darling. I'm glad.'

'Have you been out at all today? It's lovely weather.'

She didn't immediately answer but eventually said: 'I never really go anywhere, Dagur, dear. Except to visit you. I'm fine in here.'

'I'm thinking of moving,' he blurted out, though he hadn't made up his mind beforehand whether to tell her, anxious as he was not to upset her. Still, maybe it was better to be honest, and if he said it aloud that would increase the odds that he might actually do something about it.

Her reaction took him by surprise. 'I'm pleased to hear that. It's about time.'

Dagur was thrown: he'd been expecting her to try to dissuade him.

'I . . . well, nothing's actually decided yet.' It dawned on him that he might have been using his mother as an excuse, that perhaps he himself was finding it harder to come to terms with the past than he liked to admit. Did he really want to sell his childhood home and lose touch with all the memories, good and bad? Though, if he were honest, the bad ones had already eaten their way into his soul and become an indelible part of him.

'Don't delay your decision for my sake,' she said, smiling. Melancholy though her smile was, for a moment it was as though a shroud had lifted, as though he were looking back ten years in time, at his mother as she used to be.

Dagur didn't allow himself to weep; he hadn't even wept at the time. Back then, he had bottled up his feelings and found a different release for them. Yet now, suddenly, he felt as if all the suppressed tears were trying to force their way to the surface. Hastily, he changed the subject: 'Anyway, how are you feeling, Mum? Are you well?'

'I'm always tired, dear, as you know. That hasn't got any better and I don't suppose it ever will. It's always nice to see you, but in between your visits I mostly rest.'

This was exactly what Dagur had feared: that his mother had next to no contact with the other residents of the home. She had already cut herself off completely from her social circle, the women she'd worked with at the bank, old friends from school. Everything had changed and she'd closed all the doors to her past life. Her isolation was self-imposed, and so perhaps – he sometimes caught himself thinking – was the decline in her mental and physical health. Depression was the explanation most often advanced by her doctors, but the drugs they prescribed only seemed to make her lapse further into torpor.

She rarely, if ever, referred to what had happened. She seemed to feel better that way, as if it was her method of coping with the indescribable suffering. Unfortunately, Dagur hadn't yet discovered his own method, but he hoped that when he did it would be different from hers. You never knew, though; after all, he and his mother shared the same genes. He never talked about what had happened either, not even to his friends.

'You must take care of yourself,' he said. 'Why don't . . . why don't you come home for a meal?'

'Just at Christmas, dear. You've got your own life to be getting on with.'

'But—'

At that moment his phone rang.

'What's that awful noise?' protested his mother.

'My phone, Mum,' he said over the noisy ringing as he retrieved it from his jacket pocket.

'Oh, yes, one of those ... those mobile phones, of course. I don't understand why you have to carry it around everywhere. Isn't it only show-offs who use those things?'

'The bank wants me to be contactable.'

'It wasn't like that when I worked for the bank. Isn't it a nuisance when you're trying to serve customers?'

He couldn't face trying to explain to her exactly what he did at the bank, though he'd long been aware that she assumed he was a cashier like her. The banking system she'd worked in had been government owned and the arrival of the stock exchange was a recent innovation, but since she had given up her job his mother had made no attempt to keep up with what was going on outside the four walls of the home. The world of securities would be completely alien to her.

He answered the call. It turned out to be an old mate. Their relationship was still good, if no longer particularly close, as if there were some inexplicable shadow hanging over it.

'Is this a bad moment?'

Dagur glanced around the dreary, impersonal little room. His mother smiled and gave him a sign that he should go. Aware that his visits were important to her, in spite of her air of detachment, he felt ashamed that he couldn't bring himself to stay any longer.

'No, it's fine,' he said into the phone and got to his feet. When he kissed his mother on the cheek, she laid a hand on his shoulder, very gently, and again he felt the tears welling up. Christ, what was happening to him?

He hurried out.

'I was thinking, Dagur,' said his friend. 'You know, it's ages since we last got together – the old gang, I mean. The thing is, I was talking to Klara yesterday and she's just heard from Alexandra, who's in town for once, and could join us at the weekend . . .'

Dagur allowed a silence to develop as he bounded down the stairs, desperate to get back outside into the fresh summer air.

'It'll be ten years this year, you know . . .'

'Yes, I know.'

'We were thinking of doing something to mark the occasion – a sort of reunion . . .'

Dagur thought it over. Ordinarily, he would have said a flat-out no and refused to discuss it any further, but the conversation with his mother was still fresh in his mind. She had as good as encouraged him to move house. Some kind of break with the past was inevitable; he had delayed far too long, whether consciously or not.

'What did you have in mind?'

'Oh . . . er . . .'

Dagur got the feeling his friend had been prepared for a more negative reaction.

'I can arrange a great place for us to stay this weekend. It'd give us a chance to spend a little time together, just the four of us.'

'Whereabouts?'

'Are you free?'

Dagur raised his face to the sky. It was a beautiful day and he could feel his mood lifting, but he knew that if he thought about it too long he'd get cold feet.

'OK, I'm up for it. Where are we going?'

'Why not let us surprise you?'

Something was stirring, there was change in the air; he was about to take a leap into the unknown.

'Sure, no problem,' he replied. 'Look forward to seeing you guys.'

II

It was a journey that Inspector Hulda Hermannsdóttir had always meant to make one day, if not quite this literally. Her mother had died several months ago and it would be easy to think that was the reason. But this was only partly true, though not in the sense that she was fulfilling a dying woman's last wish; in fact, quite the reverse.

Hulda's mother had lingered at death's door for an unusually long time and Hulda had spent as many hours as she could by her bedside. They'd talked about the past, but her mother had no last wishes. When the end came, she had quietly slipped away, and that's all there was to it.

Sometimes, sitting by her mother's bed, watching her sleep, Hulda had tried to shed a tear, to feel some unbreakable bond, but their relationship hadn't been like that. At least, not on Hulda's side, though she knew her mother had felt differently. Hulda had read in her eyes a yearning for a closer relationship; the tiniest spark of hope, a wish that things could have turned out otherwise.

And now here Hulda was, utterly alone in the world.

Her maternal grandparents were dead and her husband and only child too. She did her best to train her mind not to dwell on that terrible period when she had lost first Dimma, then Jón, in quick succession.

Hulda supposed she had always meant to try to find out more about her GI father one day, but now at last it felt like the right time.

Her mother had rarely spoken of him, hadn't appeared to know much about him, and Hulda had judged that, as long as she was alive, it would have to be her mother's decision whether they should attempt to trace him. But she had made no move to do so. Now that she was dead, Hulda was finally free to go ahead.

All the information she had to go on was the man's first name, the rough dates of his tour of duty in Iceland and his home state.

Armed with these details, she had gone down to the American embassy, where she took the liberty of flashing her police ID, though of course she was well outside the grey area she sometimes found herself in when carrying out her duties.

She was shown into the office of a helpful young man who had promised to look into the matter for her. Several days later, he had rung with the names of two men, both called Robert and both from the relevant state, who had been stationed on the military base at Keflavík in 1947.

Acting on impulse, Hulda had booked a flight to America at short notice. As yet, only one of the men in question had been traced. For all she knew, the other might be dead, so it was possible that her journey would result in nothing more than a visit to her father's grave.

III

Benedikt

Benedikt got up from his chair, went over to the window and stretched. The view was nothing special, just faceless office blocks and a constant stream of traffic from morning to night. At times, it was actually better to keep the window closed to avoid being suffocated by exhaust fumes.

His friend Dagur had surprised him. Well, 'friend' was maybe putting it a bit strongly. They'd been close once, and the old ties of friendship didn't unravel that easily, but these days their contact was intermittent and one-sided, in the sense that it was always Benedikt who initiated it. Dagur never got in touch with him first. He seemed to be doing well at the bank but in other respects he remained stuck in a rut, still living alone in his childhood home, not getting out much. All Dagur's old mates told the same story: he was forever living in the past.

Even the traffic and the unrelieved concrete that met Benedikt's eye when he looked out of the window couldn't disguise the fact that it was a gorgeous summer's day. What a waste to be cooped up inside in weather like this.

He opened the window, despite the noise and pollution, to let in a hint of sweet, warm air.

Going back to his desk, he sat down, reached for a blank sheet of paper and pencil, and, letting his mind drift, started to draw. He often did this to relax; sometimes he didn't even realize what he was drawing until later. The action was almost unconscious, instinct guiding his pencil.

The drawers of his desk were full of these sketches, which no one else ever got to see.

Apart from these doodles, Benedikt had no time to devote to his art. His software business was going well and he had a number of exciting projects in the pipeline. He had set up the company two years ago with three other guys from his engineering course. Since then, they'd hired more employees but were still working out of the same broom cupboard of an office. It wouldn't be long, though, before they could move into a more suitable space. Although the company wasn't turning over a profit yet, they'd managed to attract some wealthy backers who were pumping money into it, which meant that Benedikt and his partners could afford to pay themselves a decent salary these days. The plan was to launch the company on the stock exchange this autumn, and there was already considerable interest from investors. Preparation for the launch kept Benedikt constantly dashing between meetings with lawyers and accountants, which left him with little time to concentrate on the proper work to be done.

He wouldn't have much time for holidays this summer either, but it would all be worth it in the end.

At least he had the upcoming trip to the island to look forward to. Everything was arranged. The last piece of the puzzle had been persuading Dagur to come. Benedikt reflected again on his friend's surprising reaction. He had been fully prepared for him to be unenthusiastic, to dismiss it as a terrible idea, but to his astonishment Dagur had sounded almost keen.

Ten years.

They had passed bewilderingly fast; indeed, at times Benedikt felt as if the events had happened only yesterday. He found it all too easy to relive that day, and the days that had followed, almost scene by scene; some of the conversations were burned into his mind. It seemed nothing would erase the memories. There were some he wanted to hold on to; others he would have given anything to forget. The intervening years had not been easy; the strain of keeping up the deception, of carrying the weight of this unbearable secret for a whole decade, had taken their toll.

Yet, oddly enough, the reunion on the island had been his idea. He had felt the need to keep her memory alive somehow, to make amends, though of course nothing could undo what had happened.

He had made a mistake, a terrible mistake, and he would just have to live with the consequences. 'Mistake' – God, what a hopelessly inadequate word to describe what he had done.

It would be painful to rake it all up, to bring everyone

together again – Dagur and the two girls, Alexandra and Klara – but in a way perhaps that was why he had worked so hard to arrange this reunion. On some level he welcomed the pain, even craved it, because it was more bearable than the corrosive sense of guilt that invariably descended when, the day's business over, he lay down to sleep and the nightmares came crowding in.

IV

It was an extraordinary feeling as the plane began its descent towards New York's JFK Airport and Hulda saw the skyscrapers of Manhattan lit by the rays of the evening sun. To be so tantalizingly close to the famous metropolis without being able to go there . . . It was Hulda's first visit to America and she had toyed with the idea of spending a few days in New York, but the cost of the trip was already prohibitive and accommodation prices in the city were steep. She couldn't afford to run up a big debt on her credit card and, besides, she mustn't lose sight of the purpose of her journey, which was to find out whether her father was alive. So it had been with a certain regret that she had checked in for the next leg of the journey, a flight down to Georgia, where the plan was to spend three days.

She only made it by the skin of her teeth. The plane from Iceland had landed a little late and Hulda hadn't left much of a gap between the flights, as she'd been keen to reach her destination that evening rather than spend her first night in America at an airport hotel. She was caught between excitement and trepidation. What if she actually met her father? How would it feel? What would she say? Would there be an instant connection or would it be like meeting a total stranger?

Before setting out, she had written to one of the two possible candidates, explaining that she was from Iceland and, since she'd be passing through his state, was wondering if it would be possible to pay him a visit on behalf of a mutual acquaintance who had known him in Iceland. He had written a nice letter back, saying he couldn't recall many people from his time in that chilly posting but that she was welcome to come and see him. The other Robert had proved more elusive: she still hadn't managed to track down any information about him. The embassy had promised that they were on the case, but she hadn't heard back from them by the time she left for America.

The internal flight to Georgia went smoothly. It was dark when she landed in the famous city of Savannah but on the taxi ride to her hotel she had an impression of heat, humidity, gracious buildings and vast, spreading trees. The hotel had an old-world grandeur about it, and when checking in she was greeted with charming warmth by the young girl at the desk. To meet with such kindness from a stranger was oddly heartening. She had been – and still was, perhaps – a little anxious about being alone in an unfamiliar city, so far from home.

She went straight to bed but, feeling in need of company,

turned on the TV with the volume on low and fell asleep to the murmuring of foreign voices.

Having slept unusually well, she woke up next morning feeling childishly excited. For once, she had been spared the nightly haunting.

V

Alexandra

Alexandra was no fan of travelling by sea. She usually avoided boats like the plague, as she felt sick and dizzy even on calm days and it could take her inner ear hours to recover once she was back on dry land. But this time she'd let Klara talk her into coming. Though the idea had struck her as misconceived at first, it was hard in the circumstances to say no. It would be ten years this autumn, and for the old gang to get together again, despite having gone their different ways, was, if nothing else, a mark of respect for the dead. They'd been inseparable as teenagers, four of them the same age and Dagur a year younger, and friendship was a powerful bond, for all its complications.

Before, when it was the five of them, they'd stuck together through thick and thin. These days, though Alexandra kept in touch with Klara, she received only second-hand news of the boys. Dagur had become a banker, which wasn't that unexpected. She could picture him in that sort of job. He had always been a matter-of-fact kind of guy, well suited to the serious business of banking. She'd been more surprised to hear that Benni had set up a software company – a company that was doing very well, from what she'd read in the papers. She'd never have believed that he would be anything other than an artist, but perhaps programming was the new art form on the eve of the millennium. She was the only member of the group who was not only married but had children as well, two little boys.

Alexandra had been born in Italy, the daughter of an Icelandic mother and an Italian father, and had moved to Iceland when she was two. She still spoke both languages fluently, thanks to summer holidays in Italy with her father's family, but always felt more Icelandic than Italian, having moved to Iceland so young. Her dad had worked in agriculture in his homeland and her mother was from farming stock in the east of Iceland, so perhaps Alexandra had missed out on the maritime gene. With a bunch of landlubbers for ancestors, was it any wonder she couldn't stand boats? For much of her early life she and her parents had lived with her grandparents in the east, before eventually relocating to the capital area. They had lived in Kópavogur for over a decade, but when the family business went bust they had moved back east to live with her mother's parents. Alexandra, just twenty at the time, had chosen to go too. Now she was married to a farmer herself and they were living with her parents, ready to take over their flourishing business when the time came. Life on the farm was good but demanding, leaving her with little time for herself, especially with two small boys tearing around the place. But this weekend she was as free as a bird for once, at liberty to rediscover her youth with her friends, far from the responsibilities of home.

It was her first visit to the Westman Islands, the little archipelago of some fifteen volcanic islands and innumerable stacks and skerries that jutted dramatically out of the sea off the south coast of Iceland. Earlier that morning she had flown with her friends to Heimaey, the largest island and the only one that was still inhabited. It had made world news in 1973, when a volcanic eruption had led to the mass evacuation of the population to the mainland. The eruption had gone on for over five months, but most of the islanders had subsequently returned and rebuilt their town, in defiance of the ever-present threat of eruption. Now, Heimaey was home to a thriving fishing industry but Alexandra could see the volcanic cone, still brown and ominously bare of vegetation, brooding above the white buildings of the town.

On arrival, they had headed down to the harbour and climbed on board a small fishing boat. Alexandra was already experiencing the first signs of queasiness, even though the boat was still moored to the dock. Thank God the sea was relatively calm today, she thought.

'This . . . this is going to be great,' Benedikt remarked, as if he felt compelled to fill the silence. It never used to be like this: all five of them used to be able to talk or be quiet together without any hint of awkwardness.

Benni had always been the one who jollied them along, but Alexandra had sometimes wondered if he was naturally that upbeat or if it was just an act. Of course, he'd been knocked sideways by the death, like the rest of them, but apart from that he didn't have much to complain about in life, as far as she could see.

Dagur, on the other hand . . . Alexandra could hardly bear to think about what he'd gone through.

'Was it your uncle, then . . . who wangled the house for us, I mean?' she asked Benni.

'Yes, he gave his permission. He's a member of the bird-hunting association that owns the lodge on the island. You can only go there if you've got contacts. I've been out with him quite often over the last few years.'

'So when's he coming?' Alexandra asked.

'He's not. Did you think he was? We wouldn't want him hanging around all weekend.'

'No, I just meant to take us out there.'

'There'd be no point. He'd only have to come back again to fetch us. It would be a hassle for him.'

'Who's in charge of the boat, then?'

'Me, of course,' Benni said, as if this were the most natural thing in the world.

A silence fell and was broken only when Dagur voiced what the rest of them were thinking. 'Do you know how to operate a boat?'

'You don't need a licence for a small boat like this,' Benedikt said airily. 'There's nothing to it. If any of you don't trust me, now's your chance to back out,' he added with a grin, though his voice held an underlying note of seriousness.

For a moment or two no one spoke. Alexandra was

longing to suggest they abandon the plan but stopped herself. Again, Dagur spoke for all of them: 'Of course no one's backing out. So, you say you've been to Ellidaey before?'

'Sure. Loads of times. But don't worry, I'm having you all on! Look, that's him now,' Benedikt said, pointing back at the docks. 'He'll take us out to the island and pick us up again on Sunday. There's a radio in the boat and another on the island so we can let him know when we're ready. It's the only means of communication while we're out there, so fingers crossed it's working OK.'

The boat pulled away from the docks and made for the harbour mouth in the capable hands of Benedikt's uncle, Sigurdur, who came across as an easy-going, cheery character.

Even so, Alexandra couldn't shrug off her sense of foreboding. Should she have said something? It wasn't the prospect of the sea voyage that was making her nervous so much as an odd premonition about the trip itself, a cold, sinking feeling that was growing ever harder to ignore. They had been good mates once, but that was a long time ago and they hadn't been together for years. OK, she'd kept in touch with Klara, but did she really know the others any more? Her thoughts flew to her little boys; that's where she belonged – at home with them, not here with a bunch of relative strangers, all engaged in a misguided attempt to recapture their youth. As if that wasn't bad enough, they'd got together for the anniversary of an event she couldn't even think about without a shudder.

In spite of her qualms, Alexandra had to admit that the view was magnificent. They glided past the fleet of colourful trawlers moored in the harbour and out through the entrance. It was a fine day with only a little light cloud, the sea was calm and the boat responded well when Benedikt's uncle finally opened up the throttle. 'There's Heimaklettur.' He pointed to the left. 'And Midklettur and Ystiklettur.' They passed close to the feet of the three craggy heights, with their green, grassy caps draped over steep, pock-marked cliffs.

Alexandra sat tight, swallowing and hanging on grimly to her seat as the boat began to rise and fall with the waves, while the boys and Klara balanced on their feet, faces to the wind, apparently enjoying the motion.

'Over there . . . look!' Benni shouted over the noise of the engine. 'There's Bjarnarey, and there, a bit further off, that's Ellidaey, where we're headed. The glacier in the background's Eyjafjallajökull.'

She followed the direction of his finger to the forbidding shape of an island, its rock walls impossibly sheer and inaccessible, rising out of the sea ahead, and beyond it another, slightly lower and more undulating but still ringed round with cliffs. She thought it resembled some humpbacked beast lying in wait for them, its head rearing up to strike. Abruptly, she looked down and closed her eyes.

A gentle hand touched her shoulder. Quickly glancing up, she saw that it was Dagur. A tiny frisson ran through her: memories of the past, hopes, expectations. There was a time when she'd thought the gang would produce two couples: her and Dagur, and Benni and . . . No, there was no point even going down that road. It was all over and forgotten long ago.

'Are you feeling all right?' His voice was kind.

'I'm not a very good sailor,' she replied ruefully.

She found herself wondering whether there could ever have been anything between them, anything more than a teenage flirtation. Of course, it was too late now – it must be. She was all too aware that the spark of romance was missing from her marriage these days, perhaps had never existed, and here she was, faced with the prospect of a whole weekend with the boy – the man – she'd fancied as a teenager ... well, more than that, she'd been in love with him. Could that be the real reason why she'd said yes when Klara suggested going away this weekend? If she were honest with herself, she had specifically asked if Dagur and Benni were both going to be there.

Ellidaey loomed up before them in all its glory, like something from another world; the golf course of the gods, a lawn of acid-green on top of vertiginous cliffs, and, nestling into a tuck in the grassy slope, a single, lonely house. It would be hard to imagine anything more remote.

'How about a quick circuit of the island?' asked Sigurdur, shooting a glance over his shoulder at his passengers.

The last thing Alexandra wanted was to prolong the boat trip, but she bit her lip as her friends welcomed the idea.

They were coming in close to the island now, to the foot of a spectacular black wall, streaked white with droppings, which appeared totally unclimbable to Alexandra. Seabirds swarmed around it in a screaming mass.

'Incredible, isn't it? Kittiwakes and gulls, mostly, I think,' said Benni. 'It's known as Háubæli. And look up there.' He pointed towards the top of the cliff. 'There's a small ledge near the top . . .'

To humour him, Alexandra peered reluctantly upwards and caught sight of the jutting crag.

'It's a good place to sit,' Benni said. 'If you really want to feel you're alive.'

'You've got to be joking,' Dagur said.

'It's no joke. We'll go over there later.'

Alexandra gulped. The boat was rocking and pitching close to the shore, making her stomach lurch. She concentrated miserably on anticipating the arrival of each wave, trying not to think about the dizzying heights above.

'You can climb up over there,' Benni went on, gesturing to a near-vertical precipice. 'Can you see the rope?'

At this, Alexandra could no longer restrain herself. 'No way are we climbing up that rope. Are you crazy? It would be unbelievably dangerous.'

'We *could* get up there.' Benni grinned. 'But there's an easier way round the other side.'

'What's that on top of the cliff – that post, or whatever it is?' asked Dagur.

'It's for lowering sheep.'

'Sheep? Are you telling me there are sheep up there?'

'Yes, a few dozen. They're lowered in a net, two at a time. There's a post up there and another down here. That's how the farmers transport them to the boats. The men string a rope between the post at the top and the bolt on that rock down there in the sea, then lower the sheep down the cliff.'

The boat chugged on around the foot of the rock walls, over the gentle swell.

'Right ...' Sigurdur said, a few minutes later. 'This is where we try to put you ashore. Over there, see?' He tried to point while simultaneously holding the little boat to her course.

Alexandra was persuaded to look up. She'd been hoping to see a jetty, but no such luck. A jumble of rocks and boulders, that was all.

'Right, you'll have to jump,' Sigurdur said, his voice sharpening.

'Jump?' exclaimed Klara. The others went very quiet.

'Yes, on to the shore, on to "the anvil", as we like to call the ledge. There's nothing to it. Just wait for the right moment. OK, Benni, you first. I'll say when.' There was a pause. 'One, two ... and jump.'

Benni didn't wait to be told twice; he took a flying leap off the boat on to the ledge, managing – just – to keep his balance. 'Piece of cake.'

Dagur followed his example.

Alexandra sat there, rigid with terror, watching as Klara jumped ashore next. They all seemed to have managed fine but, despite that, Alexandra's limbs refused to obey her.

'Get a move on!' she heard Sigurdur shouting.

Benedikt chimed in: 'Now, Alexandra, now! One, two, and jump.'

She jumped, without giving herself another moment

to think, making it somehow on to the precarious ledge. She slipped a little on landing but Dagur caught her and helped her recover her balance. At last she had dry land underfoot – if you could call it land, she thought. Now that she was here, there seemed nothing particularly safe about being ashore on this unbelievably rugged, uninhabited island. How she wished she'd never let herself be tricked into coming here. How on earth would it all end?

VI

Robert lived about half-an-hour's drive from downtown Savannah and the taxi didn't come cheap. His house turned out to be an attractive, single-storey wooden building with white walls, a red roof and a pretty porch. The garden was lush with vegetation and the temperature was suitably tropical; the taxi driver had said it was close to 100 degrees. Although Hulda had no idea of the formula for converting Fahrenheit to Celsius, she didn't need telling that it was extremely hot. As the sweat trickled down her back and sides, she prayed it would be cooler indoors.

'*Welcome, welcome!*' called an elderly man, appearing on the porch. 'Hulda?' he asked, with an American accent.

He was tall and a little overweight, but Hulda guessed he had been slimmer in his youth. Below his balding head, the deeply lined face was friendly.

'*Yes, I'm Hulda.*' Her English was a bit halting at first due to lack of use, but like most Icelanders she had a reasonable command of it, despite having travelled little and never having lived abroad. She had a good ear for languages: it was a pity she'd never had more of a chance to use them.

She walked up the path towards him, moving slowly in the stifling heat, studying every inch of his face, and for a moment she thought she caught a fleeting likeness, felt a connection, as if this man were related to her. But she was afraid it was nothing but wishful thinking.

'Shall we go inside?' he said, taking a step towards her and greeting her with a warm handshake.

'Yes, please.' Mercifully, it turned out to be much cooler in the house.

'My wife isn't home,' he explained. 'She's always out and about. But then she's a little younger than me.' Smiling, he offered Hulda a seat at the dining table.

She wondered how old he was but didn't like to ask, not straight away. It had been fifty years since he was in Iceland. Early seventies, maybe? He certainly wore his age well. His movements were quick and deliberate and he appeared to be in good health.

'But she did some baking for us, anyway,' he added, disappearing and returning almost immediately with a delicious-smelling pie.

'It's a peach pie,' he said proudly. 'Everybody here eats peach pie.'

He offered her some kind of lemonade with it.

After the first bite, Hulda had to admit it was one of the best pies she'd ever tasted. She'd long ago given up baking, could hardly be bothered to cook herself supper these days, let alone anything more complicated. There was no point when she lived alone. In the old days she would have asked for the recipe so she could bake it for Jón and Dimma, but now she made do with savouring the sweetness for herself.

'This is unbelievably delicious,' she said.

'Thank you. My wife's a great cook. It's good to have an excuse to bake, since we don't get many visitors. But here you are, all the way from Iceland!'

'It's not really that far away, as I'm sure you know. Not these days. Only five hours' flight from New York.'

'Is that all?' The old man seemed surprised. 'What the heck, maybe I should have gone back for a visit.'

'Did you never go back, then?'

'No, I was only stationed there a little while. Just short of a year. In 1947.' His eyes grew unfocused as his thoughts wandered back to that time, half a century ago.

'Do you have a clear memory of that year? Of Iceland?'

'I can't say I do, not really. I travelled a lot in those days and my stay in Iceland was just one of many postings. But I do remember the lava fields – being surrounded by all that endless lava. The landscape was incredibly barren. Just like the moon, or what you'd imagine the moon would be like.' Robert gave her a friendly smile.

'Was there anything else memorable about your stay in Iceland?' Hulda could feel herself slipping into police-interview mode, as if she were questioning a suspect, trying to trip him up, get him to confess to a crime. She had to get a grip on herself: it wasn't fair to this man.

He shook his head. 'No, can't say there was. To be honest with you, Iceland wasn't . . . how shall I put it? – the most popular posting on offer. I remember, when I heard I was being sent there, the first thing that occurred to me was: what did I do wrong?' He burst out laughing. 'Of course, that was just prejudice, but you have to admit that the country hadn't really entered the twentieth century back then. It wasn't what I was used to at home. It was so primitive it felt like going back in time. No paving on the roads, and so few buildings that the locals were living in Quonset huts. You could hardly even call Reykjavík a town then, but I expect it's a big city now. Not many of the locals spoke English either, though the young people had picked up a bit during the war, and I remember they had theatres showing American movies. I was kind of surprised by that. It was obvious that the presence of British and American soldiers during the occupation had had a big impact on the culture. That was the feeling I got, anyway.'

'You must have been young at the time . . .' she said, fishing. She was surprised at how easy she was finding it to speak English. She had studied the language at school, but her knowledge came mostly from watching subtitled series and films on TV. The Icelandic schedules were dominated by British and American programmes, so there was probably some truth even now in the old man's comment on the impact of the occupation.

'Well, yes, I guess I was about thirty . . .' He appeared to be doing some mental arithmetic. 'Yes, thirty.'

'It must have been difficult being away from your wife for a year,' Hulda commented in an enquiring tone, thinking that it would be interesting to know if he'd been single at the time. Not that this would necessarily prove anything: he could still have had an affair in Iceland.

'Yes, yes, it was – but luckily the war was over, so the danger had mostly passed. She's been kind enough to put up with me all these years. We've been married for more than half a century, you know.'

'Congratulations.'

'Thank you.' He was silent a moment, then, before Hulda had time to find the right words, added in his slow, measured voice: 'So, you said in your letter that we had a mutual friend?'

VII

Klara

Klara hadn't quite found the right direction in life. At least, that's what she told herself when trying to justify why she was still living with her parents at thirty, with no prospect of moving out any time soon. She drifted from job to job, held back by her lack of formal qualifications. For a while she'd had a temporary position at a nursery school, which she'd quite enjoyed, but that hadn't lasted. Every now and then she got work in a shop, covering for someone else, and she'd been invited to work at another nursery school, but again only in a temporary capacity. Perhaps part of the problem was that she didn't make enough effort to hang on to the good jobs when they did come up. She was comfortable living at home, where she had more or less everything she needed, since her parents let her live rent free in their basement flat.

Standing now in front of the island's lone house, she gazed out to sea, thinking back to the time when life had been simple. When she'd had these good friends and they'd pretty much spent all their free time together. They'd been so close: she remembered taking it for granted that it would always be like that, that they'd always be friends.

The light cloud had dispersed, giving way to a gloriously sunny day, and it would hardly be possible to imagine a more spectacular setting, yet for some reason Alexandra was being a real killjoy. After they'd picked their way up the grassy path beside the rough cliff face, with a bit of help from an old rope fixed to the rock, Alexandra had kept moaning that they should never have come, even turning on Klara and blaming her: 'You shouldn't have tricked me into this!' But Klara hadn't tricked her into anything; all she'd done was persuade her that they should get together to honour the memory of their old friend, the fifth member of their gang. Maybe the choice of venue was at fault, the solitary house on the uninhabited island of Ellidaey, about as far off the beaten track as you could get. But when Benni sent her a picture of the island, she had felt immediately that it was the right place. Such an unbelievably stunning setting.

Now, though, Klara was beginning to get cold feet too. Perhaps it was just the awareness of being so completely cut off from civilization. She had a sudden uneasy feeling that they were stranded, marooned on a desert island, with no way of making contact with the outside world except via the radio.

Trapped in a magnificent landscape painting.

The house, or rather hunting lodge, nestled at the foot of a grassy slope that swept up to meet the sky before plummeting vertically into the sea. Not far off was another, smaller building, a nineteenth-century bird-hunters' hut, one of the oldest buildings in the Westman Islands, Benni had said.

Someone was calling her name – Benni, probably. She filled her lungs with the fresh sea air, listening to the cries of the birds, the only sound to impinge on the silence. Then, determined to enjoy the moment, she shrugged off the creeping sense of dread and went to join the others.

Once Benni had gathered them together he announced that they were going to take a look at Háubæli. No one objected, though Klara caught the dismayed expression on Alexandra's face.

The walk took them right across the island, meeting the odd sheep on the way.

'Keep to the path. It's safest. The sheep maintain it; they usually go the same way,' said Benni.

'Safest?' exclaimed Dagur. 'Is there some reason why it's dangerous to walk on the grass?'

'There are puffin burrows all over the place and you can easily twist your ankle if you step in one by accident. So watch out.'

Klara brought up the rear, keeping as close as she could to the others. The sheep tracks had a way of petering out and, apart from them, the ground was covered with long grass and large tussocks that made walking difficult. The terrain began to slope down steeply underfoot.

'This is no place for people who are afraid of heights,' warned Benni, slowing up as they neared their destination. 'Just follow me. If you feel yourself getting vertigo, grab hold of a tuft of grass; the roots are amazingly strong.'

After a while they reached Háubæli and Klara found herself looking at one of the most breathtaking places she had ever seen. Just below the top of the cliff was a hollowed-out area under a rough rocky overhang almost like a shallow cave. And, in front of this, the ledge they'd seen earlier from the boat jutted out over the abyss. There was barely room for the four of them under the overhang and no way of standing upright unless you stepped closer to the brink.

'Who wants to sit on the ledge?' Benni invited. 'The views are amazing. And it really makes you feel alive. But then the risk of imminent death tends to have that effect. Put a foot wrong here and you've had it.'

Dagur was the first to try it, a little hesitantly, but it was clear from Alexandra's face that she had no intention of budging an inch from the relative safety of the overhang.

When Dagur came back, it was Klara's turn to perch right out on the furthest point. She gazed out to sea, up at the sky, at the white birds flying so close you could almost touch them. She felt as if she was in another world, the peace was so absolute and the view so incomparable. She could see Bjarnarey rearing sheer-sided from the sea and, beyond it, the volcanic cones of Heimaey, then nothing but ocean stretching to the far-distant horizon. Then she looked down, peering over the brink. It was like staring into infinity, like coming face to face with your own mortality. Shrinking back involuntarily, she caught her breath. No human being could possibly survive a fall like that.

VIII

Dagur

The hunting lodge, a smart wooden hut, was larger than the name suggested, almost like a summer house, clad with corrugated iron, white on the walls, black on the roof. In the kitchen past met present, modern appliances rubbing shoulders with items from another age, like the old-fashioned coffee pot, the ancient calendar and the radio that must have seen its heyday in the seventies. Dagur was immediately taken with the cosy atmosphere. The kitchen led into a sizeable living room where the four of them had already made themselves at home. Its walls were lined with old pictures of hunters, and a number of stuffed birds hung from the ceiling, like a reminder that the island was their realm and humans were only visitors.

'They say there are more birds on this island than there are people living in Manhattan,' Benni remarked. Up to now, their interaction had been a little awkward, a sign of how long it had been since all four of them had last got together, but Benni was doing his best to lighten the atmosphere. 'And you can't begin to count the puffin burrows.'

The lodge relied on a rainwater tank, as there was no source of fresh water on the island, so they'd brought along containers of drinking water in addition to the alcohol and food supplies. It had been quite a performance getting all their baggage ashore without breaking anything in the process.

'This isn't bad at all,' Alexandra said, but the tremor in her voice betrayed her. Dagur got the feeling she'd rather have been anywhere else. 'I bet they had a nightmare building this house, though.'

'Yes, I've heard the stories,' said Benni, eagerly pouncing on this conversational opener. 'I gather it was a hell of an undertaking. You can just imagine what it must have been like, having to transport all the timber and other materials out here by boat, then hauling them up the cliffs.'

'It's a real adventure, being so far away from it all,' said Klara. 'Quite a change for you, eh, Alexandra? No crying children.'

Alexandra's only reply was a faint smile.

'How are you enjoying life out east?' Dagur asked, to break the silence.

Alexandra didn't answer immediately, then said: 'Oh, fine.' When she quickly dropped her eyes, he thought he could read in her face that she wasn't telling the whole story.

He was about to turn to Klara next and ask what she was up to these days, but thought better of it. He was well aware that the last few years – the last decade, in fact – had been difficult.

Dagur caught Benedikt's eye, trying to convey the message that it was up to him to keep the conversational ball rolling.

'Shall we drink a toast . . . a toast to *her*?' Benedikt suggested, rising to his feet. It was obvious who he was referring to.

'Yes, let's,' said Klara.

She and Klara had been best friends. Out of all of them, it was Dagur and Klara who had been closest to her.

'Are you going to fetch the booze?' Klara asked, directing the question at Benni.

'What do you think?'

Opening a cupboard, he took out a bottle of whisky, poured some into three glasses, then turned to Dagur: 'What about you?' Dagur hadn't touched alcohol for years, not since the terrible events that had brought them all together now. He'd drunk as a teenager, like the rest of them, but circumstances had forced him to stop. To be precise, his father's admission that he'd been drinking when . . . when it happened . . . that he had in fact been boozing in secret for a long time, though he had hidden it from his family. After that, Dagur hadn't been able to bring himself to touch the stuff again.

At times, the temptation had been strong – perhaps it was in his genes – but he had no intention of lapsing. There was no way of knowing how far alcohol was to blame for wrecking his family, but it was clear that without it the situation wouldn't have been nearly as bad.

No, he was going to stay sober this evening, as always.

IX

'Yes, that's right . . .' Hulda hesitated over how to respond to his question about their mutual friend. Uncharacteristically, she hadn't properly prepared for this; hadn't thought how to put it into words.

'How old are you, if you don't mind my asking?' he said.

Hulda realized at once where this was going.

Then he added: 'I hope you'll excuse my being so direct but, when you reach my age, you feel you can take a few liberties with the younger generation.'

'Of course, my age is no secret . . . I will be fifty this year. A landmark birthday.'

'You're telling me. I remember when I hit fifty. I thought my life was over, but I couldn't have been more wrong.' He chuckled. 'Do you have a family, a husband and kids?'

Hulda was a little thrown by this question. At home in Iceland, most of the people she came into contact with knew what had happened, that Dimma had killed herself and she'd lost Jón not long afterwards. That she was alone in the world and had been for many years and no doubt would be for the duration. Unused to having to talk about it, she took a snap decision not to open up now to a stranger . . . which was a little unfair, considering what she wanted out of him.

'No, I live alone,' she said, deciding not to elaborate.

'Well, it's not too late to find yourself a good man,' he replied.

She didn't say anything to this.

'Won't you have another piece?' he asked then, gesturing to the peach pie. Hulda accepted the offer, if only to buy a little time.

After a brief silence, Robert spared her the effort.

'Is it maybe someone from your family?' he asked. 'Your mother, maybe? This mutual friend?'

Hulda hesitated, then said: 'Er . . . yes, exactly. My mother.'

Robert leaned back in his chair. 'Ah, I thought so.'

He didn't say anything else for a long moment, and Hulda held back, willing him to make the next move.

'You're just the right age, and I guess that's the only thing that would drag you all the way from Iceland to Georgia – a long, long way from home – just to meet an old man like me. Am I right?'

Her heart lurched. Was this her father? Was she really sitting face to face with him, after all these years? Suddenly, she found herself fighting back the tears.

'Yes . . .' she admitted diffidently, almost too choked up to speak.

'Ah,' Robert said again.

'Did you . . . were you and my mother . . . ?' Hulda couldn't find the right words.

This time it was Robert's turn to be silent. He seemed to be having difficulty finding the words himself.

X

Benedikt

Benedikt could feel the whisky going to his head, affecting him far more than he'd expected. Drinking on an empty stomach had been a bad idea.

It was funny looking round the group, at his three teenage friends, now ten years older. He'd kept in touch with Dagur and tried to meet up regularly, though Dagur seemed to prefer retreating into his shell these days. Benedikt had always believed their friendship was strong, that it had survived the adversity, but sometimes he got the impression that Dagur saw things differently. On the other hand, he hadn't seen the girls for a long time. Klara had almost vanished off the radar and Alexandra had moved away. He'd heard on the grapevine that Klara was having trouble holding on to a job and was still living with her parents. Who'd have thought it? She'd had so much promise in the old days that most people would have predicted she'd go far in whatever profession she chose. He'd always assumed that Klara would get a university degree, but it seemed she lacked the drive he'd attributed to her. No doubt he'd made the right choice . . . in fact, he'd never had any doubts on that score, regardless of the way things had gone.

Then again, he mustn't forget that the events had scarred them all in one way or another. And not just them but everyone who had known her, their friend.

They had been sitting here reminiscing about her at length, for the first time in years. It was a good feeling. High time, really.

Alexandra had just shared a poignant anecdote and Benedikt felt it was his turn next.

'There was this one time,' he began, trying to hold back the sob that threatened to burst from his throat the moment he recalled the story, 'she claimed an ancestor of hers had been burned at the stake. And as if that wasn't bad enough, he came back as a ghost as well. She swore she'd had a close encounter with him herself, that she'd sensed his presence.'

'Oh, I remember those . . . stories,' Dagur chipped in warily.

Benedikt felt warmed by the memory, while simultaneously experiencing a slight shiver at the associations it called up. 'She was full of tall stories like that – most of them made up, I expect,' he went on. 'But that was part of her charm.'

'Exactly,' said Alexandra, smiling at him. The alcohol seemed to have loosened her tongue. 'She was such a liar, but never in a bad way, don't get me wrong. She just loved embroidering the truth.'

'A liar . . .' Dagur echoed, obviously stone-cold sober and unwilling to let just anything go. 'That's a bit harsh.'

'Sorry, I didn't mean anything by it,' Alexandra said, embarrassed.

'Do you think she was telling the truth – about her ancestor, I mean?' Klara asked, oblivious to the undercurrents. She'd drunk her fair share too; more than anyone else, probably. 'Was he really burned at the stake? Did they do that sort of thing here in Iceland?'

'You know, that's exactly what I asked her . . .' Benedikt broke off, hazily aware that he had said too much. 'Anyway . . . Oh God, I don't know. I can't remember the details. It was so long ago.'

'Was this in the West Fjords?' asked Dagur.

'What? No. What do you mean? In the West Fjords?'

'I know that story. He was from the West Fjords, the man who was burned at the stake. You're right. She told me about him, *at the summer house* . . .' He emphasized the words. 'She said she was always afraid of the dark there.'

Benedikt didn't respond. He was about to change the subject when Dagur continued: 'I'd forgotten all about that. It's fun to be reminded. I expect she was exaggerating, but who knows? When did she tell you about it?'

'Me?' Benedikt reacted belatedly, as though he thought Dagur's question had been directed at one of the others.

'Yes, when did she tell you the story?'

Benedikt pretended to rack his brains. 'God, I've forgotten. All I remember is that someone got burned at the stake. It's not the kind of thing you forget!' He laughed, covertly watching his friends' reactions. He noticed

Alexandra shifting a little closer to Dagur on the sofa. Perhaps inadvertently, perhaps not. Klara didn't seem to react at all, just sat staring into space, as though she was thinking about something else entirely. And Dagur . . . Dagur, who had unquestionably been paying close attention, was staring hard at Benedikt, with an odd look in his eye. Some element of Benedikt's story was clearly bothering him.

But when Dagur spoke again it was only to say, 'Ten years . . . They've gone fast, haven't they, guys? Shall we drink that toast?'

They raised their glasses to her – who else? The girl who had been responsible for bringing them all together; who'd been in the same class as Benedikt and Klara from primary school right through to sixth form; who'd been friends with Alexandra, despite her going to a different school from them. And big sister to Dagur – 'little Dagur', as they used to call him, tongue in cheek, because he was a whole year younger than them. She would never hear of him being left out. That's how Benedikt remembered her: animated, a bit of a tease, kind-hearted, well disposed towards everyone, but single-minded when it came to getting what she wanted. She never let anything get in her way.

'I almost feel like she's here with us,' said Alexandra, slurring a little from the whisky. 'Can't you feel it? Like there's some invisible spirit in the house, making everything seem brighter – a mischievous spirit, don't you think?' Receiving no answer, she hastened to add: 'Sorry, I'm just feeling a bit sentimental. It's the drink. I'm not used to it these days. On the farm I'm always busy looking after my kids and my husband – I just don't have time to go out partying any more.'

'Sure, I can sense it, sense her, Alexandra,' Klara said, smiling. 'Definitely.'

Emboldened by Klara's encouragement, Alexandra added: 'I can't help wondering if she's trying to tell us something. If there's some message she wants to pass on to us.'

'What do you mean?' Benedikt asked, his voice involuntarily sharpening. 'Tell us?'

'Well . . . you know,' Alexandra said hesitantly.

Benedikt didn't answer; didn't know how to react.

'You know,' she began again. 'Perhaps she wants to tell us what happened.'

At this Benedikt felt the atmosphere thicken almost palpably, as if her spirit had literally come out to join them on Ellidaey.

'I don't understand,' said Klara.

Benedikt turned his head to study Klara properly for the first time. She'd aged well. Always very pretty at school, she had matured into a beautiful woman. Benedikt still found her attractive but knew there could never be anything between them now. In a way it was good to see his mates again, but at the same time he was glad they'd all gone their separate ways, except for him and Dagur, of course.

Klara persisted: 'Tell us what happened? What do you mean? We all know what happened.' She was speaking quietly but distinctly, and for a moment you could have heard a pin drop, then Dagur exploded to his feet with such violence that the glass he'd been drinking from fell to the floor and smashed to pieces.

'We *don't* know!' he exclaimed with such fury that Benedikt wondered if there had been alcohol in his glass after all. The sudden outburst was so unlike him.

Getting up, Benedikt went over and gave his friend a hug.

'Of course we don't know. Nobody knows. But you can see what she means: the case is closed, as far as the police are concerned, though of course we don't have to agree with them. We're all capable of making up our own minds.'

Dagur shoved him away, so roughly that Benedikt stumbled.

'*We're all capable of making up our own minds?* What kind of crap is that, Benni? And Klara? And what about you, Alexandra? Sitting there, quiet as a mouse. Don't you have an opinion?' His eyes bored into her.

'No. I mean . . . I agree with you, Dagur.'

'You mean to say you all believe the official version? Seriously? I thought we were friends, that we backed each other up. And now you're lying to me as well – or at least you are, Benni. You! We're friends, for Christ's sake, or used to be. Why have you been lying to me?'

'Lying? What the hell do you mean?' exclaimed Benedikt.

But Dagur had already stormed upstairs.

XI

Alexandra

Alexandra couldn't immediately work out what had woken her. She sat up, gasping, only to realize after a moment that it was the middle of the night, as dim outside as it ever got at this time of year. She shifted uncomfortably; the mattress was old and lumpy. There were no creature comforts here, but presumably most visitors didn't mind, since they'd come out to the island to get away from it all. Though Alexandra would usually have described herself as a country girl, she wasn't enjoying this. There was something in the air, something indefinably wrong, that made her wish she was back home in her own bed, back in the warm, familiar chaos of family life, far from this island and these people. The evening had ended on a sour note, with Dagur suddenly flaring up at Benedikt for no apparent reason. After this, the party had petered out, though it hadn't exactly been rollicking before that. Alexandra was hoping that the new day would bring a more positive atmosphere.

She'd had trouble getting to sleep, though she'd managed

in the end. But now she heard an eerie wail of distress and knew immediately that it was a similar cry that had woken her. It was a chilling sound that pierced her to the marrow. A woman's voice, she was sure of that. Klara?

Alexandra sat up, heavy with sleep, the alcohol still coursing through her veins after the evening's drinking. She felt woozy. It took her a moment to notice that Klara wasn't lying on the mattress beside hers. And then the cold realization struck her that she was frightened, because what on earth could have caused Klara to produce such a blood-curdling scream? The very last thing she wanted was to go and investigate, but she had to help her friend.

The sleeping loft was divided into two rooms and the connecting door was closed. The boys had taken the inner room, she and Klara the outer one.

And then she saw her. Klara was sitting in the corner, curled up almost in the foetal position, her back to Alexandra.

'What the hell's going on? What's the matter?' demanded Dagur, emerging from his room and glaring at Alexandra as if he thought she'd been the one making the noise. 'And where's Benni?'

'Isn't he with you?'

'No. Who was that screaming?'

Alexandra nodded her head towards Klara.

'Klara, are you OK?' Dagur asked in a different, gentler voice.

She turned, with dreamlike slowness, and Alexandra got the shock of her life when she saw her face.

XII

'My wife and I . . .' Robert began, then stopped, before starting again. 'My wife and I were never able to have kids. And I don't have any kids of my own with anyone else. I didn't have an affair in Iceland – I've always been faithful to my wife. I'm sorry for your sake that you've had a wasted journey, but I'm not your father. If that was what you were going to ask?'

Hulda sighed. 'Yes. I . . . I'd been hoping it was you.' She tried not to let her disappointment show. It had been a wild-goose chase after all, but for a moment there she had really believed that this kind, friendly man might be her father. And it had struck her then just how much she needed a father. She felt she had been waiting a life-time for a chance to get to know him, hug him, make him proud of her . . .

'What made you think it might be me?'

'My mother . . . She never told my father about me; that she'd had a baby, that she'd got pregnant . . .' Hulda was forced to break off to get her breathing under control.

'I see,' Robert said, jumping in. 'What's her name? Is she still alive?'

'Anna. She was called Anna. No, she's dead.'

'My condolences,' said Robert. He sounded as if he meant it.

'I've been putting off this trip, because I didn't want to do it while she was alive. It's hard to explain, but I didn't feel it was right to interfere until after she'd gone. It was her business, her decision never to try and trace . . . my father.'

'I'm sorry you haven't found him,' he said kindly. 'Not yet, anyway. But why did you think it might be me?'

'She knew his name was Robert, she told me that much. And that he came from Georgia.'

'Yes, there were two of us Roberts,' he replied thoughtfully.

'I know. But I haven't managed to trace the other guy. So I was hoping you were the right one. It was nice to meet you, anyway.' She got up slowly.

'Likewise.' He smiled.

'You don't . . . you don't by any chance know what happened to him?'

He shook his head. 'I'm afraid not, though I remember him quite well. We stayed in touch for a long time through the veterans' association, but I haven't heard from him for at least ten years. I tell you what: I could call up a mutual friend if you like? It's the least I can do.'

He got to his feet.

'I'm just going to step into my office and see if I can get hold of him. Do help yourself to more pie in the meantime. It won't finish itself, and it won't do me any good to eat it all.'

XIII

Dagur

Dagur saw Alexandra recoil as Klara turned round. He didn't blame her. Klara's face was a mask of blind terror. She was ashen too – as if she'd seen a ghost – though Dagur didn't for a minute believe in ghosts. She must have had a bad nightmare and woken, screaming the place down . . . And yet the whole thing felt uncanny. Never in his life had he seen a look of such pure, unadulterated horror on anyone's face. It was as though she was out of her mind with fear.

'Klara, are you OK?' he asked gently, slowly walking over to her, careful to make no sudden movements. Her gaze was vacant; it was as if she couldn't see him or Alexandra. When Dagur tried to make eye contact, she seemed to stare right through him.

'What happened, sweetheart? Look, come and sit down. Alexandra's here too. We heard screaming.'

Klara didn't react.

'Was it you screaming? Did something happen?'

After a minute or two she obeyed him and rose to her feet, the colour gradually returning to her white cheeks.

Dagur glanced over his shoulder and saw that Alexandra was hanging back at a discreet distance. Almost as if she didn't want to risk seeing what Klara had seen . . .

'Is everything OK?' he asked, when he judged that Klara had had time to recover.

She shook her head.

'Was it a nightmare?'

Again, she shook her head. 'No.'

'What happened?'

She didn't answer and Dagur waited patiently. He could see that she needed a little more time to get over her shock before she could speak.

At last, in a low, eerily hollow voice, she said, 'I saw her. She was here.'

Dagur felt sick and a wave of dread passed through him. There was no question who she was talking about. Even though he knew it couldn't possibly be true, a creeping sense of doubt took hold of him.

'This is bullshit!' he exploded, unable to stop himself. 'Snap out of it right now!'

Feeling a hand on his shoulder, he shuddered again, uncontrollably. When he jerked his head round, he almost expected to see *her* standing there . . .

XIV

When Robert came back into the room a few minutes later, Hulda could tell from his expression that he had bad news.

'I'm sorry, dear, I'm sorry.'

'Is he . . . dead?' she asked, though she already knew the answer. Perhaps she'd always known. Sensed it.

Robert nodded. 'Yes, five years ago. I'm so sorry.'

She felt overwhelmed by sadness over the death of a man she'd never even met. It was confirmation, once and for all, that she would never meet her father.

She silently cursed herself for having been so pathetic, for not having made the effort to trace him a long time ago.

'I . . .' Robert hesitated. 'I remember him well. He was a very nice guy, a great guy, if that's any comfort.'

Hulda nodded, trying to put a brave face on it, but she knew she wasn't fooling anyone. She fought back the tears. Crying wasn't her style, not any more. She'd gone through so much that she wasn't about to start wasting tears on someone she'd never even known.

'Thanks,' she said huskily, after a moment.

'A straight-up guy, from what I remember. When we were army buddies together, I always knew he had my back.' Then he added, and Hulda got the feeling this was purely to comfort her: 'There's a look of him about you, I could swear it. Tell you what, I could try to get hold of some pictures of him and mail them to you.'

'What, er, what did he do after he left the army?'

'He became a teacher – taught for much of his life, I believe. But like I said, it's quite a while since I last heard from him. But he was a great guy,' he repeated.

His assurances were of no particular consolation to Hulda. After all, he would be unlikely to speak ill of the dead, especially in circumstances like these.

The upshot was that she was hardly any the wiser about her father, and maybe it would be as well to leave it at that. But her curiosity got the better of her. 'Was he married?'

'Yes, but his wife died before him, that much I do know. She died long before her time, maybe fifteen years ago. I don't know if he married again.'

'Did they have children?'

'Several, yes.'

It crossed Hulda's mind to look them up. Her half-siblings . . . Not on this trip, though; not straight away. After all, she hadn't come here looking for siblings, just hoping to find her father.

Pushing back her chair, she stood up. 'Thank you so much for taking the time to meet me and being so kind,' she said, trying to smile. 'You've got a beautiful home.'

'It was great to meet you, Hulda,' he said, getting to his feet as well. 'If there is anything more I can do for you, just say the word.'

She thought for a moment, then took herself by surprise as she asked: 'Do you happen to know . . . or would you be able to find out . . . where he's buried?'

'That should be . . . sure, I should be able to find out. I can make some calls, if you don't mind waiting.'

'Of course not. Thank you so much,' she said, ashamed of making this old man waste so much time on a complete stranger.

'It'll be more fun than sitting on the deck, solving the crossword puzzle,' he said as he left the room again.

XV

Alexandra

'Calm down, Dagur,' Alexandra said soothingly. When she'd laid a wary hand on his shoulder, he'd jerked around, staring at her, and she'd read genuine fear in his wide eyes. The whole incident had got her badly spooked: Klara had been like a zombie for a moment back there.

Incongruously, Alexandra found herself taking on the maternal role, as if comforting two little children. Of course, strictly speaking, her old friends were adults, but it occurred to her now that there was a sense in which they'd never grown up. In hindsight, she'd been lucky to move away, to put some distance between herself and the hell they'd gone through. But it was becoming uncomfortably clear that Dagur and Klara hadn't got over the trauma, not really. When put to the test, they were like children. Even Dagur, that reliable, level-headed boy, couldn't take the strain.

She felt an overwhelming urge to put her arms around him, hold him close, and knew that, if she were honest, she had probably never stopped being a little in love with him. In that sense, perhaps she herself hadn't completely moved on and left the past behind either. A mature woman, a wife and mother of two children, shouldn't be thinking like this, but she felt like a girl again, like a love-struck twenty-year-old.

Dagur turned and took her hands, very tenderly, and again she experienced that warm, pleasant frisson running through her body. 'Sorry, I just got a bad shock.' He looked deep into her eyes and she thought she saw a genuine spark there. Was it possible that he had been harbouring feelings for her as well all these years? Was it too late to do anything about it?

Of course it was too late. And yet . . .

'No problem.' She waited, willing him not to let go of her hands, but after a moment he released them and turned back to Klara.

'Are you serious?' he asked. 'About thinking you saw her? It must have been a nightmare.'

'I'm serious,' she said soberly, with an edge of defiance. 'I don't *think* I saw her. I know I did. She was here!'

Dagur shook his head.

'What did she want?' Alexandra asked, wondering if it might be more effective to play along.

'I don't know what she wanted.' Klara faltered, then went on: 'Just some kind of justice . . . Like always.'

Dagur turned sharply: 'Justice?'

Klara nodded.

'Do you mean . . . er . . . did *she* mean . . . that someone else was to blame . . . or are you saying . . . ?' He floundered, unable to form a coherent sentence.

Klara didn't answer.

'It was a nightmare, that's all,' Dagur repeated after a moment, having apparently got over his initial shock. 'Let's just relax for a bit.'

He suggested going downstairs, and the three of them took a seat at the old kitchen table. Alexandra, who was sitting across from Klara, tried to avoid looking at her directly, as her gaze was still weirdly vacant. Instead, she looked out of the window. The scenery had taken on a mysterious quality in the light summer night, the colours oddly intense, the sky a clear blue vault above the darker blue, island-dotted sea and the distant silhouette of Heimaklettur.

'Why don't I put on some tea?' Dagur suggested. 'Would you both like some?' Then, in a different tone: 'Where the hell's Benni got to?'

Alexandra nodded. 'Tea would be good.' She wouldn't be able to get back to sleep anyway, not after that hair-raising scream and all the talk of ghosts. 'Didn't you hear him get up?'

'I didn't hear him go out. He was asleep upstairs earlier. Always the same bloody idiot. Doing a disappearing act in the middle of the night! Where's he gone, for Christ's sake? There's nothing out there.'

Alexandra felt a fleeting regret for her lost night's sleep. Used to waking up at the crack of dawn on the farm – the kids were an alarm clock that no one could ignore – she had been looking forward to a lie-in this weekend. But she could hardly disappear upstairs now and leave Dagur alone with Klara – not with Benni missing as well. She was starting to feel a little anxious. Where could he be?

So she sat and waited patiently for Dagur to make the tea. Eventually, he brought over three mugs of a good strong brew.

After a few sips Klara seemed to revive. 'I'm sorry. I don't know what came over me,' she said at last, breaking the silence.

'No need to apologize,' said Dagur, his usual kindly self again. He always had an air of calm authority, Alexandra thought. As if he always had an answer ready, whatever the question. 'This is all right, isn't it?' he went on. 'Just like the old days. Sitting drinking together in the middle of the night, even if it's only tea this time.'

'Well, I think I'll go back to bed,' Klara said, following an awkward pause. 'I'm so sorry I woke you.'

'Seeing as it's nearly morning anyway, I think I'll go out and take a look around for Benni,' Dagur said, his voice suddenly cheerful, as if trying to dispel the last traces of the creepy atmosphere. 'The forecast's good. It should be a great day. Maybe we can try out the barbecue at lunchtime?'

Klara had got to her feet.

'Night, you guys.'

She disappeared back up the stairs.

Once Klara had gone, Alexandra said to Dagur: 'I'll come with you.'

'With me?'

'To find Benni – if that's OK?'

'Of course it is. We ought to explore the island anyway. Make the most of our time here.'

XVI

Dagur

The air was a little chilly outside, but that didn't detract from the beauty of their surroundings. He started walking without any real idea of where he was going. Benni had told him it would take three or four hours to explore the whole island.

Alexandra had asked if she could come with him, and suddenly it was like being transported ten years back in time. When they were teenagers she was forever trailing around after him, yet although she had been a pretty, sweet-natured girl, he hadn't been interested. Later she had disappeared, moved away with her family, and that had been that. But occasionally he had wondered if they might have got together in the end, had the circumstances been different.

'Do you have any idea where we're going?' she asked in a low voice, almost a whisper.

'Oh, maybe over to the cliffs, where Benni took us

yesterday. What do you reckon? Should we wander in that direction?'

They picked their way along the sheep paths, watching their footing in the rough grass as they had the previous day, but it was harder now, in the early-morning light. The sky arched blue overhead, yet in the low rays of the sun, hovering just below the horizon, the grass cast long blue shadows over the ground.

As he walked, Dagur found himself thinking about Klara. She'd said she was going back to bed, but he doubted she would get a wink of sleep. What on earth had happened to her? That chilling scream had shocked him awake and left him breathless with fright. For a confused moment, still in the clutch of his dreams, he'd thought the sound had emanated from beyond the grave, from his sister . . . A scream of terror at the moment of her death, perhaps. Then, as he woke up properly, common sense had taken over, telling him it couldn't possibly have been her and slowing the frantic pounding of his heart.

He hoped this business with Klara was a one-off and wouldn't be repeated. People could be unsettled by unfamiliar environments, he told himself; that's all it was.

He and Alexandra walked in silence most of the way, awed, perhaps, by the mysterious beauty of their surroundings, the blue silhouettes of the islands rising out of the silvery expanse of the sea. There wasn't a breath of wind. The whole place seemed to lie under a spell of perfect tranquillity.

Paradoxically, in the midst of this dramatic scenery,

the panoramic views of sea and sky, he was aware of a creeping sense of claustrophobia.

They picked their way through the tussocky grass towards the cliffs, Alexandra leading, a few paces ahead.

'What's that?' she said, stopping dead to point at something he couldn't see.

XVII

Hulda stood by the grave. The cemetery, shimmering in the heat, was nothing like the ones she was used to at home, with its statues of angels, exotic flowers and great trees draped with streamers of moss. Used to the openness of Iceland, she found the heavy canopy of branches a little oppressive.

Almost ten years since Dimma had died, yet she still visited her grave regularly. Eight years since Jón had passed away. And now here she was, standing by her father's grave.

There he lay, Robert, the man she had in a sense been searching for all her life, though when it came to actually doing anything about it, she'd messed up. She had found him all right, but too late. Five years too late.

Or perhaps it was her mother who had died five years too late. Of course, it was unfair to look at it like that but, given the choice, Hulda would probably rather have had a year, a month, even a day with her father, than those five years with her mother. A chance to find out what he had been like, to see him smile, talk, tell stories. To tell him stories in return. Tell him about Dimma. Her father had been a fantasy figure for her all these years, all these decades; the man her mother had fallen for, at least for one night. The man who had a share in Hulda, so to speak; in her good qualities and her flaws, her talents and her failings.

And at last here he was, under this stone. She had come all this way to visit him, and now she didn't know what to say.

'Hello, Dad,' she said at last, in Icelandic, not for a minute believing that her words would be heard but feeling compelled to say something.

She and her father. Robert and Hulda Hermannsdóttir. Or Hulda Róbertsdóttir. That would have had a better ring. As it was, her patronymic, Hermannsdóttir, was ambiguous in Icelandic, meaning either the daughter of Hermann, or the daughter of an unknown soldier. As such, it was a constant reminder that she'd never had a father. A constant reminder of her loss – if you could miss someone you'd never met.

'Hi, Dad,' she tried again. 'It's me, Hulda. Your daughter. You never even knew I existed, but here I am. Several years too late. I'm sorry about that. So sorry.'

XVIII

Alexandra

Benedikt was lying deathly still on the brown rocky out-crop below the overhang, uncomfortably close to the edge.

Alexandra froze and Dagur stood motionless beside her. Then she glanced at him and they both set off warily towards Benni. Instinct told her not to call out to him, on no account to startle him.

The closer they got, the more uneasy Alexandra became, filled again with a deep foreboding that they should never have come to this island. While they had every reason to celebrate the memory of their friend on the tenth anniversary of her death, perhaps it would have been better to do so privately, each in their own way. The tragic event still felt too raw, there was still too much unfinished business, although the case itself had been formally closed. In fact, it was extraordinary how resilient Dagur had been up until now. If anyone had been crushed by the weight of those memories, it should have been him but, miraculously, he had managed to keep going. Nevertheless, she had sensed his disquiet when Klara started raving on about ghosts. Her words seemed absurd now, out here in the soft morning air, where the events of the night felt so far away.

'Benni,' Dagur said, quietly but firmly.

Benedikt didn't stir.

'Benni,' he said again. 'What are you doing out here?'

Benedikt woke with a start and for a second Alexandra was terrified he'd roll over and fall off the cliff.

'Are you awake?' he asked, surprised. 'Both of you?'

Dagur repeated his question: 'What are you doing out here?'

'I couldn't sleep, so I decided to come here, to my favourite place on the island. It's not the first time I've been here at night, but I must have dropped off without realizing. The sea air, I suppose. It's such an incredible feeling to be able to get away from it all. As if time were standing still.' He smiled.

'Benni, something rather weird just happened,' Dagur said.

Alexandra hung back, reluctant to interrupt: Dagur had a much closer relationship with Benni.

'Klara woke us up,' Dagur continued. 'She had such a bad nightmare that she screamed the place down. She's gone back to bed, but Alexandra and I were too wide awake to sleep.'

Benni's gaze travelled from Dagur to Alexandra. As he studied her, she was sure he'd guessed right: she hadn't been 'wide awake', she'd just wanted an excuse to go on a walk with Dagur. And she hadn't wanted to be left alone with Klara either after what had happened.

XIX

Hulda was sitting in her office. It was two months since her trip to America and her life had long since slipped back into its dull routine.

She'd woken up with a headache. When her alarm went off, her body had begged her not to move just yet but to go on sleeping a bit longer. She'd felt groggy when she got out of bed and, although the feeling had faded as the day went on, it hadn't gone away completely. It was getting on for 5 p.m. now and she couldn't wait to tidy her desk and clock out. If she had put in long hours before Dimma died, she had almost buried herself in work afterwards. This year would be the tenth anniversary of her daughter's suicide at only thirteen. Eight years since Jón's heart had given out. Ever since then Hulda had been alone, working all day and often late into the evenings as well, spending her free time, whenever possible, in the mountains or in the wild Icelandic interior. Doing her best to forget.

Ten years, too, since she had lost out to Lýdur in the

contest for promotion. Though perhaps there had never been any contest; perhaps she'd never been in with a chance, despite being, in her opinion, the better detective and indubitably more experienced. In the police culture of the time, it simply hadn't been the custom for women to become senior inspectors. Since his 'big break', Lýdur's success had been assured and he had risen steadily through the ranks, obtaining all the promotions he put in for, whereas Hulda had been forced to fight every step of the way. Lýdur had now progressed so high up the food chain that he had taken over from old Snorri, which meant that he was now Hulda's boss. She, in contrast, had been promoted once in the same period and had only two people working under her. Although she wasn't yet fifty, she had a strong sense that this was as far as she was destined to go.

The most infuriating part was that Lýdur was actually a pretty damn competent detective. He had a knack for getting results and knew how to blow his own trumpet. All the same, Hulda had private reservations about his working methods: he was cunning and too slick a performer. When it came down to it, she didn't trust him.

Over the years, her own work had become increasingly specialized until now she was almost entirely occupied with violent crime, a category that included unexplained deaths, though the latter were comparatively rare in Iceland. She didn't need to be told that she was good at what she did. Possibly it was because she had the ability to dismiss everything else from her mind and give work her undivided attention. In truth, it was all she lived for. The house on Álftanes – beautiful in spite of the dark shadow that had lain across it – had disappeared with Jón, sold to pay off his debts, debts she'd never known he had, and these days Hulda lived alone in a poky flat in a typical Reykjavík *bakhús*, a small building set back from the road in a yard behind another house.

Yet again she was working the weekend shift. It was Saturday, and if she hadn't been on duty she would have seized the chance to take a trip out of town. Climb one of the numerous small peaks within reach of the capital; keep herself fit. She often went alone, but from time to time she would join a walking group, though she made little attempt to cultivate the acquaintances she made in this way. She'd been single for eight years and had become worryingly used to this state of affairs – stuck in her ways – to the point where she couldn't picture herself trying to form another relationship now.

She'd agreed to take an extra shift from Friday to Sunday because the money wouldn't go amiss and because CID were having difficulty finding staff to cover these summer weekends. Her colleagues, most of them men, were taken up with their families at this time of year, especially when the weather was good. Lýdur had asked her if she could 'help them out' this weekend, since they were short-staffed. Ever obliging, she had said yes. She didn't really resent the fact either, though the weather was stunning and she was feeling dizzy and headachy, for the simple reason that in her office, with her nose buried in a pile of documents, she could lose herself for a while. Forget Dimma, forget Jón.

It looked as though it was going to be a quiet weekend, which had its pros and cons. On the one hand, it meant there wasn't enough to distract her from brooding on the dark thoughts that tended to ambush her at quiet moments, but on the other maybe it was just as well, since she wasn't feeling her best.

The year hadn't been great so far. She was dreading the tenth anniversary of Dimma's suicide, and the death of her mother had affected her more than she'd expected. She had even taken a few days' leave from work, which was almost unheard of, to mourn the fact that she was now utterly alone.

XX

Alexandra

Evening was falling and, to Alexandra, the events of the night before seemed like a distant memory. No doubt the wine had something to do with that. They'd drunk a bottle of red with lunch, raising their glasses repeatedly to *her*, and after that it was as if a line had been drawn under the past, at least temporarily. As if they'd decided, without particularly discussing it, to enjoy themselves until Sunday, concentrating on the here and now, dismissing from their minds all thoughts of the past and of Klara's bizarre night terrors. Yes, the atmosphere had definitely become more cheerful.

Alexandra was sitting opposite Klara now at the kitchen table and had just topped up their glasses.

The boys were outside, tending to the barbecue. 'The boys'. Of course, they weren't teenagers any more, but she supposed they would always be 'the boys' to her. Some things never changed. They had promised to rustle up four steaks but were taking their time over it. No doubt they had stuff to talk about, as she and Klara did.

'You know, I think this trip was a good idea, after all,' Klara remarked.

'Yes, it's been great coming out here, and getting together with you guys again.'

'No . . . That wasn't actually what I meant,' Klara said, her voice sounding suddenly unaccountably flat. 'I suppose it was time to put things straight.'

'What are you talking about? Put what straight?'

'There are too many things that aren't being said, Alexandra; too many things that we've been keeping quiet about all these years. I think . . .'

Alexandra realized that Klara was rather the worse for wear; she was slurring her words and having trouble focusing. But then Klara had never been able to handle her drink.

'I think it's time the truth came out,' Klara concluded.

XXI

Benedikt

'How's your mum doing?' Benedikt asked as he stood by the barbecue, waiting for the coals to heat up. Supper would take a while to cook, but they weren't in any hurry. They had the whole island to themselves and it wasn't as if they had anywhere else to go. The plan was to have a lazy morning tomorrow, then radio Benni's uncle to pick them up in his boat and take them back to Heimaey in time to catch the ferry to the mainland.

Benedikt knew what sort of state Dagur's mother was in, although they rarely discussed it. The traumatic events of ten years ago had hit her harder than anyone else. Dagur had been bowed, not broken, but his mother had been unable to cope with all the shocks and the resulting stress and uncertainty. She'd been in a nursing home for several years now, and Dagur had told him once, in confessional mode, that she'd just given up. He'd confided that the doctors couldn't find anything physically wrong with her: she had simply turned her back on life and retreated into her shell.

'Mum . . .' Dagur paused to think. He was sitting on the decking, leaning back against the wall of the lodge. 'She's much the same, really. On good days she's receptive but more often than not she's sort of out of it, you know. I've never really understood what's wrong with her, but that's the way it is. You just have to accept it. What about your parents? How are they doing?'

'Oh, as bossy and difficult to please as ever. I thought I'd done what they wanted by studying engineering rather than going to art school but now they're nagging me to go into banking like you. To give up messing around with computers.' He gave an exasperated laugh.

'I'm sure you'd get on well at the bank, Benni. You're much cleverer than me. To be honest, though, I envy you your company. I mean, it's the future, isn't it? Everyone's predicting that IT's only going to get bigger and bigger. You'll end up making a packet.'

Benedikt shrugged. No doubt this was right, but it didn't appeal to him, not really. He felt he was stuck in the wrong job, with no way out, since he couldn't let his partners down. Given half a chance, though, he'd quit tomorrow and go to art school instead – for *her* sake. But he knew he'd never actually have the balls to do it.

'Well, I reckon these are done,' he said, avoiding Dagur's eye and focusing on the steaks sizzling on the barbecue.

After a brief silence Dagur said, almost under his breath: 'I'm going to move. Soon.'

'Move?'

Benedikt was astonished. He'd never pictured Dagur

anywhere but in the old maisonette in Kópavogur. He'd grown up there, it was his family home – not that he had much family left. To all intents and purposes, Dagur was alone in the world these days. The house must be far too big for him, as well as being haunted with bad memories.

'Yeah, I reckon it's time. What do you think?'

Benedikt wasn't used to such candour from Dagur. He wanted to ask how his mother had reacted but decided it would be better not to trespass on to that territory.

'About bloody time,' he said heartily instead. 'You should get yourself a smaller place near the town centre. Live a little. Are you going to sell up and buy somewhere else? Or rent?'

Dagur appeared to be thinking it over.

'Originally, I was planning to find a tenant for the house and rent myself a flat in town. Mum and I own the house outright, so it should balance out . . .' He trailed off and tilted his head back to gaze at the cloudless firmament. 'But I've changed my mind. I'm going to sell. Make a clean break with the past, with all the memories associated with the house. They're . . . it's just too much.' For a moment, Benedikt was afraid his friend was going to break down; his voice sounded oddly choked up.

'Good for you,' he said hurriedly, to cover the embarrassing moment. 'After all, it was their home, really – your mum and dad's. You need to find your own place, your own niche in life. Have you viewed any flats yet?'

'Yes, sure. A couple of little places in the west of town. It's an attractive area, and convenient for the bank, of course. It would mean I could walk to work.'

'Careful you don't get somewhere too small,' Benedikt said with a twinkle in his eye.

'Too small?'

'Make sure there's room for your girlfriend.'

'I don't have a girlfriend.'

'Not yet. But it won't be long before you do, when you're no longer rattling round in that gloomy place in Kópavogur. It's a ridiculous house for a bloke of twenty-nine!'

Dagur laughed.

'Too bad Alexandra's taken,' Benedikt remarked wickedly.

'What's that supposed to mean?'

'Oh, come on. She was always into you in the old days. Surely you must have noticed? Wake up, man.'

'What? . . . OK, maybe. But it's too late now.'

'Oh, I don't know – you've still got tonight. I promise not to cramp your style. Or you could slip outside together . . .'

Dagur pushed himself upright in a sudden movement.

'For Christ's sake . . . I'm not screwing a married woman.' His voice shook as if he'd been knocked off balance. 'Or maybe you just want to get rid of us so you and Klara can . . . you know, pick up where you left off, eh? Ten years on.'

With that he stormed back inside, and Benedikt was left standing by the barbecue, prey to unsettling memories.

XXII

Alexandra

It was past one in the morning when the party, if you could call it a party, broke up. They'd been sitting in the living room òf the lodge, talking about the future, for once. The gloom that had descended earlier had gradually lifted, though the atmosphere between Benedikt and Dagur remained rather fraught, despite their efforts to hide the fact. They'd all tried to have a good time, like they used to back in the day, but of course it was hard when one of the old gang was missing.

Nevertheless, Alexandra felt as if they had managed to recapture the mood of the past, for a brief moment, a single evening. Up to now their interaction had been overshadowed by a tangible sense of how much remained unspoken between them, how much unfinished business there was.

Of course, the alcohol had played its part. Alexandra had started feeling pleasantly light-headed hours ago; she felt content to be sitting here with her old friends, so far removed from her normal life, drinking without a care in the world.

'I'm going up,' Dagur announced eventually. He sounded tired, though he was stone-cold sober. 'It's been fun, guys.'

'You can say that again,' said Klara.

'What do you make of Ellidaey then?' Benedikt asked, lying back on the sofa. 'Like being in another world, isn't it? No one to see, no one to know. Anything could happen. Nothing but us and nature. Us and the sea. We couldn't even leave if we wanted to, not straight away. It takes hours to call out a boat . . . This evening, tonight, we belong to the island.' He broke off a little hazily, then added: 'Nothing that happens here will go any further . . .'

He shot Alexandra a glance and, immediately grasping what he was hinting at, she flushed scarlet and avoided his eye, looking anywhere but at Dagur.

'Nobody knows anything,' Klara said pensively. 'That's the problem.'

Dagur paused on the stair ladder, as if waiting for her to go on, but her words were followed by a heavy silence. With a sudden shiver, Alexandra felt the shadow passing over them again.

She got to her feet, hoping the flush had left her cheeks. 'It's been fun, but I'm shattered too.'

It was true. She *was* tired, but what she longed for more than anything else was a night with Dagur. She didn't dare make the first move but decided that instead of going straight to sleep she would lie awake for a while and see what happened.

'I can't go to bed yet,' Klara said, more to herself than to the others. 'It seems such a waste of a beautiful evening . . . night, I mean. I'm still wide awake. We haven't even finished the booze.'

'I'll sit up with you for a bit,' said Benedikt, though he looked more in need of sleep than any of them. 'Just for a few minutes . . .' He broke off to yawn. 'Then you can have the island to yourself, Klara, dear.'

Alexandra woke with a gasp. At first she thought she'd been disturbed by Klara's blood-curdling screams again, then she realized that this time it must have been a dream.

She hadn't a clue what time it was or how long she'd been asleep. These light nights were so disorientating. But when she checked her watch, she saw to her surprise that it was morning. Half past eight. Sitting up, she stretched and looked around.

Klara was nowhere to be seen. Surely she couldn't still be downstairs. Still drinking?

Alexandra got up, unable to sleep any longer, in spite of her plans for a lie-in. She badly needed caffeine.

As she started down the ladder she heard someone moving about in the inner room where the boys were sleeping. Dagur appeared on the landing.

'What time is it?'

'Half past eight.'

'Damn, I could have done with more sleep.' He sounded tired.

'Do you know where Klara is?' Alexandra asked.

'Klara? Isn't she in with you?'

At that moment they heard Benni's protesting groan: 'Stop making all that racket, I'm trying to sleep.'

'No, she's not up here,' Alexandra said, ignoring Benedikt. Peering down into the living room, she called, 'Klara?' There was no answer.

'I don't think she's inside,' Alexandra said. 'But surely she can't have slept outside, can she?'

At this point Benedikt made an appearance. 'Bloody hell, now you've woken me up too. We can't have lost Klara?'

XXIII

Hulda had been half hoping that an interesting assign-
ment would land on her desk that Sunday morning.
Having nothing to work on but minor cases for days on
end didn't suit her at all. However, it seemed her luck was
in, since her shift began with a phone call from the Westman Islands.

'Inspector Hulda Hermannsdóttir.'

'Hello . . . We may need assistance from CID in connection with a fatal incident.'

'Don't you have any detectives at your end?'

'Our officer on duty isn't available at the moment. He's off
sick. I was told to try and get someone from the mainland.'

'A fatal incident? Are we talking about a crime?' asked
Hulda, thinking about the Westman Islands, where several
years ago she had gone on a walking tour that involved
climbing all the peaks on Heimaey, the main island, in a
single day. She had given up on the last, having completely run out of steam after scaling Heimaklettur, the
steep-sided rock that rose nearly 300 metres above the

port. Despite this failure, she had happy memories of the trip – and happy memories were always welcome – as it had been a brilliantly sunny day, warm and still, and she'd been in good company, a small group of walkers from here and there. One of the men, who was around Hulda's age, had stuck close to her and tried to strike up a conversation, apparently keen to get to know her better, but she hadn't given him the chance. She wasn't ready for anything like that.

'Hmm . . . I couldn't say, but I've got a bad feeling about it. Some youngsters on a weekend jaunt. I'm guessing there was booze involved. Have you got anyone available to come over today?'

Hulda took a moment to think about it. She could send one of the team; there was no reason for her to go. Then again, she had nothing better to do and she was feeling brighter today than she had been yesterday. Perhaps the trip would turn out to be a waste of time, but anything would be better than another stultifying day in the office.

'Of course,' she replied, making up her mind. 'I'll come.'

There was a silence on the other end, then the policeman from the Westman Islands said respectfully, 'You mean you're coming yourself? There's really no need . . . not as things stand. All we need is one of your people to sail out there with us and take a look at the situation.'

Hulda couldn't help feeling rather flattered. Although she had a couple of officers under her command, her title of inspector sounded rather grander than it really was. No one would have addressed her with that deferential note here at the Reykjavík office.

'Nevertheless, I think I'll come myself. It would be good to get out of the office.' Then, remembering belatedly that he'd said 'sail out there with us', she asked, 'Where do we need to sail to? Can't I just hop on a plane to Heimaey?'

'No, sorry . . . well, yes, I mean you can fly to Heimaey but after that we'll need to take a boat out to Ellidaey.'

Ellidaey? The name conjured up images of a craggy green island with a lone white house on it, seen no doubt in some newspaper, TV documentary or tourist brochure. She'd certainly never been there herself.

'Yes, it's one of the biggest islands in the archipelago, north-east of Heimaey. It's quite famous, because of the house.'

'And we'd need to take a boat out there? Isn't that a bit of a palaver? Can't we use a helicopter?'

'Well, there's no landing stage, but there are several places where you can bring a boat right in to shore. It's not that inaccessible, but it's probably not for everyone . . . At least, not for anyone who's scared of heights.'

And then the suspicion crept up on Hulda that perhaps his reaction hadn't been prompted by respect for her as a senior officer from Reykjavík but simply by a reluctance to take a woman out to the island.

'That won't be an issue,' she said crisply.

XXIV

Hulda could feel herself getting increasingly irritated over how long the journey was taking. If something suspicious had happened on the island, those involved would have had ample time to destroy any evidence.

According to the information she'd been given, the group were in their late twenties or early thirties, and one of them, Benedikt, had some link to the island.

The police – Hulda, accompanied by two local officers from the Westman Islands and a forensic technician – were ferried out to Ellidaey by a man called Sigurdur, who had taken the group of friends over there on Friday. He didn't speak much on the way, and it was clear that the news had hit him hard. All Hulda heard him say, more to himself than to anyone else, was: 'Those bloody kids, I warned them to be careful. You have to watch what you're doing out there.'

As they chugged with frustrating slowness over the gentle waves, the small boat dwarfed by the cliffs of first Heimaey, then Bjarnarey, Hulda reflected on the unexpected turn that her Sunday, which had begun so unpromisingly, had now taken. It was looking increasingly unlikely that she would make it home this evening. At times like this she often thought back to the days when, if she had to work late, she'd have rung home to tell Dimma or Jón that she wouldn't be back for supper, or back at all that night. Even now, after all these years, she still experienced that nagging feeling that there was someone she ought to call.

Ellidaey appeared ahead, looking just like the pictures she'd seen; the single white speck shining amidst the green pasture gradually resolving itself into a house. Behind it the grassy slope reared up like the crest of a wave. As they drew closer, the black cliffs with their splashes of white bird droppings didn't look as if they offered the visitor any way up from the sea.

'Not for anyone who's scared of heights', the policeman had said on the phone, and as she clambered over the boulders on the shore, then slogged up the steep, grassy path beside the cliff, she acknowledged the truth of this.

For an experienced climber like her, the ascent naturally presented no problem. What left her momentarily speechless was the view from the top – the volcanic peaks of the islands jutting out of the vast, flat expanse of the sea, the Eyjafjallajökull glacier hovering white above a line of dark slopes on the mainland – but there was no time to linger and enjoy it. Speed was of the essence. She followed her colleagues through the tall, rough grass; the silence was all-encompassing, overwhelming. Then the building came into view, two buildings in fact, some way apart, one small, the other larger. They headed for the larger one, which turned out to be quite an impressive house. As Hulda drew closer she was hit by a wave of something approaching loneliness. While she could understand why people would be tempted by the idea of spending a weekend on the island, she doubted she could handle it herself; the isolation would get to her. Although she was the outdoorsy type and loved being in the mountains, this place was too cut off, even though, as the crow flew, it wasn't that far from Heimaey.

The older, more senior of the local policemen halted and turned to address her. 'Do you want to do the talking, Hulda? If they've got something to hide, they'll probably be more intimidated by a detective from Reykjavík CID.'

Hulda nodded, slightly taken aback by his request. She'd have expected the local police to want to run the show, at least to start off with.

The hunting lodge was surrounded by a fence, which, the officer explained, was to keep out the sheep. It was news to Hulda that there were sheep here, as they hadn't spotted any on their way across the island, but he assured her that they were there. 'And so many birds you can't even guess at their number. They're the main draw for visitors, apparently. I heard there were some ornithologists here the other day, tagging swallows.'

Hulda didn't answer, too busy focusing her mind before knocking on the door. She wanted to savour the tranquillity, the unique sense of isolation, for a few more seconds before embarking on the grim task of establishing what had happened here.

Finally, she knocked lightly, then, without waiting for a response, opened the door.

Inside, two young men were sitting at an old kitchen table, hunched over cups of coffee. Neither stood up to greet the police.

'Hello,' Hulda said quietly. She was working on the assumption that what they were dealing with here was an accident, or, failing that, a suicide. She was reluctant to believe that a murder had been committed, though nothing could be ruled out. In a situation like this her first reaction was always to be considerate to the people involved.

After a brief silence, one of the men rose to his feet. He was tall and very thin but athletic looking, with one of those brutally short haircuts that Hulda found so off-putting. She supposed it was the fashion these days but, if so, she didn't think much of it. When she was their age, men had worn their hair long, often their beards too, and that's the way she liked them.

She went over, holding out her hand.

'Hello, I'm Hulda. From CID,' she said calmly, without drama. 'We were informed that one of your party had died.'

The young man nodded dumbly; perhaps he was trying to pull himself together.

'Hello,' he croaked at last, taking her hand, then cleared his throat and tried again: 'Hello, I'm Dagur, Dagur Veturlidason.'

'Dagur, could you fill me in briefly on what happened?'

'Well . . . the thing is . . . she just went over the cliff, on the other side of the island . . . I don't know what happened, whether she jumped or fell or . . .'

'When was this?'

'Last night, I think. I mean, it must have been last night. She was alive yesterday evening, but then . . . she must have fallen. There's no way of getting down to her but we could see her body at the bottom . . . It's horrible, she's just lying there, not moving. There's no way she could have survived that fall.' Dagur gestured at his companion, who was sitting at the table as if his mind was miles away. 'Benni, here, ran back to the house to radio his uncle on Heimaey – it's the only way of communicating with the outside world.'

Hulda nodded. Dagur's words came out in a rush, tumbling over themselves. His distress was obvious.

She turned to the young man he'd called Benni. 'Are you Benedikt?'

He nodded, standing up as well.

'Yes.' They were both equally tall and quite good-looking, but this one had a noticeably fuller head of hair. Beneath the springy mane, his eyes were hard.

'Can you confirm that what your friend just said is correct, Benedikt?' Hulda asked in a slow, measured voice.

He nodded again.

'We'll need you to show us the way,' Hulda said. Her colleagues from the local police were still hanging back. 'I was told there were four of you?'

'That's right,' said Benedikt, who gave the impression of being more composed than Dagur, as if he were better equipped to cope in a crisis. 'She's upstairs – there's a sleeping loft. She . . . couldn't cope and had to lie down.' He added in a low voice: 'She went completely to pieces.'

'We'll talk to her later. I'm afraid it can't be avoided,' said Hulda. She was beginning to feel uneasy. Perhaps it was her intuition telling her that something was wrong; that something untoward had happened. But that might just be the effect this remote place was having on her. 'And her name is?'

'Alexandra.'

'Alexandra,' Hulda repeated. 'And the dead woman was called Klara. Am I right?'

There was a pause before the reply came, as if by answering the question the friends were admitting to themselves for the first time that their friend was really dead.

'Yes,' Benedikt said at last, in an undertone. 'Her name is . . . was Klara. Klara Jónsdóttir.'

'Would you show me where you found her, please?'

XXV

'It's called Háubæli,' Benedikt said, showing Hulda the
spot at the top of the cliff, hollowed out by erosion, from
which it seemed the woman had fallen. Hulda shivered
and felt her knees grow weak at the thought. The ledge
was designed for birds, not people; the drop was so sheer
you couldn't even see the bottom. Getting down on her
hands and knees on the rough, eroded rock, she eased herself forwards to peer over the edge, sucking in her breath,
and snatched a glimpse far below of the pale shape of the
girl's body against the dark rocks. Head spinning, she withdrew to the safety of the overhang and got to her feet again.
The two local officers were conferring about how best to
reach the body from the sea. Better leave the practical side
for them to solve while she concentrated on establishing
how the girl had ended up there in the first place.

'What possible reason could Klara have had for coming out here?' she asked.

'I . . .' Benedikt hesitated, then went on: 'I showed them
this spot on the first day. It's my favourite place.'

'Did all three of them come here with you?'

He nodded. 'Yes, and then I came back by myself during the night – Friday night, that is. I wanted to be alone for a while, to unwind, and ended up falling asleep out here. They found me – Dagur and Alexandra, I mean – in the morning.'

'So every member of your party would have known how to find this place?'

'Yes.'

Hulda found herself hoping fervently that none of these kids would turn out to be implicated in the girl's death. Of course, she mustn't let her judgement be clouded by personal sentiment, but she liked these two young men, on first impressions at least. She couldn't help thinking that Dimma would have been twenty-three this year – probably quite a bit younger than these boys, but still. Unlike them, she hadn't belonged to any particular gang at the time of her death – her suicide – because by then she'd isolated herself from her friends and classmates. She had only been thirteen. Why the hell hadn't Hulda realized sooner, seen the signs piling up and intervened?

Oh God, why did everything have to remind her of Dimma? She must snap out of it, try to banish these thoughts to the back of her mind, though she knew they wouldn't go far. They'd return with a vengeance the moment her head touched the pillow that evening.

At least this incident could probably be wrapped up quickly. The odds were that the poor girl had lost her footing and fallen – an accident, in other words. No doubt alcohol had been partly to blame.

'Had you been drinking?' Hulda asked aloud, beckoning to Benedikt to accompany her back to the house.

He hesitated, as if he suspected Hulda of trying to lead him into a trap, then answered: 'Yes, there's no point denying it, but no one was seriously drunk. We know how to have a good time without getting wasted.'

'What about Klara? Was she drunk last night?'

'Yes. That is, she'd had a bit to drink . . . but I don't understand how it could have happened. After all, it's not like it's even properly dark at night, not at this time of year. She didn't go to bed at the same time as the rest of us, she wanted to stay up a bit longer. Then . . . then she . . . I'm guessing she must have gone out for a walk to enjoy the peace and quiet. It's an incredible feeling to be out here on a light summer's night. All I can think of is that she must have gone too near the edge and misjudged it – lost her balance because she'd been drinking . . . It's the only explanation.' More quietly, he repeated: 'The only possible explanation.' As if he was trying to convince himself. Or Hulda.

When they got back to the lodge, Alexandra, the girl who'd been asleep upstairs, had appeared. She was standing in the corner, head drooping, and didn't even look up when they came in, but Hulda could see that she was small and slim, with raven hair.

'I expect you're keen to leave here as soon as possible,' Hulda said, addressing the three of them, 'and I can assure you that the same applies to me. There's been a tragic incident, but when something like this happens we need to try and piece together the circumstances that led to it, and that requires cooperation. I haven't come here looking for someone to blame,' she continued, not entirely honestly. 'So far, everything suggests that your friend, Klara, slipped and fell to her death. A terrible accident. But in cases of unexpected death, I'm afraid there always has to be an inquiry. I hope you understand?'

She scanned their faces.

Benedikt had sat down in the same chair as before. Dagur didn't appear to have moved at all in the interim. They both met her eye and nodded without a word. Alexandra, on the other hand, didn't react at all.

'What made you come out here in the first place?' asked Hulda.

After a lengthy pause it was Benedikt who answered: 'My uncle's a member of the bird-hunting association that owns the lodge. He set it up for us. It was only meant to be a weekend trip. We were – we all used to be friends in our teens when we lived in Kópavogur.'

'And hopefully still are,' Hulda commented, watching their reactions closely.

'What – what do you mean?' He was taken aback. 'Oh, right, sure, of course. We're still friends. It's just that people go their separate ways, you know? We haven't met for ages, not all of us together, I mean.'

'So why now?' asked Hulda.

Another awkward silence. Benedikt glanced at Dagur, apparently waiting for him to reply, then his gaze shifted to Alexandra, but she remained perfectly still.

In the end it was Dagur who answered. 'Well . . . Why not?'

Hulda suspected that there had been some specific reason for their reunion, but perhaps she was reading too much into it. These young people had just undergone a shattering experience: you couldn't expect them to provide coherent answers to all her questions straight away. But she would have to interview each of them individually before leaving the island. If they did have something to hide, this would be her best chance of catching them out.

XXVI

In practice, it proved tricky to take a statement from each of them in private as the house was too small and there was nowhere that could function as a separate interview room. The only option was to go outside, so Hulda resorted to inviting Benedikt for a little walk. She decided that it would probably be most useful to talk to him first. As well as being more familiar with the island than the other two, he appeared to have his feelings better under control.

'I'd like you to describe for me briefly what happened yesterday evening, Benedikt,' she said. They were standing by the older hut, at a discreet distance from the main house. As she spoke, a puffin flew right overhead with a frantic whirring of wings, which certainly wasn't what she was used to when interviewing a suspect. This setting was as different as it was possible to imagine from the sterile interrogation rooms at the police station. There the walls echoed only with fear and gloom, whereas the current surroundings felt like a celebration of life, in spite of the grim event that had brought Hulda there.

'There's nothing much to tell. It was a perfectly normal evening . . . until . . . of course . . . until this morning. We had a barbecue, then sat around drinking beer and a bottle or two of wine. It's a long time since we've spent an evening together like that.'

'Did Klara say or do anything out of the ordinary? Did you have a fight?' Hulda asked, watching Benedikt. Then her gaze shifted beyond him to the view, the grassy humps and hollows, and beyond them a glimpse of blue sea. Staying here, far from civilization, would feel very liberating, she was sure, but the dread of being stuck here, of being cut off from the outside world, was making her feel claustrophobic.

'A fight? No, of course not,' said Benedikt, sounding surprised at the question. 'We're not in the habit of coming to blows when we meet up.'

'I didn't necessarily mean physically. Were there any tensions? Did you fall out?'

'No, we've known each other for fifteen years, longer . . . there are no tensions, we're friends. I can assure you that nothing happened between us yesterday evening that could explain Klara's death. It was just a horrible accident,' he finished, his voice suddenly thickening with distress. 'Absolutely horrible . . . You have to let us go home. Christ, do you have any idea what this is like for us? Do you think it's easy?'

Hulda didn't answer. She knew only too well that it wasn't easy, but what could she say that wouldn't sound empty and insincere? She could hardly start talking about her personal experience of sudden death.

'Well? Do you think it's easy?' Benedikt repeated angrily, revealing a new, harder side of himself. He was in danger of crossing the invisible line of what could be considered acceptable behaviour for a member of the public when talking to the police.

'We'll leave as soon as possible,' she assured him calmly.

'I may put a brave face on it – after all, I'm used to coping with stuff, but . . . you know . . . I'm worried about Dagur. I don't think he's as tough as he looks. And Alexandra . . . we've got to get her home. I don't think it's even really sunk in yet for her.'

'I'm well aware of the gravity of the situation, Benedikt,' Hulda replied firmly. 'And I never forget to consider the feelings of those who get caught up in situations like this, but I also have a duty to the victim. Let's not forget that a young woman has lost her life. We need to establish what happened.'

'What happened? Come on, it was an accident.' His voice trembled a little and, to Hulda, it seemed blindingly obvious that he was holding something back; that he thought differently but wasn't letting on.

'Was there nothing . . . nothing at all that could explain what happened?'

Benedikt shook his head.

'So you think she just walked out and had a fatal accident in the middle of the night?'

'She was quite drunk the last time I saw her. We'd all gone up to bed, but she wanted to stay downstairs a bit longer. I don't think she wanted to go up . . .' He broke off mid-sentence.

'Why didn't she want to go up?' Hulda asked, pouncing on this. 'Was she trying to avoid one of you?'

'What? No. God, no. Nothing like that. All I meant was . . .' He paused for a moment. 'All I meant was that she didn't want to go to bed straight away. Maybe she just wanted a nightcap to help her get to sleep. How should I know? I haven't had much contact with her in the last few years. All I know is that she's had a bit of a tough time. Money troubles. You know the sort of thing.'

Hulda certainly did. Life in the police involved endless haggling over pay and conditions, and she had far too big a mortgage on her little flat, which kept rising relentlessly with inflation.

'So what are you saying, Benedikt? That she might simply have given up? Thrown herself off the cliff?'

'Who knows?' he said, his voice more confident now. 'Maybe that's exactly what happened. But, as you can imagine, it's not a suggestion I want to make. I can hardly bear to think about it . . . that my friend, our friend, should have been so desperate that she – that she went out in the middle of the night and threw herself in the sea, deliberately, knowing what she was doing, while we were asleep nearby . . . I can't actually imagine anyone deliberately throwing themselves off that cliff. It's a horrific thought – horrible.'

Hulda had no answer to this. Before she could come up with anything, Benedikt asked, 'Have her parents been informed?'

At this she nodded. There was nothing more to be said.

Dagur was clearly devastated. Hulda surprised herself by having an impulse to give him a hug and tell him not to worry, that it would be all right, though she didn't know if this was true. He was only a boy, caught up in a deeply distressing situation.

She had escorted him a safe distance from the house, though in a different direction from the one she'd taken with Benedikt, closer to the sea. The horizon was almost unreal, endless, like in a dream. She stood still for a moment or two, listening to the muted booming of the waves far below, the wingbeats of the birds, and realized that, slowly but surely, the island was winning her over. It was a question of letting yourself slip into a different tempo from what you were used to.

At length, she broke the silence. 'How old are you?'

'Sorry?' He'd clearly been bracing himself for a different question. 'Twenty-nine . . . I'm twenty-nine.'

'Are you all the same age?'

'Yes, or thereabouts,' he said, the tremor again audible in his voice. 'The others are a year older, or were . . . or, you know what I mean.'

'Klara, Benedikt and Alexandra?'

'Yes.'

'Did you come here because of Benedikt?'

'Because of him? How do you mean?'

'Because he organized it? I imagine it's not easy arranging a visit to Ellidaey.'

'Oh, I see, yes, that's right . . .' A pause. 'Yes, because he fixed it for us.'

'Were you meeting up for Klara's sake?' It was a shot in the dark, but Hulda had nothing to lose at this stage.

Dagur seemed taken aback. 'Klara? No, how do you mean? No. I mean, sure, she'd been having a few problems, had trouble holding down a job and that sort of thing, granted. But that was none of our business. The trip wasn't arranged specifically for her benefit, if that's what you're asking. Definitely not.'

He sounded sincere and Hulda believed him.

'Do you know what happened last night?'

He shook his head.

'Can you hazard a guess?'

Dagur hesitated. 'No, we'd all gone to bed. Before Klara, I mean.'

'Do you know why she stayed up?'

'No, I've no idea.'

'Did you hear anyone moving about in the night?'

'No, I slept like a log. Didn't hear a thing,' he said emphatically.

'Did you all sleep upstairs?' Hulda had climbed up into the loft and ascertained that it contained two sleeping compartments, with more than enough room for four people; it could have accommodated far more.

'Yes, us boys in the room at the back, and the girls were in the one at the front, by the top of the ladder.'

'Wouldn't you have heard if someone had gone downstairs?'

'No,' he said. 'I . . . I'm a heavy sleeper.'

Hulda allowed a silence to develop, before continuing: 'What do you do, Dagur?'

'Me?' Again, he seemed thrown by her question.

'Yes, what do you do for a living? Do you work?'

'Oh, yes. I work for a bank.' He added, as if for emphasis: 'An investment bank.'

'An investment bank? What does that involve?'

'This and that ... I'm a stockbroker, I trade in securities.'

This surprised Hulda, as she wouldn't have pictured Dagur in a job like that. Probably because to her mind he seemed no more than a boy, far too young for that kind of work. Dealing in shares – presumably that meant handling large sums of money. Here, on this godforsaken island, he came across as so vulnerable and confused, not at all like Hulda's stereotypical image of stockbrokers as brash young men in sharp suits who exuded self-confidence.

Her thoughts flew involuntarily to her late husband, Jón. He'd been in investments, but Hulda had preferred not to know too much about it. In those days there were no investment banks in Iceland, just the old state-owned banks and mortgage companies. No doubt Jón would have become a stockbroker if he'd belonged to Dagur's generation. He certainly hadn't lacked the self-confidence.

'What about your friend, Benedikt? Is he a banker too?'

'God, no, he'd never go anywhere near a bank. He's ... um ... he runs an IT company.'

'An IT company? Computing, you mean? I may not be that old, but I must admit I've never really understood what IT involves.'

Dagur smiled. 'It's hugely popular with the banks. Everyone wants to own shares in an IT company nowadays.'

'Not me,' said Hulda under her breath. It would never have occurred to her to gamble her meagre life's savings on the stock market. After a moment, she added: 'And Alexandra?'

'She's a farmer.'

Hulda almost blurted out that this was an unusual job for a young woman, only to realize just in time that she was no better than the men who'd said the same of her when she first joined the police. 'Where?'

'What?'

'Where does she farm?'

'Out east,' Dagur replied. 'She's married with children. We don't stay in touch, not really.'

'And yet . . .' Hulda said, breaking off for a moment to study Dagur's reaction. 'And yet you all came out here, to the edge of the world, to spend the whole weekend together. Just the four of you.'

There was no answer. Dagur merely nodded awkwardly and stared out to sea.

'I have to say I find that a little strange, Dagur,' she said sternly, while trying not to lose sight of the fact that he'd just had a traumatic experience.

'Well . . . yes, I can see why you might . . .'

'And there was no special occasion? It wasn't a celebration of some kind?'

'No, absolutely not, nothing like that,' he said quickly.

'Do you know each other better than you're letting on?'

'What? No, we know each other well. I already told you that.'

'But you never meet up?'

'No, not any more. I suppose it would be more accurate to say we used to be close. But old friendships last.'

'Right,' said Hulda, though she wouldn't actually know. She'd made a few friends at primary school but never formed a particularly strong bond with them. In hindsight, she was sure that coming from a poor family had affected her chances of getting to know the other kids well. She and her mother had lived with her grandparents, all four of them crammed into a small flat, with never enough to go round. New clothes and nice toys were something other children had. Only later did she realize that her teachers' attitudes to her had also been influenced by her family circumstances. To make matters worse, her mother had worked all the hours of the day to put food on the table, which meant she hadn't been around much. Hulda had been much closer to her grandfather. By the time she started secondary school, convinced that she would never be popular, Hulda had made little attempt to get to know her classmates. She'd been guarded and withdrawn, making acquaintances but no real lasting friendships. The same was true of her time at college. As there hadn't been many girls there in those days, they'd tended to be a bit cliquey, and she was always the outsider. The girls still met up regularly and Hulda used to invite them round for coffee or the odd meal, but after she met Jón she had gradually lost contact with them. He'd had little time for her old classmates. He was a quiet man and not very keen on socializing, so they had gradually fallen out of the habit of inviting people round. It had been just the three of them alone together every evening and weekend: Hulda, Jón and Dimma. At first, Hulda had found their little family unit cosy. It wasn't until later that she realized something was wrong.

'When can we go home?' Dagur asked, abruptly dragging Hulda back to the present.

'Soon,' she replied.

'All the way home or . . . ?'

'We've missed the ferry for today so we'll have to sort out accommodation for you on Heimaey. We may need to take more detailed statements from you all.'

'Why? Isn't it clear what happened?'

'Let's hope so,' Hulda said, and she meant it.

XXVII

Alexandra appeared to be in no fit state for a conversation with the police but, however genuine Hulda's sympathy for her, the interview was unavoidable. It was vital to assess the initial reactions of all three friends so she could gauge whether the case warranted further investigation.

The two women sat down together in the lodge. Hulda had sent Benedikt and Dagur down to the boat, escorted by the local police.

'I just can't believe it,' the girl said for the third time in short succession. 'That she's dead.'

'Have you any idea how it happened?' Hulda asked.

'No . . .' Alexandra answered, but her voice wavered. 'Please, I need to make a quick call. I need to ring home.'

'There are no phones here.'

'What about the radio? Could I try—?'

'We'll go down to the boat in a minute. You'll have plenty of time to call once we're back on Heimaey with access to a phone.'

'Could we go now, at once?' Alexandra was breathing fast. 'Please?'

'Did you see anything last night?'

She shook her head.

'Hear anything?'

She shook her head again.

'What do you think happened?'

'I don't know!' Her voice rising, on the brink of hysteria, she repeated: 'I don't know! Look, I've got to get to a phone!'

'Won't be long now,' Hulda repeated calmly. She wondered if it would make sense to cut short the interview and pick it up again later, if necessary. Let Alexandra and the boys go home as soon as possible to recover from their shock. Although she had a feeling they weren't telling her the whole truth, she was still inclined to give them the benefit of the doubt. Maybe they'd had an argument with Klara and were feeling bad about it. But actively guilty of manslaughter or murder? No, she didn't believe it. 'News of the death hasn't got out yet,' Hulda stated with a confidence that wasn't entirely justified, 'and we'd rather keep it that way for now. There's no need for you to call home until we get to Heimaey.'

'But I need to talk to my little boys, to make sure everything's OK and that they're not worried.'

Either Alexandra had been so badly affected by last night's incident that she couldn't take in what Hulda was saying or this was a cunning ploy to avoid answering questions. It almost worked; Hulda was ready to give up.

Deciding at the last minute to change her tactics, she

abandoned the soft touch: 'What brought you all out here? What was the reason for your visit?' This time her voice was that of a police interrogator.

Alexandra flinched. 'What? We . . . well, we . . .' She faltered. 'Nothing. No special reason.'

'Did something happen here last night?' Hulda demanded, realizing, as soon as the words were out of her mouth, that the question was unfortunately phrased.

Alexandra shook her head yet again.

'Do you know what happened to your friend?' Hulda asked, raising her voice, confident that the others were well out of earshot by now. She and Alexandra were quite alone in the house; they had the island more or less to themselves.

But Alexandra remained stubbornly mute.

'Do you know what happened, Alexandra?' Hulda fixed the girl's gaze with her own, and then, as she had feared, Alexandra disintegrated.

Chest heaving, the girl pleaded, through uncontrollable sobs, 'Can I go? Please!'

Resigned, Hulda got to her feet. Their conversation was over – for the moment.

XXVIII

Hulda had lain wide awake in her bed at the guesthouse in the little town on Heimaey, waiting for sleep to come, but her old adversary, both longed for and dreaded in equal measure, had kept her waiting. While she desperately needed to catch up on her rest, worn out as she was by the day's travelling, all too often sleep only added to the strain, exhausting her with nightmares and memories that she would give anything to forget. Why could she never dream all night long about the natural beauty of Álftanes, the birdsong and the sea?

Yes, it had been a long day, much longer than expected. She'd planned to spend Sunday evening outdoors, maybe stroll into town to make the most of the midnight sun and balmy weather. But she didn't really mind, since work always took priority: it was the only thing that kept her going.

As always when she lay awake at night, her thoughts slipped into a familiar groove of brooding on the past or worrying about the future. This time it was the future that won out. Sooner or later she would have to face up to the fact that she would be fifty this year. The idea was hard to get used to. It was much easier to bury your head in the sand, preoccupy yourself with other people's problems, take on too many cases, work evenings and weekends. She had few hobbies; well, if she were honest, she only had one: walking in the mountains. And she still wasn't ready to start dating; she wouldn't even know how any more and, besides, there was no guarantee that she'd meet Mr Right. As for travel to exotic countries, that was nothing more than a pipedream, given the state of her finances.

Of course, she was still a long way off retirement, but she couldn't help worrying about it, with the milestone of her fiftieth birthday looming. She hadn't a clue what she was supposed to do with her time once she stopped working, and then there was the problem of money; the prospect of being stuck in her poky flat on a low, fixed pension. At present she did at least have the possibility of eking out her salary with overtime.

It was no good: sleep refused to come. Admitting defeat, Hulda got out of bed and went over to the window, where she gazed out into the sunny night at the forest of white masts rising against the distinctive rocky walls and green cap of the Heimaklettur rock. Instead of taking in the scene, her mind was preoccupied with the problem of the three young people . . . or four, rather; the dead girl, Klara, and her friends. While they plainly weren't telling Hulda the whole truth, that didn't necessarily mean they were guilty of manslaughter or worse. Hulda had learned the hard way that people could withhold information from the police for a variety of motives, not always sinister, and she could sympathize. You couldn't expect them to reveal all their secrets to a stranger, especially one who turned up in the middle of a highly distressing situation. But the investigation had to be completed.

Before Jón and Dimma died, Hulda used to be able to relax in the evenings by reading, taking refuge in the cosy world of trashy romances with their happy endings, as far from the depressing, messy reality of her job as could be imagined. How she missed falling asleep over a book. These days, she didn't have the patience to read for pleasure; she was too restless. The only time she could properly unwind was out in the wilderness. Then her mind would empty. Apart from that, her thoughts would return obsessively to Dimma and Jón. And she would blame herself for everything that had happened. The months leading up to Dimma's death preyed on her mind. How could she not have known . . . ?

She forced herself to stop thinking about the past and tried to focus on the case at hand. Those poor kids. She could tell from their reactions that they all felt a measure of responsibility for their friend's death. Perhaps they hadn't been there for Klara when she needed them; perhaps they'd treated her badly. Or perhaps they had no idea what they could have done differently, only that there must have been something. Some past decision that could have brought about a different outcome, a decision that wouldn't have led to Klara's shocking fate. Just like it had been with Dimma: the knowledge that her terrible fate could have been avoided.

Were those kids' guilty consciences of any interest to Hulda? Not really. Not unless one of them had, quite literally, pushed the girl over the edge.

Hulda got back into bed and closed her eyes. She had to get some sleep. As for the nightmares, she would just have to let them in.

XXIX

Hulda stopped off at her flat after a frustratingly slow journey home, first by ferry to the port of Thorlákshöfn on the south coast, then by car to Reykjavík. There was nothing more for her to do on Ellidaey or Heimaey. If the death turned out not to have been accidental, the case would be handed over to Reykjavík CID anyway, which meant it would land back on her desk.

She felt wiped out after her bad night at the guesthouse and was now kicking herself for having decided to make the trip in person instead of delegating it to one of her subordinates. Normally, she'd have used Sunday evening to recharge her batteries for the week ahead, but now Monday had crept up on her. Of course, she should have taken a nap, as no one would have noticed if she'd turned up to work an hour later, but it wasn't in her nature to shirk her duties. So she jumped in the shower, changed her clothes and set off for the office in her trusty green Skoda.

She got straight down to writing the report about the incident on Ellidaey to get the dreary task over with as soon as possible. She had informed her head of department before leaving for the Westman Islands and had his permission to charge the trip to expenses. He had urged her to go, as supportive as ever – on the surface, at least. 'Of course we're happy to lend our colleagues on the islands a hand. They'll be lucky to have you.' Hulda knew the praise was hollow.

She had travelled back on the same ferry as Benedikt, Dagur and Alexandra, but once on board they'd huddled together and kept their distance from her, apparently wanting nothing to do with the policewoman. Alexandra had spent much of her time gripping the rail, green with misery, and the boys had stayed protectively beside her. Hulda had made no attempt to approach them. She'd already asked the obvious questions and obtained enough material to write a thorough report, concluding that it had been a case of accidental death.

Now that her little adventure on Ellidaey was over, Hulda tried to settle back into her daily routine. Her days were almost indistinguishable one from another. This was how it had been ever since she'd made a clean break with her old life by selling the family house on Álftanes – actually, it had been repossessed by the bank – and buying herself a place of her own. To begin with, she had lived with her mother, then in a rented flat, while she was scraping together a tiny deposit, so little had Jón left on his death. Living with her mother had been an odd experience, to say the least. Though it had long been obvious that they weren't temperamentally suited, Hulda had seen this as an opportunity to become better acquainted.

Her mother had pulled out all the stops, doing her best to wrap her daughter in love and affection after Dimma and Jón died. At times, Hulda had felt she must be a bad person because she found herself unable to respond in kind, to accept her mother's solicitude or return it. Since she had carried on working long hours, the time she spent with her mother tended to be in the evenings and at weekends, when Hulda's greatest desire was for solitude, preferably up a mountain in the middle of nowhere. Her mother, on the other hand, had been convinced they could talk their way through the trauma, but Hulda knew it wouldn't work. She was doomed to live with the fallout.

In the end, she had moved out. The event had passed without drama. She had simply told her mother one day that she'd found herself a flat and thanked her for her hospitality. Her mother's reaction was politely friendly, no more. But then they never quarrelled; it was as if their feelings weren't strong enough. Hulda had settled into a small rented flat and, from then on, she'd had her leisure time to herself.

These days, she was at least living in a property of her own, paying interest instead of rent.

At work she was entrusted with fairly serious cases and had a high success rate. Her methods were not always conventional, but she got results. And although she didn't receive the praise she felt she deserved, her colleagues knew she was tough enough to handle difficult investigations.

More from a sense of duty than curiosity, she decided to look up the individuals involved in the Ellidaey incident in the records. The deceased, Klara, hadn't come to the attention of the police in any capacity, nor had her friend Alexandra. The two girls appeared to have a completely clean record. Benedikt, on the other hand, the young man with the IT company, had got into a fight in Kópavogur when he was fifteen. The report was brief and sketchy on the specifics, but it was clear that there had been no repercussions.

Dagur's name turned up as well.

In 1987, when he was nineteen, he had been reported for threatening behaviour towards a police officer, but no detail was provided and the matter had been taken no further. This was a little unusual in itself: as a rule, people weren't let off that lightly after threatening a member of the police. Still, there could be various explanations. Hulda was acquainted with the officer involved but saw no reason to dig any deeper into the long-ago fracas, since it could hardly be of any relevance now. If anything suspicious came to light in the course of the Ellidaey investigation, she could always get in touch with the officer in question. But at this stage she didn't feel it was any of her concern. Better let it lie.

XXX

Hulda was woken from a peaceful slumber by the ringing of her phone. She'd nodded off in the sitting room but the damned phone was in the hall, which meant she had to drag herself up from the comfy old armchair she'd inherited from her mother.

She half hoped it would stop ringing before she could pick up. After all, it was bound to be a sales call; no one ever rang her in the evening and it was nearly nine o'clock. She'd fallen asleep over the British wildlife documentary that had come on after the news. Since she couldn't afford a subscription to Channel 2, she had to make do with the offerings on the State Broadcasting Service.

Levering herself out of her chair with a groan, still dog-tired after the long day and the eventful weekend, she walked stiffly into the hall. She was conscious of being a bit slower these days. It took her longer to recover from any sort of physical effort, like hiking or her exercise class – or getting up out of a chair after nodding off.

'Hulda,' she answered, trying to sound alert.

'Hulda? Hello. Did I wake you?'

'What, no, of course not. Who is this?'

'Sæmundur.'

'Oh, Sæmundur, hello.' Sæmundur was around Hulda's age, or a couple of years younger, and worked in the lab at the University Hospital's Department of Pathology. Since he seemed to work all hours of the day and night, Hulda might have guessed the call was from him. She pictured him: a friendly, rather tubby figure who'd been bald for as long as she had known him, which was a decade at least.

'Sorry to ring so, er, late.'

'That's all right.' She sometimes got the suspicion Sæmundur was keen on her, though he'd never done anything about it. He was the eternal bachelor, good-natured and kind, but, alas, just not Hulda's type. 'Are you ringing about the girl on Ellidaey?' Some of Hulda's colleagues would have said 'the body' on Ellidaey, but she always tried to personalize the deceased, so as not to lose sight of the fact that a human life had been lost.

'Yes, that's right, I am.'

'You haven't finished the post-mortem already? That's good going.'

'No, we haven't got that far yet, I'm afraid, but you couldn't miss it – well, I couldn't. I noticed it at once and wanted to let you know. I've no idea how the investigation's progressing but I assume any evidence will help.'

Not for the first time, he wasn't making a lot of sense.

'Absolutely,' she said encouragingly. 'What was it you noticed?'

'Oh, right, yes, sorry – the marks on her throat.'

Hulda could feel her heart beating faster. 'Marks on her throat?'

'Yes, you know, where someone tried to throttle the deceased – before she died, that is. It looks pretty obvious to me.'

'You mean—?' Hulda was given no chance to finish.

'Yes, all the signs indicate that violence was involved. Does that fit in with your initial findings?'

Hulda was silent a moment before answering, 'Yes, more or less.' A white lie never hurt. 'Was that the cause of death?'

'I doubt it, given the severity of her head injuries. It was a long fall. Obviously I'm no detective, Hulda, and it's just speculation at this stage, but my initial impression is that there was a struggle and the attacker grabbed her round the neck and squeezed tight, cutting off her airways, after which she fell to her death. I can't tell you how it happened, but it seems fair to conclude that . . . er, that . . .'

'. . . that she was murdered?' Hulda finished.

'Exactly.'

XXXI

Hulda cursed herself for not having been more suspicious on the island. Her instinct had failed her in her hour of need, with the result that she had failed the poor girl. Perhaps she should have conducted the investigation differently, not let the three friends go straight home without grilling them harder. She couldn't decide what to do. It was getting on for ten in the evening and, although still tired, here she was behind the wheel of the Skoda. The whole thing could probably wait until morning but, after the news Sæmundur had given her, she felt an urgent need to act.

She had taken down the young people's details at the scene but had left the information at the office. Almost before she knew what she was doing she had reversed out of the tight parking space, squeezed past her neighbour's car and was on her way to the CID offices. The sky was clear and blue, the sun still relatively high above the horizon; you would never have guessed it was so late.

Once Hulda reached her desk, she sat there for a while, staring at the page of addresses and phone numbers.

Alexandra, Benedikt and Dagur. She tried to visualize the scene: could one of them really have killed Klara? Half strangled her, then pushed her off the cliff? None of them seemed to fit the role of murderer. In a country with a murder rate as low as Iceland's, this was going to cause a huge stir. She should probably have phoned her boss to keep him abreast of the situation, but that could wait until morning. The question now was whether she should try and use the time to question Klara's friends again. Pay them a surprise visit.

Hulda didn't need to think twice about who to tackle first; the answer was staring her in the face. Alexandra had been planning to spend the night with relatives in Kópavogur. Hulda had earmarked her as the most upset of the three and consequently the easiest touch. She had come close to going to pieces on the island. Of course, it was unfair to exploit her weakness, but the case had just become a lot more serious.

Alexandra's relatives in Kópavogur left Hulda in no doubt that she'd ruined their evening. They kicked up a fuss when she turned up on their doorstep, explained who she was and asked to speak to the young woman.

'She's asleep. It's all been a terrible shock. I don't see why you have to disturb her now,' said the middle-aged woman who had answered the door, her manner uncompromising. A thickset man was standing behind her, his gaze dodging Hulda's; presumably the husband. He nodded in vehement agreement while the woman was speaking. 'You'll just have to come back in the morning.'

Hulda wasn't in the habit of backing down in circumstances like this. 'It won't take long,' she persisted, undeterred. 'I'm afraid I need to sit down with her and go over the events of the weekend in more detail.'

'Why? Why her?' asked the woman, still not budging from the doorway. Her husband continued to nod along.

'As you're aware, a young woman has lost her life, and I need to speak to Alexandra and the two men who were with her on Ellidaey. In an investigation like this, we have to prioritize the interests of the deceased, even if it means inconveniencing innocent people' – she was careful to stress the word 'innocent'. 'Would you let me in, please?'

At this the woman relented and stepped aside, and her husband followed suit. When they showed Hulda into the sitting room, she asked if there was somewhere more private she could speak to Alexandra. It was obvious from the couple's expressions that they were disappointed at not being allowed to sit in on the interview, but in the end Hulda was shown into a small room that was a cross between a study and a sewing room. There she waited as the minutes ticked by.

Finally, Alexandra appeared in the doorway. Judging by the puffiness of her face, it was no lie that she'd been asleep. Hulda wouldn't be surprised if she had done a lot of crying that evening as well. Certainly, she didn't appear to have got over her initial shock and distress yet.

Having first made sure that the door was properly closed and Alexandra was sitting down, Hulda launched into her questions.

'I'm sorry to have to inform you, Alexandra, but all the evidence suggests your friend was murdered.'

Alexandra's reaction was immediate. The news left her visibly stunned, then she seemed to crumple, suddenly overwhelmed by grief, as if she were hearing the news of Klara's death for the first time. But, of course, it was possible to fake an emotional reaction like that, and Hulda didn't yet know the girl well enough to tell whether she'd be capable of putting on such a convincing act.

Hulda waited, and waited.

At last Alexandra broke the silence: 'It . . . no, that's impossible. Why? Why do you think that? Why would someone . . . have done a thing like that?' She shook her head, her voice rising hysterically: 'No, no, no!'

'The evidence points in that direction, I'm afraid.'

'Murdered? Killed? Seriously? What . . . what evidence?'

'I need you to tell me what happened that night, Alexandra. We have to get to the bottom of this together.'

'It . . . it . . . nothing happened.' She began to cry. 'Nothing.'

'It's time to stop covering things up, Alexandra. If she was murdered,' Hulda said, letting the word hang in the air for a moment, then repeated: 'If she was murdered . . .'

Alexandra nodded.

'. . . there are only three people who could have done it: you, Benedikt or Dagur.'

The girl looked away, wiping her eyes with the back of her hand.

'I know you didn't do it,' Hulda lied smoothly. 'So

which of the others do you think is the more likely killer, Benedikt or Dagur?'

Alexandra didn't answer.

'Have you any idea what could have been behind it? An old grudge, for example?'

'No, you don't understand . . .' Alexandra trailed off. 'It's impossible . . . None of us . . . neither Dagur nor Benni would ever . . . kill anyone. You don't know them. I just . . . I refuse to believe it.'

'Strictly speaking, I can't rule you out either, Alexandra. I'm sure you understand.'

'What do you mean? You just said . . . I . . . that you knew . . .'

'What I think is irrelevant. Of course, I don't believe you'd be capable of murdering your friend, but I can't eliminate you from the inquiry. You have to cooperate with me.'

'But . . . yes, of course, I just can't . . . I don't want . . .'

'What is it you don't want? To be a suspect in a murder inquiry?'

'God, no! Of course not.'

Tears started rolling down the young woman's face again.

'You need to pull yourself together and try to help me, Alexandra.'

'Yes . . . I know, I know,' she wailed between her sobs.

At that moment there was an angry knocking on the door and it opened to admit the woman who'd greeted Hulda, her face like thunder. 'That's enough! All I can hear is the poor girl sobbing her heart out. This is totally unacceptable. How dare you treat her like that? She's just lost her friend.'

Hulda responded sharply: 'I need a minute to finish taking her statement.'

'No, this stops right now or I'm ringing my brother-in-law, who's a solicitor. It's totally unacceptable.' She turned to Alexandra: 'Come here, dear. The woman's leaving.'

Alexandra shot a glance at Hulda, then, standing up, obeyed her aunt.

Hulda could tell from the girl's expression that she was concealing something. She was sure of it.

XXXII

Yes, it was the right place: Dagur's name was the only one on the bell, but Hulda was a little surprised to find such a young man living alone in a large maisonette like this. After ringing the bell and waiting for a minute, she knocked on the door, first quietly, then louder, but got no response. Dagur appeared to be out. Hulda made one last attempt, keeping her finger pressed on the bell for a long time. No answer. She would have to drop by again later tonight or first thing in the morning.

Benedikt turned out to live in a much more conventional place for a thirty-year-old bachelor, a small basement flat in the town centre.

The flat was in a traditional wooden house painted blue and white and was entered from the rear, via a garden that was rank with weeds. Unable to see a bell anywhere, Hulda banged on the door.

She heard a noise inside, then the door opened and

Benedikt appeared in the gap. He was visibly startled when he saw who it was.

'Good evening, Benedikt.'

'What, oh, hello . . . Hang on, were we supposed to be meeting again?'

'Can I come in?'

He hesitated a moment. 'Actually, I'm not alone, but . . . I suppose . . .'

'Thanks.' She stepped inside without asking again. 'We need to have a word.'

The moment she entered she caught sight of Dagur standing in the middle of the living room and got the impression she had walked straight into the middle of a fight or a quarrel. The air was thrumming.

'Hi,' said Dagur in a low voice, dropping his eyes to the parquet floor.

The room was minimally furnished, containing only a worn leather sofa, a television and shelves full of videos. No books, no paintings on the walls and only a naked light bulb hanging from the ceiling. Hulda noticed that there were no refreshments on the table either, no drinks or snacks, a detail that had probably helped alert her to the fact that Dagur was not here on a social call.

'Hello, Dagur,' she said. 'I've just come from your place in Kópavogur.'

He looked up again, his face registering surprise: 'Were you looking for me?'

'Yes, I need to talk to you both.' After a brief silence, she added: 'I wasn't expecting to find you here, Dagur.'

'What, oh, no, I . . . er . . .' He looked embarrassed,

unnaturally so, Hulda thought. There shouldn't be any difficulty in explaining why he was visiting a friend, yet for some reason Dagur was lost for words. Yes, there was definitely something more going on here than met the eye.

Given the choice, she would rather have spoken to the young men separately, but in the circumstances that would be difficult.

'Sit down,' she said firmly; 'this won't take long,' and, obeying her, they both plumped down side by side on the sofa. Hulda fetched a stool from the small kitchen that opened off the living room and perched on it, facing them.

She studied them both for a while, cranking up the tension, making them sweat a little. Their discomfort was plain to see.

'Your friend,' Hulda began. 'Your friend, Klara, appears not to have fallen off the cliff by accident.'

'What do you mean?' Benedikt asked sharply.

'She was attacked,' Hulda replied.

'Attacked?' Dagur sounded incredulous.

'What are you implying?' Benedikt asked. 'That someone killed her?'

Hulda nodded. 'It certainly looks like it. And that's the assumption we're working on for now,' she continued, deliberately giving the impression that she wasn't alone in her suspicions, that she had the whole of CID behind her.

'You're working on the assumption . . . that she was killed?' Benedikt sounded both shocked and angry. 'For Christ's sake, you're not insinuating that either of us – or Alexandra – could have killed her?'

'Was there anyone else on the island?' Hulda enquired in a matter-of-fact voice.

It was Dagur who replied: 'No. No, there wasn't.'

'Then there's no one else in the picture, is there?'

Benedikt shook his head.

'Is it possible that someone else could have come to the island without your knowledge?'

'Hardly. Though I suppose it's not totally out of the question.'

'Would you have heard if a boat had arrived in the night, for example?'

'No, probably not.'

'So for the moment that leaves us with no alternative but to focus on you three,' Hulda said. 'Unless evidence to the contrary comes to light.'

'This is bullshit,' said Dagur. 'You can't seriously believe that . . . that we murdered our friend?'

'You've got to be joking,' chimed in Benedikt.

'I wish I were,' Hulda said, her expression severe. 'Look, it's time you told me the truth. What happened that night?'

Dagur flicked a glance at Benedikt, then answered, 'For crying out loud, what more do you want us to tell you? We don't know what happened. Klara didn't come up to bed at the same time as the rest of us.' He stopped, getting a grip on himself, then added: 'Anyway, what makes you think someone . . . killed her?'

'I'm not at liberty to tell you that, not at present.'

Benedikt shot to his feet. 'You can't expect us to answer questions about something that's not . . . I mean, something you don't have a shred of evidence for. You're just trying to trap us. Trying to frame us for murder when all that happened was that our friend either slipped and fell . . . or threw herself over the cliff.'

'Surely we have a right to have a lawyer present?' Dagur said unexpectedly.

Hulda smiled. 'That's entirely up to you. Let's just calm down a minute. No one's under arrest, no one's a suspect . . . not officially. We're just having a chat, but, like I said, it's up to you. We'll see tomorrow morning whether I need to summon you formally for questioning at the station. It's within your rights to bring a lawyer with you then, if you like.'

Benedikt stood there, dithering. Dagur sat tight.

'Anyway, what exactly are you doing round here, Dagur?' Hulda asked, fixing her gaze on the young man on the sofa.

'Sorry?' The question caught him by surprise.

'And don't lie to me that it was a social call,' she added sharply.

Dagur just sat there without saying anything.

'Were you two making sure your stories matched?' She shifted her gaze back to Benedikt.

He shook his head violently, seeming at last to be genuinely worried about the turn the conversation had taken rather than simply annoyed and angry at the way Hulda had walked in unannounced and started casting accusations.

'Absolutely not,' he said. 'No way.'

'Dagur?'

'What? God, no. Nothing like that. You've got it all wrong. We don't need to make sure our stories match. Honestly.'

She believed them, almost. Yes, perhaps they were telling the truth. But she still didn't entirely trust them.

She got to her feet.

'In that case, what *are* you doing here, Dagur?'

He thought, for longer than necessary. 'Our friend just died,' he said at last, 'almost under our noses. I couldn't face being alone, and I didn't know who else to talk to apart from Benni. Alexandra and I aren't that close, but me and Benni have always been good mates. We've never kept any secrets from each other . . .'

Hulda had the feeling from Dagur's tone that this last remark was charged with a peculiar significance, that it concealed some deeper meaning that she had every intention of bringing to light.

XXXIII

Hulda had instructed the three young people not to leave town until further notice. Neither Benedikt nor Dagur had raised any objections, but Alexandra had protested that she needed to go back east to her family. Eventually, however, she had been persuaded to wait another night or two.

Hulda's next step, the following morning, was to go and see Thorvardur, the policeman who had taken Dagur's statement a decade ago when he had been cautioned for threatening a police officer. Thorvardur was in his mid-thirties, honest, down to earth and easy to talk to.

Having requested a meeting with him, Hulda was now sitting in his office.

'So, what can I do for you?' he asked, his smile genuine.

'This is probably a waste of time,' she said, 'but I found an old report dating back to 1987, relating to a minor incident you reported.'

'Oh, right, 1987, hmm. I'd have been just out of training school then. I joined the police in '86.'

She handed over a copy of the report on Dagur.

'I don't suppose for one minute that you'll remember it . . .'

'Hmm, let's see.' He skimmed the report.

'Ah . . . hang on, yes, 1987 – though I'm not absolutely sure.' He continued to peer at the report. 'Let's see. How old was he? Only nineteen. Is he a repeat offender or something?'

Hulda shook her head. 'No, just an ordinary, respectable kid, as far as I can tell. This is the only time he crops up in the records, his only offence.'

'Dagur . . . Dagur Veturlidason . . . ?' A light bulb seemed to go on in Thorvardur's head: 'Ah, yes, of course. Dagur Veturlidason, of course. Sorry, I didn't immediately twig. You should have told me the context, Hulda.' He smiled at her.

'The context?'

'Yes, wasn't it in connection with his father? Why are you looking into that now?'

'His father? What did he do?'

'Veturlidi Dagsson, don't you remember him?'

Although the name was vaguely familiar, Hulda had to admit she couldn't place it.

'He killed his daughter, remember?'

And then Hulda remembered all right. She hadn't been involved in the investigation at the time, but the events had been headline news, so no one could have failed to be aware of them. An absolutely sickening case, in which an outwardly respectable accountant from Kópavogur was accused of killing his own daughter at their summer house in an isolated spot in the West Fjords. Hulda couldn't remember the specifics, since she'd only followed the investigation via the news and from gossip overheard in the corridors of the police station. The man had committed suicide in custody before the verdict was announced. What did stick in her memory, however, was that this was the case that had cemented Lýdur's success. There had also been indications of an underlying history of abuse, and that felt rather too close to home for Hulda, although she hadn't realized it at the time.

Come to think of it, the fact that the accountant lived in Kópavogur would fit: the maisonette that was a couple of sizes too big for Dagur must be the old family home. He appeared to be living there alone nowadays, though. Which begged the question: what had become of his mother?

'God,' Hulda breathed, more to herself than Thorvardur. 'Are you saying Dagur's his son?'

'Didn't you know?'

'No, I hadn't . . . put two and two together,' she said.

'Then why are you looking into it? Surely it's ancient history – the fact the boy kicked up a bit of a fuss at the time.'

'You remember, then?'

'Yes, I felt sorry for him. He was always coming down to the station, raging about his father's arrest. He refused to believe he was guilty. Mostly, he just demanded to see Lýdur, but sometimes he'd start ranting and yelling at the rest of us. We . . . well, we felt sorry for him, you know. We didn't take any action. Once, though, on the occasion in question, he overstepped the mark, went too far and started making threats, so we were forced to arrest him and have a bit of a chat with him to calm him down. It wasn't taken any further. The kid was in a terrible state. But that was only natural.'

'Right . . .' Hulda answered distractedly. She was having trouble taking it all in . . . that this was the son of a man who had murdered his own daughter. Damn it. Surely there couldn't be any connection, though?

'So, out with it, what's going on – why the interest in the boy?'

'He's a suspect in a murder case. You know, the girl who fell to her death on Ellidaey at the weekend.'

'You're kidding? Bloody hell!' Thorvardur banged his fist on the desk. 'Are you serious?'

Hulda nodded.

'And you reckon he could be guilty?'

'I don't really know what to think any more.'

'Well, it could run in the family, couldn't it?'

Hulda raised her eyebrows. 'Oh, come on.'

'Yes, really. Tendencies of that sort. If I were you, I definitely wouldn't rule it out.'

'I can hardly arrest him for the sins of his father. Is that what you're suggesting?'

'You could be dealing with a chip off the old block, Hulda.'

XXXIV

The press had begun sniffing around the case and when Hulda got back to her desk she found several messages waiting for her, enquiring about what had happened that night on the island. Instead of wasting time on them now, she decided her day would be better spent dealing with other matters. Fortunately, the news hadn't yet leaked out that the police were treating the death as a potential murder.

In light of the latest information, she urgently needed to speak to Dagur, but first she wanted to make sure she was familiar with all the details in the Veturlidi case. The quickest way to do that would be to ask Lýdur to fill her in. It wasn't a prospect she relished, given her aversion to the man – a feeling that was no doubt mutual. But he had been in charge of the investigation; it had been his big break, the case that had given him a push up the ladder. He had even achieved a degree of celebrity at the time, since he had been diligent about appearing in the media to discuss the investigation, assuming the role of a man in whom the public could place their trust. He was good at it, she'd give him that, but Hulda still didn't trust him. She could never put her finger on why.

But now, at last, Hulda had a big case of her own; she knew it in her guts. This was her chance and she would have to use it to her advantage if she wanted to break through the barrier to greater prestige and better pay. Come to think of it, maybe this was the moment to overcome her reluctance to appear in the spotlight by calling a press conference. She wasn't a natural performer like Lýdur, but she needed a success and, if she got one, her achievement mustn't be allowed to pass unnoticed.

In the event, after she had braced herself to go and talk to him, it was an anticlimax to discover that Lýdur was out of town. He'd gone to his summer house in Borgar-fjördur after work yesterday, she was told, and didn't have a phone there. Like Hulda, Lýdur hadn't yet got into the habit of carrying around a mobile phone, though the way things were going, they would be required to before long. Until then, Hulda meant to make the most of the free-dom of not being permanently accessible to her bosses.

On reflection, this seemed like a good opportunity to take her car for a spin in the fine weather. The Skoda had recently come back from an expensive service, which meant it shouldn't be any problem to zip up the west coast to Borgarfjördur. No, it wasn't a bad idea at all.

Hulda never tired of the road north up the coast from Rey-kjavík, with its incomparable views of some of her favourite mountains: the dish-like Akrafjall standing alone on its peninsula, the great flat-topped hulk of Esja, the almost alpine peaks of Skardsheidi. She didn't even resent the length of time it took to drive around Hvalfjördur, aware that this would soon be a thing of the past. The tunnel across the mouth of the fjord was due to open next year, which would cut the journey time from an hour to seven minutes. But she would miss the panorama of mountains and sea, the neat farms and hayfields dotted with round, white bales, the familiar landmarks of the old whaling station and the Nissen huts left over from the war.

As she rounded the shoulder of Hafnarfjall, she got her first views of Borgarfjördur, surrounded immediately to the north and east by flatter, more open country, with the mountains forming a distant backdrop. Dominating the fjord was the little town of Borgarnes with its pretty white church, but that wasn't her destination today. Lýdur's summer house turned out to be located in the middle of a holiday colony that appeared to have been designed with the express intention of making life difficult for visitors. Despite having a reasonable sense of direction, Hulda found herself driving round and round in circles, before finally she found the right cul-de-sac and spotted the summer house, partially obscured from the road by birch trees and bushes.

As she parked the Skoda behind Lýdur's big four-by-four, she reflected again that he must be several rungs higher than her on the salary ladder, more than could be justified by his position, age and experience.

Her tentative tap on the front door went unanswered, so she wandered round the side of the property to see if

Lýdur was out the back. She was in luck. He was standing over a gas grill, all bare chest and sunglasses, and appeared extremely startled to see her.

'Good grief, Hulda! What in God's name are you doing out here?' he asked, his initial surprise giving way to amusement.

'Hello, I'm so sorry to barge in like this,' she said insincerely. Inside, she was reflecting bitterly that there he was with his smart holiday home and that swanky jeep parked out front, while she had to make do with a ten-year-old Skoda, a rabbit hutch with a crippling mortgage and, every few years, her allotted week in the police union's summer house in Hvalfjördur, not far from Reykjavík . . . It was bloody unfair.

'I'm just amazed, that's all. The wife went for a lie-down. I'll have to introduce you two later. Have you met?'

'Yes, often.'

'Oh, right. Anyway, I assume it must be urgent. I just hope you haven't come here to drag me back to the office.' He laughed.

'No danger of that. Have you got a few minutes?'

'Sure. Want a hamburger? I've got plenty.'

She was about to decline when she realized she was starving. 'Er, yes, thanks. That would be great.'

'One hamburger and Coke, coming up,' he said, and the fake laugh she'd heard so often rang out again. Everything about this man was fake, yet that hadn't stopped his meteoric rise through the ranks. Could it be that she was envious?

He went inside and returned immediately with a big

juicy burger which he slapped on the grill. There was a hissing and spitting of fat.

'OK then, fire away. What on earth brought you out here, Hulda?' The jokey note had gone and his voice was businesslike.

'I . . . um, actually, I wanted to ask you about an old case. You remember Veturlidi Dagsson?'

She noticed his involuntary start at Veturlidi's name, despite his attempt to cover it. There was a silence that seemed to last longer than the question warranted.

'Veturlidi, yes, of course I remember him,' he said eventually, his voice giving nothing away. 'Shocking case, absolutely shocking,' he added, without looking round. 'Why are you interested in that?'

'I ran into his son at the weekend. His name's Dagur. Did you encounter him at the time?'

'Er . . . yes,' Lýdur answered, with apparent reluctance. 'I'd forgotten his name, but I did meet him at least once, probably more. He totally freaked out when we arrested his father. We went round at the crack of dawn and the boy woke up and started yelling and making a scene. He wasn't that young at the time either; he must have been at least eighteen, nineteen.'

'Nineteen,' Hulda confirmed.

'Right. I don't think he . . . that he was ever willing to face up to the truth.' Finally, Lýdur turned and met Hulda's eye, his own face well under control. 'Of course, it's understandable. It was a terrible time for the family, an appalling situation.'

He turned back to the barbecue again, asking casually, 'Where did you run into the son?'

'He's involved in a case I'm working on.'

There was presumably no way Lýdur could know that the inquiry into the incident on Ellidaey had been upgraded to a murder investigation, not yet, cut off out here at his summer house without a phone.

'Oh, what case is that?' he asked after a pause. 'The death in the Westman Islands?'

'Yes. Evidence has come to light that suggests the girl was murdered.'

'Murdered? Hell. I'd better get back to town.'

'I'm dealing with it,' she said, her voice rising sharply.

'Damn,' he said, as if he hadn't heard her. 'I'll have a word with the wife, then shoot back to the office. Anyway, Hulda, what was it you wanted to ask?'

'All I wanted to know,' she replied, trying to recover from her momentary burst of anger, 'was whether you'd ever considered Dagur at the time?'

'*Considered* him? How do you mean?'

'Was he ever a suspect?'

'What?' Lýdur's head snapped round. 'For his sister's murder? No, of course not. Never. It was an open-and-shut case, as I'm sure you'll remember. Veturlidi did it, no question.' Lýdur was emphatic, convincing. Convinced.

'Can you give me a brief rundown of the facts? It was your investigation, wasn't it?' she asked, though she already knew the answer.

'Just give me a sec,' he said, removing the burgers from the barbecue. He waved Hulda to a chair on the decking and took a seat facing her. For an instant, Hulda forgot everything but the pure pleasure of the moment as she savoured the smell of freshly grilled hamburgers, the warm summer air, not a breath of wind. This is how life should be – how her life used to be.

Lýdur got to his feet again almost immediately. 'I'll fetch that Coke for you.'

He went inside and quickly returned with the drink. Once he'd settled back in his chair, he answered her question: 'Sure, I handled the investigation from start to finish. And it went like clockwork, I might add. Hell of an ugly crime – a father killing his own daughter like that. What kind of father would harm his own child?'

The question sent a shiver down Hulda's spine.

'Remind me, where was her body found?'

'In the West Fjords,' he said, taking a big bite out of his burger and chewing vigorously. 'It was a gory scene. Happened at the family summer house. At first sight, she appeared to have been up there on her own but Veturlidi's jumper was a dead giveaway. She was clutching it. He couldn't deny that it was his, though of course he denied he'd been there with her. But no one could explain why the girl would have been there alone, especially since she and her father often used to travel up to the summer house together. All we can do is fill in the gaps by guesswork.' He took another bite, polishing off half the burger in one go, and stopped talking while he was chewing. Hulda took the opportunity to taste her own food. She had to hand it to Lýdur: he certainly knew how to use a grill.

'I mean,' Lýdur continued, swallowing, 'they regularly used to go up there alone together, and it's not hard to guess what went on during those trips – what he was doing to her. But by the time of that last weekend away she had grown up and must have decided to resist him. At least, that's how I pictured it. He pushed her and she hit her head on the sharp corner of a table, then died of blood loss. It's hard to tell how much of a struggle there was. It might have been possible to save her, though, if he hadn't left her alone to bleed to death. Unsurprisingly, the case caused an outcry. It was no joke having to arrest a father for a crime like that, as I'm sure you can imagine.' He looked at Hulda but, in spite of his words, she couldn't detect any compassion in his face.

'Yes, I can.'

'He drank as well. Used to go on benders, disappear for days at a time. He'd been to rehab and gone on the wagon at least once before, but clearly he'd started again because it turned out that he'd been using the summer house for his secret binges. We found bottles stashed around the place. My theory is that he must have been drunk when he killed her. We couldn't prove it but, naturally, it provided ammo for the prosecution.'

'Were there no grounds at all for reasonable doubt?'

'None,' Lýdur answered with finality. 'Veturlidi was guilty as hell. The way he ended it put paid to any remaining doubts about that. It didn't take a genius to work out what it meant when he hanged himself. He'd been charged; the game was up, but he wanted to finish it on his own terms. End of story. Of course, I'd have liked to see him found guilty, but obviously he couldn't live with what he'd done. Which is understandable, I suppose.'

'Going back to his son, is there any chance he could have been there too – at the summer house, I mean?'

'His son? The teenager? No, definitely not. There was zero evidence to suggest that.'

'Was the possibility ever examined?'

'Not really. He was just a kid. Look, it was a no-brainer. Veturlidi was alone that weekend, drinking in secret. He claimed he'd been in town, but he didn't have an alibi. His wife was off on a trip with friends and his son wasn't home either. He pleaded with us to believe him . . . But the truth was that they were both at the summer house together. His daughter would hardly have gone there alone.'

'What was she called, the daughter?'

'Katla. She would have been about twenty at the time. No one had anything but good things to say about her. She'd been a happy girl, high-spirited, bit of a tease.'

'When was this again?'

Lýdur thought back. 'Um, late eighties . . . '87, yes, that was it. Ten years ago.'

'Did Katla have a boyfriend?'

'Apparently not. I asked around. Talked to some of her friends.' She could see that he was losing patience with her questions.

'Do you happen to remember who they were?'

'What? No, I've forgotten.'

'Would there be a note of their names in the file?'

'I doubt it. I just made a few informal inquiries.' He sighed heavily.

'Dagur didn't mention a word about this when I talked to him. Links to two murders . . . that's bound to raise questions.'

'Oh, come off it, Hulda. Saying he's linked to two murders is putting it a bit strongly. It was his sister who was killed. He was just an innocent victim.'

Lýdur stood up abruptly.

The message was unmistakeable so Hulda followed suit. 'Thanks for your help, Lýdur.' As an afterthought, she asked: 'Did he ever confess? Veturlidi, I mean.'

'No, not formally. But it was as plain as day. Believe me, Hulda, you're barking up the wrong tree. There's no connection between the two cases. It's totally implausible, out of the question.'

XXXV

Katla.

Twenty when she was found dead at the summer house.

Hulda spent the rest of that sunny day shut up in her office, reading the old case files. Lýdur's insistence that there could be no link between Katla's death and the incident in Ellidaey ran directly counter to Hulda's own instincts. She needed to find out more about Katla's murder, and the most obvious way to do that would be to have another talk with Dagur.

Lýdur's summary over their burgers turned out to have been pretty accurate. The events had happened ten years ago. Katla's body had been found in the autumn of 1987, at the family summer house, which was located in the remote valley of Heydalur, off Mjóifjördur, an uninhabited fjord on the south coast of Ísafjardardjúp. The local police inspector from Ísafjördur, one Andrés Andrésson, had made the discovery. Hulda reflected that it might be worth tracking him down as well, to hear his version of events.

The scene had been an ugly one, judging by the pictures.

There had been a lot of blood. Katla had sustained a head injury by falling backwards on to the corner of a table, as Lýdur had said. Her body hadn't been found for several days, and Hulda shuddered at the thought of what it must have been like for the first people on the scene.

According to Lýdur, it had been Veturlidi's *lopapeysa* that gave him away. Katla had been clutching it to her. Oddly, it wasn't visible in any of the pictures, but Andrés had given a statement confirming the detail and explaining that it was possible he had moved the jumper out of the way when he was checking the girl's pulse for signs of life.

If so, his behaviour would have been highly irregular – moving evidence at a crime scene. Yes, it was becoming increasingly clear that Hulda would have to have a word with this Andrés.

The last page in the thick bundle of papers contained a brief statement reporting that the prisoner had taken his own life.

'I'm terribly sorry to bother you,' Hulda said in her gentlest voice. Klara's parents lived in Kópavogur, only a couple of streets away from Dagur's place, in a detached house that looked as if it had been built some time in the seventies. 'Could I possibly have a word, just very quickly?'

Soon after Klara had been reported dead, representatives of the police, accompanied by a vicar, had gone round to inform her parents. It was clear from the couple's haggard appearance that they were still in shock.

'Oh . . . all right, come in, then.' The woman, presumably Klara's mother, looked to be in her fifties. She was pale, with short hair and old-fashioned glasses. 'I'm Agnes. This is my husband, Vilhjálmur.'

'Can't you lot leave us alone?' the man said after a slight pause. He spoke with feeling yet his tone was apologetic. 'Are you investigating her death?'

'Yes, I've taken on the case,' Hulda answered quietly. She followed the couple into the sitting room, noting the atmosphere of silent desolation; all the lights out, the curtains drawn. Hulda felt deeply uncomfortable intruding on their grief like this.

'Are you . . . ?' Vilhjálmur asked hoarsely, then, clearing his throat, tried again: 'Are you any closer to finding out how she . . . fell?'

Tactfully, to soften the blow, Hulda replied, 'We're examining various angles. It's possible . . . just possible there was some sort of struggle.'

Klara's father gasped. 'What . . . what do you mean? A struggle?'

'It's possible she was pushed.'

'What? No, that can't be true,' Agnes protested. 'No, I don't believe it.'

'How well did she know the people with her on the island?' Hulda asked.

'They've been friends for years. They used to be inseparable when Klara was in the sixth form.'

'Could you tell me who was in the group of friends then?'

This time Klara's father pre-empted his wife: 'The same people . . . Dagur and Benni, and Alexandra. And Katla, of course.' His voice flattened as he pronounced the last name.

'Ah, right,' said Hulda. 'Katla. The girl who died in the West Fjords.'

'Was murdered, you mean,' said Agnes. 'It was a dreadful, dreadful business.'

'Can you take me through what happened?'

This request was met by a heavy silence.

Then Klara's mother shook her head. 'I'd rather not.'

Hulda hesitated, unsure how far she ought to press them.

'It's not our story,' Vilhjálmur said eventually. 'You should talk to her . . . to Katla's family.'

'Were they close, Klara and Katla?'

There was another lengthy pause, then Klara's mother said, 'They were best friends.'

Hulda waited, sensing that there was more to be said.

'Everything changed after Katla died,' the woman went on in a low voice.

'How do you mean?'

At this point Klara's father got to his feet and laid a gentle hand on his wife's shoulder. 'This isn't the moment,' he said. 'We need to be left alone.'

There was nothing Hulda could say to this. She'd been hoping for something more concrete, but the last thing she wanted was to cause Klara's parents any further distress.

'I'm so sorry to have disturbed you,' she said, standing up. 'Please accept my heartfelt condolences. I'll make sure you're kept informed about the progress of the investigation.'

Everything changed after Katla died, Klara's mother had

said. Hulda was more convinced than ever now that Katla's murder might hold the key to solving the case.

What were the odds? Two girls, Katla and Klara, from the same group of friends, murdered ten years apart. In Iceland, too, where murder was rare. And this time the friends of the first victim had been the only people present. Yes, damn it, the cases had to be connected. Not only that but, logically, she had to allow for the possibility that the same killer was responsible for both deaths.

Was it conceivable? Could one of the friends have murdered both girls?

Benedikt? Hulda couldn't work him out; all she knew was that he wasn't telling her the whole truth.

Alexandra? Superficially shy and nervous, but could she be a very different person underneath?

Or Dagur? Katla's brother. That likeable, self-possessed young man who had endured seeing his father arrested for murder, and protested repeatedly and vehemently, going so far as to threaten a police officer. Was it conceivable that he had murdered his sister and that his father had shouldered the blame? And what was his mother's part in all this? Yes, that was another person Hulda needed to track down.

She couldn't rid herself of the idea that Dagur might have been guilty of Katla's murder and Veturlidi therefore innocent. As shocking as this theory was, it fitted the facts more neatly than any other explanation. None of the other friends would have had as strong a bond to Katla as her own brother. Added to that, he would presumably have had access to the summer house, like the rest of his family. And, most significantly of all, if Veturlidi was innocent, might the reason for his suicide have been that he wanted to protect his son? But why on earth would Dagur have wanted to murder Klara?

It was time to act, time to call Dagur in for a formal interview and leave him to sweat overnight in the cells. Maybe that would bring some old secrets up to the surface.

XXXVI

On her return to CID, Hulda was greeted by the unwelcome news that Lýdur had come back to town and wanted to see her as soon as possible. She approached his office with a heavy heart, her mind working overtime as she wondered what he could want, afraid above all that he would try to wrestle the case away from her. But the fact was that Lýdur's boss had entrusted her with the investigation and it was almost unheard of for a detective to be taken off an inquiry halfway through, except in the case of misconduct or a serious mistake.

'Hello,' she greeted Lýdur, rather coolly, as she entered his office. He was on his feet, glowing lobster red from too much sun.

'Hi, Hulda,' he said and, perhaps in response to her tone, immediately reassured her: 'Look, although I'm back, that doesn't mean I'm trying to muscle in on your turf. You're still in charge of the investigation, but I'm here to lend a hand, should you want it. After all, I'm familiar with some of the characters involved from my work on the inquiry ten years ago. What do you say?'

'Fine . . . er, fine,' she said, struggling to sound sincere.

'Great, great. You know, I've always wanted to work with you, Hulda – learn from the master, so to speak. It's amazing, actually, to think we've never worked on a case together before.' He grinned. 'So, where do we go from here?'

'I want . . . I'm going to call Dagur in for a formal interview.'

'Right, excellent. Let me know when he's coming in and I'll join you. We'll be questioning him here at CID, I assume?'

She nodded, far from happy at this turn of events.

Lýdur evidently meant to keep them waiting.

Dagur was sitting across the table from Hulda in the interview room. He'd turned up punctually, but his face was drained of colour and he hadn't said a single word beyond what was required.

'Sorry about this,' Hulda said. 'But we've got to wait a few more minutes for my colleague to join us.'

Dagur nodded.

They sat in silence for what felt like a long time.

Dagur grew conspicuously more nervous as the minutes ticked by. It occurred to Hulda that the delay might be a deliberate tactic on Lýdur's part.

Finally, there was a light tap on the door and the man himself came in.

'Sorry I'm so late. Hello, Dagur,' he said with easy authority, and held out his hand.

Dagur looked up and did a double-take. 'What's *he* doing here?'

'I believe you two are acquainted?' Hulda said.

'We met way back – ten years ago, wasn't it?' Lýdur said, withdrawing his hand, since Dagur plainly had no intention of taking it.

Hulda's eyes remained fixed on Dagur.

He nodded. 'Oh, I remember you. I remember you all right. You were the one who arrested Dad.'

'Yes,' Lýdur said. 'It wasn't easy for either of us.'

'You know he was innocent,' Dagur retorted, with sudden force.

'Lýdur's going to sit in on the interview, Dagur,' Hulda intervened, in a voice that brooked no argument. 'Because we need to have a chat about what happened when your sister died.'

Dagur nodded, seeming suddenly deflated, as if he had no more energy to object.

Before going any further, Hulda pointed out to him that, since he was being questioned as a possible suspect, he was entitled to have a lawyer present.

He shook his head. 'I've done nothing wrong.' Then, in a lower voice: 'And neither had my dad.'

'You and your friends lied to me on the island.' Hulda launched in before Lýdur could react, determined not to give him a chance to take over the interview.

'Lied to you?'

'You didn't mention that you'd been linked to another murder case a decade ago.'

'You never asked.'

'Was it because you have something to hide?'

'No, not at all. We just thought we'd have a reunion. Mark the fact that it's ten years since Katla died. But apart from that it wasn't really about her.' He added, rather lamely: 'In any case, none of us had anything to do with Katla's death.'

Hulda allowed a silence to follow his words.

As if compelled to continue, Dagur added: 'Sure, Katla was my sister, and friends with Alexandra, Klara and Benni, but that was all. Why do we have to drag the whole thing up again? It has nothing to do with what happened to Klara.'

'But surely you should have mentioned it when we first spoke?' said Hulda, though she had some sympathy with Dagur's point of view. She could understand why he wouldn't have wanted to bring up the upsetting episode from his past.

'But we . . . I haven't done anything,' Dagur repeated, wiping the sweat from his forehead.

'Why do you say your father was innocent?'

'Because he *was* innocent,' he answered forcefully. 'Do you know what they claimed? Do you? That he'd been abusing my sister for years, then taken her to the country-side and killed her! I knew my dad. He was a good man.' Dagur's voice came close to cracking. 'A good man. Sure, he drank – he'd quit but started again in secret, but he never took it out on us. And alcohol didn't turn him into some kind of monster. It just made him vulnerable, an easy target for the police, because they did such a shit job of investigating the case. They couldn't find anyone else to blame.' As he said this he glared at Lýdur, his face twisted with loathing.

Ignoring his outburst, Hulda asked in a tone that invited confidences, as if she were chatting to a friend, 'What happened last weekend, Dagur?'

'It . . . nothing happened. Klara died. How many times do I have to tell you? It's got to have been an accident.'

'Don't you find it an extraordinary coincidence that two girls who were friends should have been murdered, even if it was a decade apart?' Hulda asked.

'I don't believe . . .' After a momentary wobble, his voice gained strength: 'I don't believe she was murdered. Think what you like. There were only the four of us on the island. I know the others, I know my friends. They're not murderers!'

To give him his due, he certainly sounded sincere.

Hulda let the silence hang, then said: 'And you're quite sure, Dagur, that your father didn't murder Katla?'

'A hundred per cent positive.'

'Then who did?'

'How am I supposed to know that?' His voice trembled.

'Could it have been one of you, Dagur?'

He shook his head violently. 'God, no!'

'Alexandra or Benedikt, for example?'

'No . . .' But this time he didn't sound as confident.

'Or maybe you, Dagur?'

This attack shouldn't have taken him by surprise, but he flinched and protested feebly: 'I didn't lay a finger on—'

Hulda interrupted: 'Suppose we accept, Dagur, that your father didn't murder Katla; that instead we're dealing with someone who killed her and got away with it, then killed again last weekend. Someone who was close to Katla and was on the island as well . . . I have to tell you that you'd be top of my list.'

He exploded out of his chair. 'You can't be serious!'

'I'm afraid I am. What do you think, Lýdur?' Hulda turned to look at him.

He met her gaze, his face unreadable, but didn't answer.

'Who were the other main suspects for Katla's killing, apart from Veturlidi?' Hulda prompted him.

'Veturlidi was guilty,' Lýdur stated flatly. 'There's no point suggesting anything else. The case against him was watertight.'

Hulda looked back at Dagur. 'Sit down. We need to discuss this properly.'

'There's . . . there's nothing to discuss,' Dagur said, but he sat all the same.

'I have to say, Dagur, that the way you lot kept quiet about the earlier murder looks extremely suspicious. You all knew Katla; you were all connected to her in one way or another, weren't you?'

He nodded reluctantly.

'You must have known the police would have considered it relevant information.'

'I find it painful to talk about, you must be able to understand that. And . . . and, to be honest, I assumed you knew, or would soon find out. But there's no link, there can't be.'

'You seem very sure that your father was innocent,' Hulda said, her eyes boring into him. 'Have you made any attempt to get the case reopened or——?'

'Or what? Investigated it myself? I'm no detective. And, remember, I was only a boy at the time. All I had the energy for back then was to support Dad, to believe in him. And I'm proud of that. Of course . . . of course I want to know who . . .' He broke off and Hulda could see that he was close to tears. He coughed. 'Of course I want to know who killed my sister, but I don't suppose I'll ever find out now. It . . . Katla's death wrecked all our lives. Dad was arrested and Mum . . .'

Hulda waited, but Dagur didn't go on.

'What were you going to say about your mother? Is she still alive?'

'Yes.'

'She doesn't live with you?'

'No, she's in a nursing home. She just sort of gave up after Katla and Dad died. Withdrew into herself. Stopped going out, stopped talking to people. Lost interest in living. The doctors can't find anything medically wrong with her, but that makes no difference. It's hard to explain . . .'

Hulda nodded. 'I understand.' She had stood on the brink herself and stared down into the abyss after Dimma died but had decided – after a huge internal struggle – to go on fighting. To get her revenge, as far as that was possible, then do her best to live her life. But her days were often empty; her attempts to keep busy had a hollow, oppressive echo. Yet she stubbornly kept going. She had no intention of giving up: what good would that do anyone?

'Do you have any idea why your mother reacted the way she did?' Hulda asked.

'What? No, or . . . actually, I've often wondered if it was the drugs.'

'The drugs?'

'Yes, they put her on all kinds of pills after . . . Katla and Dad died . . . She hit rock bottom, as you'd expect. I was left to cope with everything – our finances, the house, everything. She just sank into depression and the doctors started pumping her full of drugs, trying to help her snap out of it. I've sometimes wondered if all those pills messed up her system. But maybe she's simply never recovered from the trauma.'

'Is there any chance . . .' Hulda began, trying to be diplomatic: 'Is there any chance that she retreated into another world – if I can put it like that – because she couldn't face the fact that your father murdered your sister?'

'No!' Dagur snapped. 'Because he didn't.'

'I'm not necessarily saying he was guilty, only that your mother might have believed he was. Is that possible?'

'No,' said Dagur, though not as angrily this time. 'She . . . she believed in Dad. Just like I did.'

'Have you ever discussed it – whether he was guilty, I mean?'

Dagur shook his head. 'No. We were all sure he was innocent.' He was silent a moment, then resumed: 'I suppose it's not impossible . . . not impossible that she had her doubts. Thanks to him!' He jabbed a finger in Lýdur's direction. 'He . . . they did their best to make Dad look bad. They just made up their minds that he was guilty. And Mum, she was shattered and she began to have doubts. I could tell. She didn't know who to believe any more.' Tears had started trickling down Dagur's cheeks. Embarrassed, he wiped them away with his sleeve.

'And your friends?' Hulda asked, after an interval when no one said anything. 'What impact did Katla's death have on them? On Alexandra, Benedikt and Klara?'

Lýdur intervened before Dagur could answer. 'I think we're done here, Hulda,' he said, and this time it was unmistakeably a command. 'Could you and I have a quick word outside?'

He got up and Hulda had no alternative but to follow him, leaving Dagur alone in the interview room.

'Hulda, it's not on,' Lýdur said in a firm but not unfriendly voice.

'What do you mean?'

'We're investigating the death of the girl on the island, not a decade-old murder case that was solved at the time. I can't just sit meekly by while you cast doubt on my findings. And it sounds to me as if that's exactly where you're going with this line of questioning.'

Hulda bit back a powerful urge to object, aware that it wasn't worth it. He had a point. Besides, she had no good reason to antagonize Lýdur, and he was clearly taking her questions personally.

'OK,' she said after a pause. 'We'll wrap it up for now.' Then she added, without stopping to think, perhaps purely from a desire to get in the last word: 'But we won't let him go immediately.'

Lýdur didn't comment.

'We can hold him for twenty-four hours. Let's use that to our advantage.'

'Do you really think that's justifiable?' Lýdur asked, his voice still level and reasonable.

'I want to question his friends again before he has a chance to speak to them. And, all right, maybe put a bit of pressure on him too. He's the main link between the two cases, after all. We need to find out what he knows. I have a hunch he's not telling us the whole truth.'

Lýdur shrugged. 'Fine, have it your own way, Hulda.'

He walked off without another word.

As Hulda re-entered the interview room she caught the apprehensive look in Dagur's eyes.

'Thanks for waiting,' she said in a friendly tone. She wasn't at all sure that they had the right man. Dagur hadn't had an easy life and, under normal circumstances, she would have let him go at this point and investigated the matter further. But, although she felt sorry for him, she was going to stick to the plan she'd outlined to Lýdur. Because she couldn't back down now. They probably wouldn't even need the whole twenty-four hours; just a few would do, unless new details emerged from her conversations with Alexandra or Benedikt, details which would give them grounds for applying to a judge to extend custody.

She explained to him, as gently as possible, that he was under arrest on suspicion of being involved in Klara's death and that she strongly recommended he get himself a lawyer.

'But I've done nothing!' he objected desperately.

'I hope we'll be able to sort this out as quickly as possible so you won't have to stay with us too long,' said Hulda. Even as she spoke, her instincts were screaming at her that they'd arrested an innocent man. And perhaps the same had been true in Dagur's father's case.

XXXVII

Alexandra had come down to the police station in obedience to Hulda's request. This time Hulda faced her alone across the table in the interview room. Lýdur had gone home, half threatening that he'd be back. She doubted he would be. The weather was too good to be stuck inside.

'Thank you so much for coming in,' she said warmly.

Alexandra merely nodded and shifted restlessly in her chair, transparently anxious about being there.

'We need to have another little chat about what happened last weekend.'

Again the girl nodded.

'Why did you four go to the island?' Hulda asked, her voice sharpening.

'We . . . we . . . just for a reunion, you know . . . a reunion . . .' Alexandra stammered.

'So it had nothing to do with your friend Katla?'

'What? . . . Oh, yes . . . she died ten years ago.'

'Was that the reason for your reunion?'

'Yes . . . I suppose so.'

'You suppose so?'

'It gave us an excuse to get together, because we . . . we hadn't seen each other for ages . . . It would have been a good idea, even . . . regardless of Katla.'

'Why didn't you mention her earlier?'

Silence.

'Why, Alexandra?'

'Just . . .'

Hulda waited patiently.

'Because I got the feeling the boys didn't want to bring it up.'

'Oh?'

'I don't know. I just . . . I just got that impression when we were on the island because neither of them mentioned Katla to you.' Then, still looking nervous, she elaborated: 'You . . . surely you can understand? She was Dagur's sister. It was incredibly difficult for him . . . And his father . . . you know about his father—'

'I know,' Hulda cut her short. 'Have you ever discussed among yourselves whether his father was innocent?'

'No, not really. We didn't talk about it much. The subject's so difficult. But I do know that Dagur never believed he was guilty, and I can understand why. It was his dad, after all. And Veturlidi was such a lovely man. I remember the family so well – they were nice people, Veturlidi and Vera – great people. Of course, it turned out that Veturlidi was . . . that he drank . . . but I could never in a million years have imagined him murdering anyone, let alone his own daughter.'

'Did Dagur's parents have a good relationship? With each other and with their kids?'

'Yes, really good. It was the kind of family everyone wanted to be a part of, they always looked so happy . . . The whole thing was totally unbelievable.'

'And now there's been another murder,' Hulda said, watching her intently.

Alexandra's eyes flickered, avoiding Hulda's gaze.

'Another murder, the same group of friends . . . And you didn't think there was any reason to mention her?'

'Of course, of course I did . . . I hope you don't think I was trying to hide anything.' Alexandra's voice trembled. 'But I can't believe, just can't believe that Klara was . . . that she was pushed.'

'I'm afraid we have to accept that she may have been, Alexandra. The question is, who did it?'

XXXVIII

Hulda could have put a lot more pressure on Alexandra, but she felt a little sorry for her. She thought it made sense to go gently on her for now. Wait and see what happened, then crank up the pressure later, if necessary.

Since Lýdur had made himself scarce, Hulda decided to drop in on Benedikt on her way home rather than summoning him to the station. She didn't expect to learn anything new from him, but it was worth keeping him on his toes.

But he appeared to be out. Hulda rang the bell and knocked on the door, to no avail. It was past 9 p.m. by now, so she decided to leave it for the moment and surprise him first thing in the morning instead. There was a risk that Alexandra might contact him to tell him what she'd been asked in her interview, but Hulda hoped not: she had the impression that the two of them weren't particularly close.

When she got home, a mood of despondency descended on her, not helped by the fact that she'd forgotten to have supper and there was virtually nothing in the fridge. Her stomach growled and she briefly toyed with the idea of ordering a takeaway pizza, something she'd never done before, but she couldn't face the hassle this late in the evening. In the end, she made do with a yoghurt that was two days past its use-by date.

At a loose end after her meagre snack, she had the idea of ringing directory enquiries and requesting the number of Andrés Andrésson, the police inspector from Ísafjördur who had found Katla's body a decade ago. She'd never had any dealings with him before and didn't even know if he was still alive, but his role in Veturlidi's case had roused her curiosity. Better grab the chance now to do a little digging, find out whether there could be any link between the two girls' deaths, and Andrés might be just the man to shed some light on the matter.

The phone rang for a long time before it was eventually picked up.

'Yes,' a man answered. He cleared his throat and said again: 'Yes, hello?' A deep, hoarse voice.

'Andrés Andrésson?'

'Yes, speaking,' he answered gruffly.

'My name's Hulda Hermannsdóttir, I'm ringing from CID in Reykjavík,' she said, deciding not to apologize for calling at such a late hour.

'What . . . CID, you say? Oh? Has something happened?'

'No, no, nothing like that. I just wondered if I could have a word with you about an old case. I am speaking to the right person, aren't I? You're the police inspector from Ísafjördur?'

'Yes – ex-inspector, that is. I'm retired now.'

'I see. Well, I'm sure you'll remember the incident. It was ten years ago. A young girl was found dead in a summer house on your patch.'

There was silence at the other end and for a moment Hulda thought the man had hung up on her.

'Are you still there?'

'Yes.'

'Do you remember the case?'

'I remember it,' he said, slowly and heavily.

'I just wanted to ask you—'

He interrupted before she could go any further: 'Why?' Then, more roughly: 'Why are you dragging that up?'

'It's connected to a fatal incident that occurred last weekend.'

'Oh? What incident?'

'A girl fell to her death on Ellidaey.'

'How . . . what's the connection?'

'It so happens that the dead girl was a friend of Katla's, the one who—'

'Yes, damn it, I haven't forgotten her name.'

'Right, well,' Hulda said, still in a polite tone. 'They knew each other. She was on the island with three other friends, all of them linked in one way or another to Katla.'

'Are you serious?' His voice was shaking now.

'Yes, and we've arrested one of them. His name's Dagur Veturlidason.'

'Veturlidason? The son—'

'Yes, Veturlidi's son.'

'But how are they linked? You don't think . . . ?' He trailed off.

'Of course,' she said, 'the same person can't possibly have been responsible.'

Andrés didn't react.

'Since, as I'm sure you know,' she went on, 'Veturlidi killed himself not long after murdering his daughter.'

'Damn it, I don't need you to tell me that. But . . . Look, I don't want to talk about it. You can read about it for yourself in the old case files.'

With that he put the phone down.

His rudeness left Hulda slightly stunned. Why had he reacted that way? She thought of ringing back, but it didn't seem very wise. Not straight away. Perhaps she should leave him to cool down and try again later.

Or perhaps she'd simply got on the wrong side of him by calling too late in the evening.

Whatever the reason, she was gripped once again by a powerful intuition that they had the wrong man in the cells. Her thoughts flew to Dagur, to how he must be feeling, and she wondered whether she'd made a mistake by psyching herself up to arrest him and lock him up, purely to show off to Lýdur . . . Hell.

Admittedly, there was nothing to prevent her from ordering his release, but that would definitely be a sign of weakness. No, it had to be like this. And she still needed to talk to Benedikt again.

Before going to bed, Hulda got out the envelope Robert had sent her, which she kept in a safe place in the chest of drawers in the sitting room. It was two months since her visit to America. After learning that her father was dead, she had asked a small favour of his namesake: could he possibly get her a picture of her father, old or new – it didn't matter – seeing as he used to know him? Robert had said he didn't have any photos himself, as far as he could recall, but he promised to do his best to get hold of one for her. Just over a month later an envelope had arrived from the States. It hadn't looked like much but what it contained proved infinitely precious to Hulda. The picture wasn't an original but a good copy of an old photo showing a man in uniform. There he was, as large as life: Hulda's father. A young man, barely thirty, exceptionally handsome, with thick, dark, wavy hair. He was smiling more with his eyes than with his mouth, looking off to one side rather than meeting his daughter's gaze. Every evening since the picture had arrived, Hulda had taken it out to look at, the tears pricking her eyelids, wondering how her life might have turned out if she'd known her father all her life. Would she perhaps have moved to America, never met Jón, never given birth to Dimma, never experienced the sorrow that now defined her life . . . ?

She was woken by a loud ringing.

Reacting quickly, since she wasn't deeply asleep, she leapt out of bed and ran to the phone.

'Hulda, you need to get here now.' It was Lýdur.

She was alarmed. For some reason the first question that sprang to mind was: had something happened to Dagur?

But all she asked was: 'What's up?'

'It's Dagur. He's gone completely nuts. We had to call a doctor out. Being locked up is doing his head in. We managed to calm him down a bit, but he insists on speaking to you. He won't talk to me – it's got to be you. He's still not too – er – happy about the fact I arrested his father back in the day.'

'OK, I'll be right there.' She hung up and began hurriedly pulling on her clothes.

XXXIX

'I want to talk to you alone. Not with him here.' He sounded defiant.

Hulda had no intention of letting the prisoner dictate conditions. 'Lýdur stays, Dagur. No discussion. You wanted to talk to me. What is it you have to say?' They were in the interview room.

Dagur remained mulishly silent for a moment or two, then burst out: 'I . . . I can't do this . . . I can't cope with being shut in like this! I just . . . I keep thinking about my dad, about that time he was arrested in front of me. He ended up in a cell like this and he couldn't take it. Somehow he got hold of that bloody belt and hanged himself. I can't breathe in there . . . I feel as if I'm suffocating.'

'I sympathize, Dagur; I know it's not easy. But it was my understanding that you had something new to share with us.'

Another silence, then: 'Yes.'

Hulda waited.

'I wasn't going to mention it . . . but I've got to get out

of that cell. I can't stand it!' His voice had taken on an edge of hysteria.

No one spoke.

'It's about Benni,' Dagur continued eventually. 'Of course, I wouldn't for a minute want to land him in trouble. We're . . . we used to be friends but . . .' He paused. 'Look, I don't know if he's mentioned it to you, but he stayed up with Klara the evening she died. She didn't want to go to bed so he, you know, he offered to stay up a bit longer with her. I don't know what they did or how long he was with her . . .'

'Interesting,' said Hulda. 'This is the first time any-one's mentioned this.'

'Of course, that doesn't necessarily mean he . . . that he . . .'

'Of course not,' Hulda agreed.

'But there's something else. Something else more import-ant I wanted to tell you. When you came round to Benni's and found me there, you walked right into the middle of a fight, a row, about—'

'What?' Lýdur demanded roughly.

'I'm talking to *her*, not you,' Dagur retorted, pointedly turning to Hulda. 'When we were on the island Benni started talking about my sister, repeating an old story Katla liked to tell. About one of our ancestors who was burned at the stake and supposedly came back as a ghost, about how she'd sensed him. I'd heard the story myself, more than once. But I never remember her telling it to Benni. You see, she always used to bring it up when we were in the West Fjords, at the summer house. My sister could be a bit of a drama queen. The whole thing was made up, must have been. Sure, the man was burned at the stake, but the summer house wasn't haunted. Katla used to love telling visitors it was, though – exaggerating for effect. And then suddenly there was Benni saying he'd heard the story. Now, as far as I'm aware, Benni never *went* to the summer house. So I had a go at him, demanding to know when she told him the story, and the bastard became all evasive. And then I knew . . .'

After a brief pause he went on: 'Then I knew he'd been up there with her when she died. I confronted him when I went round to see him – that's what we were quarrelling about. He didn't exactly deny it, though he didn't admit it either. He obviously couldn't bring himself to lie to my face. And *you* . . .' He broke off to glare at Lýdur. 'You arrested the wrong man, like I said all along. Because if Benni was there with Katla, my dad can't have been there. And that means there's a chance . . .' He hesitated. 'I hate to admit it, but there's a chance it was Benni who killed my sister.' He buried his face in his hands, his breathing fast and ragged. When he looked up again, he couldn't hold back the tears.

XL

Officers from CID had been sent round to Benedikt's flat to bring him in for questioning. After the interview, Hulda would make up her mind whether to let Dagur walk free. In the meantime, he was being detained outside the cells, on compassionate grounds. He was now sitting in a meeting room at the police station, guarded by a junior officer.

Lýdur, who seemed to have more stamina now than he had earlier, showed no signs of leaving. He and Hulda were sitting facing Benedikt in the room where they had interviewed Dagur. Same set-up, different man. Perhaps this time they'd got their hands on the right person – a man guilty of possibly more than one murder.

'What do you want from me?' Benedikt asked for the third time. Hulda hadn't answered yet; she'd been waiting for the right moment to begin the conversation, but now at last she raised her eyes from the pile of papers in front of her, explained the situation to Benedikt and read him his rights. Like Dagur, Benedikt had refused the offer of a lawyer, stating that he was innocent and that this was 'some stupid bloody misunderstanding'.

'Where were you this evening, by the way?' Hulda asked. 'I dropped by your flat but you weren't home.'

'I went out for a beer. Is that against the law?'

'Benedikt, I understand you stayed downstairs with Klara on Saturday night after the others had gone to bed.' She watched his reactions closely.

He gave no sign of being wrong-footed by the question. 'Yes, for a short time. Just for one more drink. I didn't want to leave her on her own.'

'You didn't tell us about that.'

'I didn't think it was important.'

'You were the last person to see her alive.'

'What, you seriously think *I* killed her? I didn't kill her!' His voice had risen.

'What did you two talk about?'

'Oh God, I can't remember. Just some drunken nonsense. We were both a bit pissed. I went up to bed after one more glass. After, I don't know, quarter of an hour, half an hour, something like that. I wasn't in too much of a hurry because I wanted to give Dagur and Alexandra a chance to . . . you know, give them a bit of space.'

'Was there something going on between them?' Hulda asked.

'No, but there was definitely chemistry between them when we were younger. She's always been crazy about him. In love with him, I reckon. But I don't think anything happened. After all, she's married now; she wouldn't have let herself. And Dagur's always so polite and diffident.'

'Were they asleep by the time you went up to bed?'

'Yep. In separate beds. Everything was quiet.'

'And Klara? Did you leave her alone downstairs?'

'Yes. She was going out for a walk, to clear her head and enjoy the beauties of nature. I couldn't stop her from going.'

'Then what?' asked Hulda.

'Then what? I fell asleep, I was dead tired. I don't know what happened, as I've already told you repeatedly.'

Hulda took a sip of water and made a pretence of leafing through the documents in front of her, choosing her moment to shift the interview up a gear.

'I want to talk to you about Katla.'

This time, he was obviously flustered.

'Katla?' A pause, then he repeated: 'Katla?'

'Yes. I assume you remember her?'

'Of course I remember her. I just can't work out why you should bring her up. It's ten years since . . . since she . . . died.' It was clear he found the subject difficult.

'I'm mainly surprised that not one of you has seen fit to mention her,' Hulda said in a matter-of-fact voice. 'It would have sped things up considerably if we'd been informed that you all had a connection to the earlier murder.'

'But we weren't connected to her murder. Why on earth would you think that?'

'Oh? I was under the impression you were friends – you, Dagur, Alexandra, Klara and Katla?'

'Yes, sure, but what's that got to do with anything?'

'And you and Katla, weren't you . . . ?'

Benedikt quickly averted his gaze and, when he looked

back at Hulda, she guessed from his expression that she had hit the nail on the head. Or rather, that Dagur had.

But he didn't answer.

'Were you and Katla seeing each other?'

'No,' he said, unconvincingly. 'I don't know where you got that idea from or why . . . why I should have to answer that. It's a personal question.'

'Were you at the summer house together when she died?'

Benedikt dropped his eyes to the table, then suddenly, without warning, buried his face in his hands. He didn't say a word and a long silence followed. Hulda wasn't in any hurry.

At last, Benedikt lowered his hands, looked up and nodded.

XLI

Hulda had felt some sympathy, or at least some kind of fellow feeling, for Dagur when he had cracked under the pressure of questioning. Now that Benedikt was in the same position, she watched his torment with a cold detachment. Perhaps it was because Dagur was easier to warm to than Benedikt, a more likeable character; perhaps it was simply that she felt sorry for Dagur because of the tragedies he'd been forced to endure. He'd lost his sister in an unspeakable manner, then his father in no less harrowing circumstances, and now, to all intents and purposes, he'd lost his mother as well. He was alone in the world, just like Hulda.

'I think . . . I think I'd like that lawyer you mentioned earlier,' Benedikt said at last in a strained voice.

Hulda stood up. 'Of course.'

'But don't get the wrong idea: I didn't kill her.'

Hulda glanced at Lýdur, but he sat there impassively.

'Shall I fetch a lawyer for you now or would you like to go on talking to us?' she asked.

'I'll talk to the lawyer afterwards. I just don't want you to get the idea . . . that I killed her.'

'Killed who?'

'Katla, of course.'

'And Klara?'

'Klara? No, I didn't kill her either!' He was shouting now. 'I swear I haven't killed anyone!'

'But you were at the summer house with Katla?' Hulda asked sharply, giving him no time to think.

'Yes . . . yes, look . . .' he said, clamping his hands over his eyes again. When he took them away there were tears running down his cheeks.

'Why the hell didn't you come forward with this before?' Lýdur intervened, banging his hand on the table. 'Are you lying to us, boy?'

'Lying . . . ? No, I . . . you see, we were in love, me and Katla. It was our first weekend away; we'd only just got together, so no one knew. It was . . . it was our secret. But . . .'

He broke off, unable to continue for a moment, then drew a shuddering breath and resumed. 'I went out for a walk – this was in the morning, the day after we'd got there. I hiked up the valley, as far as I could go, taking my time because Katla was having a lie-in and I wanted to give her plenty of time to sleep. I don't know how long I was away from the hut, probably about three hours, because I stopped at the hot tub on the way back and was in there for ages. No, not a tub, I mean a natural pool, a hot spring . . .'

Hulda nodded, encouraging him to carry on.

'And . . .' He drew a gasping breath, the tears pouring down his face. 'God, it's a relief to be able to tell someone at

last, after all these years. Dagur found out last weekend –
he worked it out . . . But . . . the thing is, when I got back
to the summer house she was just lying there, dead . . .'
His voice cracked, then he repeated: 'Dead.'

'Did you two fall out? Did you have a fight?'

Hulda's question seemed to stun Benedikt.

'A fight? God, no. No, I didn't do anything to her. I'd
never have laid a finger on her. Never. You've got to
understand. You've got to believe me.'

'You didn't come forward ten years ago,' Lýdur cut in,
frowning grimly. 'How are we to know if you're telling
the truth now?'

'Of course I am. Why would I lie?'

Hulda got in before Lýdur this time. 'Were you aware
of anyone else in the vicinity?'

'No. We were alone. But clearly someone else must
have been there. It was autumn, so it got dark at night and
the summer house was fairly tucked away; you wouldn't
necessarily have been able to see a car approaching. I certainly didn't notice any from where I was, higher up the
valley – I was too far away. But somebody had been
there – somebody had come to the summer house and
killed Katla. And I've thought about it every single . . .
Christ, every single day of my life since then. In spite of
everything, I believed, up to a point, that Veturlidi must
have done it because the police were so sure they'd got
the right man. I had to believe it, you see? I had . . .'

He broke down, crying in great, tearing sobs, but persisted: 'Because if Veturlidi didn't do it, he may have killed
himself because of me . . . because of what I *didn't* say,

because I didn't dare come forward for fear that I'd be blamed. I didn't dare . . . I was so young, just a stupid boy . . . The whole situation just sort of snowballed. You see, I thought Veturlidi would be released because I knew he hadn't been there with Katla, not unless he'd turned up unexpectedly . . . I knew the police had got it wrong, but as the days and weeks went by it became harder and harder for me to come forward. I didn't . . . didn't have the guts. And I still feel responsible for Veturlidi's death – I see him at night, in my dreams; see Dagur, poor Dagur . . . And I saw the hatred in his eyes yesterday. He knew I'd been lying, which meant he knew I was partly to blame for his dad's suicide. And because of his dad's death his mum lost her will to live . . . He's lost them both, all because of me.'

After this, he clammed up and wouldn't say any more.

Hulda tried to persuade him to go on talking, but it was no good. In the end, she told him that he would be taken to the cells and provided with a lawyer: there was no way they could let him go after this revelation. And Lýdur had a point: the boy had lied once; what was to stop him lying again?

Perhaps they'd caught Klara's killer.

And not just Klara's killer but Katla's too. If so, the uncharitable thought occurred to her, Lýdur's biggest triumph in the police would be converted, in one fell swoop, into the most ignominious failure.

XLII

The only possible response in the circumstances was to release Dagur and turn the spotlight on to Benedikt instead. They needed to establish beyond a doubt whether Benedikt had been telling the truth about the events leading up to Katla's death.

The thought that Veturlidi might have been wrongly accused, and that this had led directly to his suicide, was deeply disturbing. It would be an understatement to say that Lýdur was stressed out by Benedikt's revelations. Ever since the interview, he had been extremely jittery, giving Hulda no peace to concentrate on the investigation.

The plan was to summon Alexandra for further questioning first thing in the morning. Since it wasn't worth going home to bed at this stage, Hulda grabbed a few hours' rest on the sofa in her office, not for the first time. The experience was as uncomfortable as ever, since the sofa was too short to stretch out on.

She did manage to get a couple of hours' kip, though,

before being woken in the morning by the phone. It turned out to be an operator from the police switchboard. 'Hulda, I've got a man on the line who wants to talk to you. He asked for you by name. He's called Andrés Andrésson. Shall I put him through?'

'Andrés? Oh, yes, please do,' she said, rubbing the sleep from her eyes and stretching. 'Hello, Hulda Hermanns-dóttir.'

'Yes, hello, Hulda.' The man sounded a lot less gruff this time. 'I'm sorry to bother you. And . . . sorry I was so short with you on the phone yesterday, but I was completely thrown by your questions. You see, it's years since I've spoken to anyone about that case.'

'No need to apologize,' she said, and waited for him to explain the reason for his call.

'I was wondering if we could meet.'

'Meet? Why?'

'Um, there are certain facts I'd like to bring to your attention. Face to face, if possible.' He sounded tense.

'Are you coming to town any time soon?'

'No, that's the thing. I was wondering if you'd mind coming up here? I . . . I've been awake all night. I really think it's time to come clean. To tell someone. Is there any way you could fly up here and meet me?'

'That could be tricky,' she said, but promised to think about it before hanging up.

The last thing she wanted to do right now was drop everything and traipse all the way to the West Fjords, but something told her that Andrés might be in possession of key information. His choice of words and his tone of voice; the fact he'd asked her to come to him rather than discuss it over the phone . . .

Damn it, she thought and, digging out his number, rang him back.

'Hello, Hulda here again. I might be able to come after all. When's the next plane?'

'There's a flight at nine o'clock. You should still be able to make it.'

She sighed. 'All right, I'll try.'

Hulda wasn't used to taking domestic flights. When going on trips to the mountains, she invariably went in her old Skoda or took the bus. It was years since she'd last flown to Ísafjördur, and then it had been in nightmare conditions, in the middle of a blizzard, but this time the weather was good and the flight went smoothly. They had a magnificent view of the West Fjords coming in, of great flat-topped mountains plunging sheer into deep fjords, and, away to the north, the uninhabited Hornstrandir peninsula, still white with snow. Below, the rocky ground fell away as if carved out with a knife, and at the end of a green valley she spotted the blue fjord with the old town of Ísafjördur clinging to its narrow spit, the newer settlement a geometric pattern of streets and houses lying some way off at the head of the fjord. Then the plane began its descent, coming in at what seemed an impossible angle. Hulda caught her breath and braced herself, clutching the armrests as they appeared to be heading straight for the mountainside. All she could see was a wall of rock, scored with gullies and skirted with screes and tongues of green.

Heart in her mouth, she felt herself impotently braking with her feet until, at what seemed like the last minute, the plane executed another turn and there was the road running like a ribbon across the fjord and the runway ahead, on the narrow strip of lowland between mountain and sea. It looked alarmingly short. She closed her eyes, every muscle tense, but they landed with scarcely a bump and taxied to the small terminal, dwarfed by the imposing scenery.

Andrés turned out to be a fairly short, stout man with glasses. He was almost entirely bald apart from a fringe of white hair. Instead of driving her into town, he offered to take her to the place where Katla had died and she accepted, not realizing until too late just how far it was from Ísafjördur. At first she tried to winkle out of him what his call had been about, but he remained tight-lipped, merely insisting that all would be explained when they got to the summer house.

In normal circumstances, Hulda would have relished this journey, despite the rough gravel roads. They snaked in and out of the sparsely populated fjords along the south coast of the Djúp, the pure elemental forms of the mountains and the low green islands of Ædey and Vídey providing a picturesque backdrop. She was aware from the news that the last couple of farms on the north coast of the Djúp had recently been abandoned, leaving the entire northern peninsula of the West Fjords, from Hornstrandir to Snæfjallaströnd, uninhabited. It was an area she had always wanted to go hiking in, and she tried to distract herself with plans for a walking trip next summer, but it was no good: all she could think about was hearing what Andrés had to tell her then getting back to town as quickly as possible to pick up the investigation where she'd left off.

As time wore on the sun went in and the clouds gathered low and grey over the landscape, rendering it increasingly forbidding. After they'd been driving for an hour, Hulda asked Andrés, with rising impatience, how long they had left, and he told her it was still over half an hour to the valley. Apart from that he proved uncommunicative, playing the cassette of an opera in preference to talking. 'Puccini's *Turandot*,' he answered tersely when Hulda asked what it was.

Lýdur had been very surprised and disapproving when Hulda told him she was taking a quick trip up to the West Fjords to talk to Andrés. He had pressed her hard about what Andrés wanted but she said, as was true, that she didn't know what exactly it was about. After that, Lýdur had done his best to dissuade her from going by saying it was a waste of her time when she should be focusing all her energy on investigating Klara's death. This wasn't the first time Hulda had stood up to him, though, and she stuck to her guns, calmly informing him that she'd already booked her ticket and wasn't going back on the promise she'd made Andrés. Lýdur had given up in the end. Changing tack, he'd said ominously that he would 'take care of her job while she was away' by interviewing Alexandra and perhaps questioning Benedikt again. All she could think about now was what he was up to while she was being carted off to the middle of nowhere. She couldn't decide which would be worse: for him to mess up her investigation or to solve the case in her absence.

When Andrés and Hulda finally reached the valley and bumped their way up the rough track towards the summer house, it struck her at once that Benedikt's description of the place had been pretty accurate. The hut was invisible from the parking place, so presumably it would be impossible to see anyone approaching from the road.

'It's a beautiful spot,' she remarked, when they got out of the car.

'It was a beautiful spot,' Andrés said heavily. 'Now when I come here all I can see is the dead girl. I remember it like it was yesterday.'

'Does anyone use the summer house now?'

'I don't think so. The family still owns it, as far as I know, but I've never heard of any visitors coming here, not after what happened. I suppose it's possible that people use the hut, though. It's so secluded that the locals wouldn't be likely to notice.'

'One of Katla's friends mentioned that there's a natural hot pool nearby. Is that right?'

'Yes, but it's a bit of a walk. We can't see it from here.'

'Would you be able to see from the pool if someone drove up the road to the house?'

Andrés shook his head. 'No, it's out of sight. Why do you ask?'

'I'm just trying to get to grips with the geography.'

They walked up to the A-shaped hut, which looked shabby with neglect, and halted in front of it. Andrés seemed unwilling to approach any closer.

'You can . . .' He coughed and tried again: 'You can look in the window if you like. I'd rather not myself.'

Hulda rubbed at the dirty glass of the window beside the door and peered inside, trying to visualize the scene from her memory of the photographs taken at the time. She couldn't sense the ghosts that seemed to haunt Andrés, but seeing the actual place where the murder had happened made it seem somehow more real to her.

A cold breeze sneaked in through her light summer clothes. A rain cloud hung low over the valley. The contrast with the heatwave she'd left behind in Reykjavík couldn't have been starker, reminding her that here in the far north-west the Arctic sea ice often drifted close to shore, breathing its chill breath over the land. She shivered.

'There's something I have to tell you,' Andrés said at last, in a low voice. 'I felt this was the right place to do it, out of respect for those who died.'

'Those who died?'

'Katla and her father. You see, I feel partly responsible for what happened to him.'

'How come?' Hulda asked, astonished.

'It's a long story,' he said. 'Well, maybe not that long. I never thought I'd be telling it to anyone. I was determined to take it to my grave, but when you rang and said you were investigating a case that might be linked to Katla's murder, I realized there was no going back. I had to right the wrong. And, you know, whatever happens, I reckon I'll sleep better tonight than I have for nearly a decade.'

'Tell me what happened, Andrés.'

They stood face to face in the chilly summer breeze under the brooding cloud.

'The whole thing was Lýdur's fault. I assume you know who he is?'

'Yes.'

'He asked me to tell a lie.'

'He asked you to tell a lie?' Hulda couldn't believe she was hearing this. She had always known that Lýdur was ruthlessly ambitious, but if this were true he had crossed a line a policeman should never cross.

'Yes. Politely at first, but then he went too far. I didn't mean to cave in – I knew it was the wrong thing to do. He wanted me to testify in court that the girl, Katla, had been holding her father's *lopapeysa* when I found her body. It's true the jumper was lying on the floor, but I'm fairly sure she wasn't touching it when I found her. He was an ambitious young man, Lýdur, and I reckon he was determined to get a conviction, come what may. He was utterly convinced of Veturlidi's guilt. And I trusted him; I believed what he said. He persuaded me that the man's suicide only confirmed his guilt – that my action had made no difference. But of course it made a difference; maybe it was the deciding factor. I gave a false statement. I was going to correct it at the time – I got in touch with Lýdur shortly afterwards, all ready to head back to Reykjavík and tell the truth, but before I could, the wretched man killed himself. So I kept my mouth shut. And then you ring up, all these years later, and rake the whole thing up again. And this time I just can't keep silent any more.'

'For God's sake, why did you lie in the first place? I . . .

I'm finding this hard to believe, Andrés. Why would you give in to Lýdur over something like that?'

'For very selfish reasons. I don't expect you to understand but maybe you could try to put yourself in my shoes . . .' He broke off for a moment. 'The thing is, I was heavily in debt at the time, to a loan shark. You remember them? They pretty much had you over a barrel. Well, my loan shark went and got himself arrested and started squealing about how much he'd lent me, a cop from the West Fjords. Somehow Lýdur got wind of it and threatened to publicly expose me. I couldn't face it – I was thinking of my family's reputation, my wife, my children. You must be able to understand that?'

He closed his eyes, then opened them again, looking up at the sky to avoid Hulda's gaze. 'I betrayed the girl. Betrayed her father. Betrayed everyone, when it comes down to it.'

'I can understand, to a certain extent, why you acted the way you did,' Hulda said carefully. 'I had a family myself once, so I can easily put myself in your place.'

'But Lýdur didn't leave it at that,' Andrés hastened to explain. 'He hinted that he would make sure my name was removed from the case and my debts disappeared as well. I don't know how he fixed it but after that I never heard from that bloody loan shark again. Of course, I know what I did was unforgiveable . . .'

'Would you be willing to provide a signed statement of this, Andrés? You shouldn't have to shoulder the blame alone if what you say is true.'

'Yes, I'm willing. I can drive you back to Reykjavík, if you like. It'll take hours, but it should still be quicker for you than going all the way back to Ísafjördur and waiting for the next plane. I want to come with you and give a statement. It's time.'

'What about . . . ?' Hulda hesitated, but felt compelled to ask: 'What about your family? How will they react?'

Andrés met her eyes, his own bleak. 'My wife left me – several years ago. I don't think I was much fun to live with by the end. Those events . . . that case, it changed everything, you know.'

'And your children?'

'The kids . . . Well, they're ten years older now. They're adults. I hope they'll understand. It's worse for the grand-children, of course. But I have to do this, I have to be able to live with myself.'

Hulda had the sudden impression that Andrés had aged twenty years in front of her. For a moment she thought of her own future, jumping twenty, twenty-five years ahead in time. Would she still be alone? Tortured by guilt and regrets? Would she end up like this poor, broken man? Would she ever confess her sins to anyone?

XLIII

Hulda and Andrés made it back to Reykjavík by evening. After his confession at the summer house, Andrés had lapsed into sombre silence again, which had made the slow drive south even more of an endurance test. Once back, Hulda took the precaution of avoiding the CID offices so there was no risk of their bumping into Lýdur. Instead, she rang Lýdur's superior and asked him to be present for the taking of Andrés's statement. Andrés repeated the whole story, leaving out nothing of importance.

Afterwards, Hulda promised not to discuss the matter with Lýdur, as it needed to go 'through official channels'. She had no intention of keeping her promise.

The moment she got back to the office, she knocked on Lýdur's door, conscious that she would have to tread carefully and avoid saying too much. But she was dying to see the look on his face when he heard the news. The accusation was so serious that it was clear he faced immediate suspension or dismissal, and possibly criminal charges as well, which would create an opening for Hulda. The job she had been eyeing up for so long might become available at last. She felt a twinge of conscience at her own ruthlessness – but only a twinge.

If she managed to find Klara's murderer as well, that would make her position even stronger.

'Have you got a minute, Lýdur? Just for a very quick word.'

He looked annoyed. 'Yes, but make it snappy. I've been run off my feet all day, thanks to you bunking off to Ísafjördur. I had a word with Alexandra, but nothing doing. In my view, we've got the right man in custody. As far as we can tell, Benedikt was the last person to see Klara alive. He also lied about the old case and—'

'Lýdur,' Hulda cut in, taking a chair facing him. She had closed the door behind her. 'This conversation must remain absolutely confidential. I just wanted to warn you . . .' She paused, spinning out the moment.

'Warn me? What the hell are you on about?'

'It's about Andrés. He's brought some very serious charges against you.'

Lýdur turned white.

'Serious . . . serious charges?' he stammered, then, rising abruptly from his desk, started pacing back and forth across his office. 'What do you mean?' he threw at her.

Hulda allowed herself to savour the feeling of vindication. Her instincts about this man had been right all along: his record *had* been too good to be true. She thought about all the years of watching him effortlessly claim the positions that should have gone to her. She wouldn't have been human if she hadn't gained a certain satisfaction from watching him squirm. 'It's about the investigation into Katla's death.'

'What? The investigation, the investigation . . .' It was as if he was obscurely relieved, though surely that couldn't be right. Perhaps it was the involuntary response of a man on the edge.

'He claims you – how shall I put it? – exerted pressure on him to give a false statement.'

Lýdur didn't confirm or deny it.

'To increase the chances of a conviction. Is that correct, Lýdur?'

'Of course not,' he shot back, but his voice betrayed him. He resorted to bluster. 'That stupid old sod would say anything – he was in a hell of a mess at the time, under the thumb of some loan shark. Was that all?'

'All?'

'All he said?'

Isn't it enough? Hulda thought privately. 'Yes, that was all,' she said coolly, and walked out of Lýdur's office without another word.

XLIV

By that evening, Lýdur had been suspended pending an inquiry into Andrés's accusations. Hulda, meanwhile, was given additional manpower to work on the Klara case, as well as being asked to take care of matters arising from the flawed investigation of Katla's murder ten years ago.

The pressure was considerable and, in spite of the adrenaline coursing through her veins, she could feel the fatigue beginning to get the better of her. In the old days she could have sought refuge at home with Jón and Dimma, escaping the demands of the inquiry for a while to recharge her batteries, even if it was only to snatch a quick supper with her family. But now there was no solace to be found in her empty, dreary little flat. Instead, she tried to fight off her tiredness by flogging herself to even greater efforts.

Benedikt would remain in custody for now. He had admitted to having been at the summer house with Katla. He had also been on the island and was the last person known to have seen Klara alive. The question was: had

Klara discovered the truth about his relationship with Katla? Had he been forced to silence her? It was the most plausible theory at present and would mean not only that the wrong man had been arrested for the earlier crime but that Veturlidi had killed himself as the result of a police blunder or, rather, a miscarriage of justice.

Hulda took out the telephone directory with the intention of ringing Klara's parents to let them know about Benedikt's arrest. At the last minute she changed her mind and decided to go round and talk to them in person. Her previous visit had been rather inconclusive; maybe she would get more out of them this time.

Agnes, Klara's mother, opened the door to her and invited her into the sitting room. Her husband was nowhere to be seen, a fact that came as a relief to Hulda, since she suspected it would be easier to deal with the mother alone. Together, the couple had been rather unforthcoming.

'I'm so sorry to bother you again,' Hulda began, once she had sat down. 'I just wanted to give you a progress report.'

'No need to apologize. We'll do anything we can to help. I'm afraid my husband's not in – he had to pop out. I hope that's all right with you, but if you'd rather talk to us both together, I can let you know when he comes home.'

'No, no, it's fine.'

'I'll make you some coffee. It was so rude of us not to offer you any last time,' the woman said, and vanished into the kitchen before Hulda had a chance to decline.

The coffee, when produced, turned out to be on the

weak side, but Hulda drank it anyway. 'I won't keep you longer than necessary,' she said.

Klara's mother seemed more relaxed this time. 'It's not as if I've got anything better to do. Like I said, I want to help.'

Her distress was still obvious in the pinched cheeks and the dark trenches under her eyes, but this time she was at least neatly dressed and had done her hair and make-up in an attempt to hide the tell-tale signs of grief, perhaps in the expectation of visits of condolence from friends and relatives.

'We're still trying to get a clear picture of what happened,' Hulda explained. 'We had a long conversation with Klara's friend Dagur.'

'Right, Katla's brother.'

Hulda nodded.

'He was always such a nice boy – I can't believe he'd do anything bad.' After a little pause, Klara's mother asked: 'You don't think he . . . ?'

'No, we released him after . . . er, after interviewing him. We're now holding Benedikt.'

'Benedikt? Really? He's a hard one to read. I was never that taken with him.'

'Oh?'

'Yes, I never knew what to make of him when he was seeing Klara.'

'Seeing Klara? What do you mean? Were they an item?'

'Didn't you know?'

It was the first Hulda had heard of this. Every time she

thought she was getting the hang of how the pieces fitted together, another was added to the puzzle. 'When was this?'

'A long time ago. Ten years.'

'Ten years? Exactly ten years ago?'

Agnes thought. 'Yes, shortly before their friend died – Katla, who we talked about last time. The one who was murdered by her father.'

'Shortly before Katla died, you say? As it happens, I've been looking into her case in connection with your daughter's death.'

'Oh? Why?' Agnes leaned forward, her drawn face wearing a look of intense curiosity.

'Well.' Hulda thought quickly. 'We can't rule out a connection, you see. Two mysterious deaths among the same group of friends.'

'I find that very unlikely. Anyway, I thought the case was solved when Katla's father killed himself.'

Hulda nodded non-committally.

'Of course, I trust the police – you know what you're doing. And I'd just like to repeat that my husband and I will do everything we can to help. You can't imagine how important this is to us.' Agnes was choking up, her voice suddenly emerging high and strained. 'We have to know what happened.'

'I'll do my best, I promise,' Hulda said, then waited, giving the woman a chance to recover slightly, before putting the next question. 'Were your daughter and Benedikt going out with each other when Katla died?'

'No, actually, they'd broken up just a few days before. I remember it so well because of the murder – it's like a reference point for when everything happened. Not that the two things were related.'

'Right.' Hulda delayed asking the next question while she considered what line to pursue. She took a mouthful of watery coffee and breathed in the bleak silence in the house, properly taking in her surroundings for the first time. The walls were hung with old paintings of landscapes, familiar motifs by artists Hulda should probably recognize but couldn't immediately place. The furniture was handsomely carved – classy furniture, as Hulda used to call it – of the type she and Jón would have bought in due course for their house on Álftanes. Then, remembering what Klara's mother had said at their last meeting, she asked, 'The girls were best friends, weren't they?'

'Best friends, yes,' Agnes confirmed.

She clearly hadn't the faintest suspicion that, when Katla died, she had been enjoying a romantic weekend in the countryside with Benedikt – her best friend's boyfriend, or rather ex-boyfriend. How many days had passed between Klara and Benedikt's break-up and his getting together with Katla? Had Klara discovered what was going on? And if so, when . . . ?

'You mentioned the other day that Katla's death had changed everything,' Hulda said, allowing her words to hang in the air. It was a statement rather than a question, but she waited for Agnes's reaction.

'Yes . . .' the other woman said, with apparent reluctance.

'It must have been a terrible shock for Klara, losing her best friend like that,' Hulda prompted.

'It was,' Agnes replied, rather hesitantly.

'Not only that but—'

'You're right, it was more than that.'

Hulda waited.

'They were like sisters. Almost like twins, you could say. They did everything together; it was like they were joined at the hip, even though they were such opposites: Klara was affectionate and friendly but never as popular as Katla. Katla used to wrap people round her little finger. She could be cold too – you never really knew where you were with her. But they were inseparable, you know? Klara and Katla, Katla and Klara . . .' Agnes chanted their names almost as if she were in a trance, her voice petering out.

'What happened?'

'It was all very odd and unsettling . . . I know my husband would rather I didn't talk about it, but I trust you.'

Hulda nodded gravely.

'I *can* trust you, can't I?'

'Of course.'

'If she was . . . if our daughter was . . . murdered . . .' Agnes was speaking quietly, a nervous tremor in her voice '. . . You have to find out who did it. So I'm going to be honest with you.'

Hulda waited.

'Klara took Katla's death to heart – far more than was healthy. Her life was turned upside down, she was shattered, suffered a complete breakdown. But the worst part was that she started seeing Katla everywhere. She couldn't sleep at night, used to wake up drenched in sweat, saying that Katla had come and spoken to her. She would scream in her sleep. And it got worse . . .'

'In what way?'

'She actually started . . . being Katla. It's hard to explain, I know, but sometimes she talked to us as if Katla was there, as if she was still with us. I'll never forget the first time we heard about it happening.' Agnes broke off to take a deep, shuddering breath, obviously finding it a strain to tell the story. 'She used to babysit for a family who lived nearby, neighbours of Katla's, in fact; a very nice couple with a little girl. They lived in the block of flats next to Katla's place. They may still live there, for all I know. Anyway, she was babysitting for them as usual, not long after Katla died, and when she came home that night it was like nothing had happened. But next morning the little girl's father rang me to say his daughter had been terrified because . . . because Klara had been "pretending to be Katla" off and on all evening. The girl was only six or seven, from what I can remember. I was horrified. When I tried to talk to Klara, she refused to discuss it; just retreated even further into her shell.'

Agnes was silent for a moment or two before carrying on: 'Of course, it was beyond a joke. It wasn't healthy. We sought the advice of doctors, but they just blamed it on the trauma, saying she'd get over it.'

'And did she?'

'It took different forms, stopped being as noticeable, but Klara had Katla on the brain right up to her death. She had problems sleeping, couldn't hold down a job and carried on living at home with us. She gave the impression of being totally normal on the outside. You had to spend a bit of time with her to realize something was wrong. To be honest, I don't think she'd ever have managed on her own.' Agnes's eyes filled with tears and she paused to clear her throat before continuing: 'We always looked after her, kept her with us at home . . . I never gave up hope that she'd get over it one day.'

'Why do you think it affected her so badly?' Hulda asked, carefully watching Agnes's reaction.

'I simply can't imagine,' the woman said, with apparent sincerity. 'They were as close as sisters, that's the only explanation I can think of.' There was a naive innocence in the gaze she turned on Hulda, but also such profound despair.

'I'm very sorry to hear this,' Hulda said. 'I had no idea she'd been suffering like that. Do you know how she felt about attending the reunion on Ellidaey?'

'She was excited – she had her good days, you see. Most days were good, actually. It was the nights that were difficult. And stress – she couldn't really cope with being under any sort of pressure. That's why most of her employers gave up on her sooner or later, and in the end she stopped even applying for jobs.'

'Had she discussed Katla's death with you at all recently? In connection with the trip, for example?'

There was a silence. Then Agnes said, 'Well, now you come to mention it . . . She said it would be good to see the gang again and have a chance to reminisce about the past. Settle . . . oh, how did she put it? Something about old secrets. Yes, she talked about everyone putting the record straight. Said they'd been keeping quiet about the truth for too long, or something. I didn't know what she was referring to. To be honest, I didn't always understand her; she was often lost in a world of her own, if you know what I mean.'

'But she felt up to making the trip?' Hulda asked. 'And you were OK with her going? Was she capable of travelling alone, given the state she was in?'

'She wasn't alone,' Agnes answered, rather sharply. 'She was with her friends. Her best friends. They're all good kids. It wasn't their fault that Veturlidi was a murderer.' She rose abruptly to her feet. 'Anyway, I think that's enough. I've been talking too much. You must be able to see that we couldn't possibly guess what would happen on Ellidaey. You must see . . .'

Hulda got up, too, but took her time before answering, choosing her words carefully: 'No one's suggesting for a moment that you should have done. All we're concerned about is getting to the bottom of what happened and catching the person who . . . pushed her, if our suspicions prove correct.'

Agnes seemed reassured. 'Thank you. But I'm afraid you'll have to go now. I need a rest. And I don't want . . .' She faltered. 'I don't want my husband to see you. He doesn't like me talking about it. Doesn't want it to get out – doesn't want people to find out what had happened to Klara, how she'd changed. I think he's ashamed. No, I shouldn't say that. Please don't get me wrong – of course he wasn't ashamed of her but . . . it was hard, it's been hard for him, for both of us.'

'I'm grateful for your honesty,' Hulda said. 'I promise to treat what you told me in confidence.'

'Thanks for coming to see me. Can you find your own way out?'

XLV

Things were finally falling into place. Hulda could feel it in her gut: she was getting close to the truth; old secrets were coming up to the surface at last. She was confident that the case was about to be solved, perhaps that very night. It would be her greatest success to date: two murders solved in one fell swoop. The bonds of silence were breaking; all she needed to do was dig a little deeper.

Benedikt had been at the summer house with Katla, his girlfriend, at the time of her death.

And shortly before that, Benedikt and Klara had been seeing each other.

Now both girls were dead. Murdered.

According to Lýdur, nothing of interest had emerged from his questioning of Alexandra, but Hulda put little faith in his interviewing skills, especially since he had been unaware of the latest information to come to light. It was clear that she needed to see Alexandra for herself. And, this time, the gloves would be off. Alexandra had withheld a vital fact from Hulda last time they met. She was sure of it.

The girl's aunt came to the door in her nightie and made no attempt to hide her anger when she saw who it was.

'Do you know what time it is?' she hissed furiously, without bothering to greet Hulda.

'I need to talk to Alexandra.'

'She's already spoken to one of your colleagues today. I warned you, I'm going to call a lawyer. My brother-in-law's a solicitor with a practice near here. I'm ringing him now; I tell you, I'm ringing him right this minute. You can talk to him instead of harassing my niece like this. It's totally unacceptable.'

'Alexandra's an adult,' Hulda replied in a voice of cool authority. 'I assume she's still staying with you, and I need to talk to her. Would you fetch her, please? Otherwise, we'll have to arrest her and take a formal statement from her at the station. Your brother-in-law's welcome to come along, too, if that's what Alexandra wants.'

That stopped the aunt in her tracks.

'She's asleep. Can't you come back tomorrow?'

'I need to speak to her now,' Hulda insisted.

'Oh, right, well . . . in that case, I'd better get her,' the woman said, with bad grace. She went back inside and, after a short delay, Alexandra appeared at the door, suppressing a yawn. It was clear she'd just woken up. She was barefoot, in a T-shirt and pyjama bottoms.

'Hello again.'

'Hello, Alexandra. I hope you're feeling better. I need to speak to you in private. Is that all right with you?'

'What, now?'

'Yes, now.'

'Oh, OK. Come in, then.'

She showed Hulda into the same room as before and Hulda closed the door, confident that, this time, they wouldn't be disturbed.

'We've arrested Benedikt, as I assume Lýdur told you,' she began without preamble.

'Yes, but I don't see why. I'm so confused. Benni wouldn't hurt a fly.'

'We suspect him of having murdered Klara. They were both drinking downstairs when you and Dagur went up to bed. Am I right?'

'Yes, that's what I told, um, Lýdur. That's right . . .' She broke off, but Hulda got the definite feeling that she'd been about to say something else. That she wanted to say more, admit something . . . confess, even? But as the silence dragged on it became evident that Hulda would have to give her a nudge.

'We also suspect him of having murdered Katla.'

'What?' Alexandra was utterly thrown. 'Katla? You mean at the summer house? No . . . No, that's impossible. Dagur's dad did it; it was proved at the time.'

'Not necessarily. Did you know that she and Benedikt had got together?'

'Benni and Klara? Yes, of course, but that was years ago.'

'I meant Benedikt and Katla.'

'No, you're getting mixed up. Benni used to be with *Klara* in the old days. They broke up after . . . after the murder.'

'No, actually – their relationship ended before that. Benedikt was at the summer house with Katla,' Hulda said in a level voice, watching Alexandra intently.

'At the summer house? When . . . when she died? No, you must be making it up! I don't believe it.' Alexandra certainly gave the appearance of telling the truth; her astonishment seemed genuine.

'That's why we believe he murdered both girls, Alexandra. Both Klara and Katla.'

'No, no, you're wrong, you must be. Did he say he'd done it?'

'No, he denies it, naturally.'

'Veturlidi, Dagur's father, he . . . he killed Katla. He even committed suicide because of it.'

'Then who killed Klara?' Hulda asked, fixing Alexandra's eyes with her own. In that moment, she was sure the girl knew the answer.

But, infuriatingly, Alexandra went silent on her.

'What happened on Ellidaey, Alexandra?' Hulda demanded. 'What is it you're not telling me?'

There was a long pause, then Alexandra said, as if talking to herself rather than Hulda: 'I got the feeling there was something wrong with Klara.'

'Oh?' Hulda said, though the news didn't come as any surprise after what Klara's mother had told her.

'She was behaving weirdly on the island. She woke up screaming in the middle of the night, claiming she'd seen

Katla. She was so scarily convincing she frightened me. She genuinely seemed to believe that Katla had been there, that she'd seen a ghost. She told us Katla wanted justice. As if, well, as if she thought someone other than Veturlidi had murdered her. No, that's wrong – it wasn't just like she thought so, it was like she *knew* it for a fact. Do you understand what I mean? It was so strange. Up until then I think we'd all, deep down, assumed Veturlidi was guilty, as horrible as that sounds. All except Dagur, of course. He's claimed all along that his dad was innocent. But that night I suddenly got the feeling Klara knew for certain that it wasn't Veturlidi.'

'What do you think?'

'I'm not sure any more . . . But I don't believe Benni did it; he's just not capable of something like that. He's a good guy.'

'But you were always keener on Dagur, weren't you? In love with him, I was told.'

Alexandra nodded. 'Though I never did anything about it. But . . . yes. There's something about him. We've always had a special connection, you know?'

Hulda hardly needed to continue the conversation. The whole thing was plain to her now. She knew who had killed Katla. There was only one person it could have been: all the evidence pointed the same way. And the same was true of the incident on the island. She knew who had attacked Klara and pushed her over the cliff; could even picture 'the hatred in his eyes' that Benedikt had described.

'Is there anything else you need to tell me, Alexandra?'

'Yes, I suppose there is. In the circumstances, I have no choice but to tell you. Benedikt wasn't the last person to see Klara alive.'

'Who was, then?' Hulda asked, purely for form's sake. She already knew the answer.

XLVI

Hulda was alone, though she should probably have taken someone else along, both as a witness to a potential confession and as back-up in case the situation turned violent. But instinct told her there wasn't going to be any violence. Although she was going to meet a murderer, she wasn't afraid. She knew she wasn't in any danger.

She had stood here before, ringing the bell and knocking on the door without getting any response. This time, he came to the door almost as soon as she pressed the bell.

'Hello, I was half expecting you.'

Dagur was fully dressed, though it was past midnight.

'Can I come in?'

'Please do.' As she did so, he added: 'This is where they arrested Dad, at the crack of dawn. The detective – your mate Lýdur – was standing here in the hall when they dragged him out in his pyjamas. I was up there, at the top of the stairs ...' He turned to look over his shoulder, pointing at the landing. 'There I stood, hardly more than a kid, yelling and crying, begging them to leave my dad alone. Of course, Katla's death was the turning point when everything changed, but that moment when they arrested Dad . . . that was the beginning of the end. That's when my family began to fall apart. Before that, we had a chance, you know? We had a chance of getting through it, of working through the grief. But then they took Dad. And he died. And Mum, she couldn't cope. And now I'm the only one left . . . All alone in this big, empty house. You've come to arrest me, haven't you?'

'Yes, that's right, Dagur.'

'At least I'm not wearing my pyjamas. And I'm not going to resist or make a scene. There's no kid standing on the stairs protesting this time. In a way, that kid died that day as well. So this time the neighbours won't find out until they read it in the papers. You're not even in a marked vehicle. Are you in your green car?'

She nodded.

'The cop in the green Skoda. That's really something.'

'Shall we go inside and have a chat?'

'There's no need. I'm going to sell the house, you know; I don't really want to go back inside. Can't I just come with you now?'

She was aware, in that instant, of a powerful urge to let him go, give him a second chance. She pitied him and understood him only too well. She knew that some crimes are so despicable that revenge is justified. She could understand why he had gone for Klara and pushed her over the cliff, no doubt in a moment of blind rage. But of course there was no question of letting him off, not least because Alexandra had confirmed that Klara had come to see him that night and the two of them had gone downstairs together, Klara and Dagur. Alexandra hadn't been able to sleep because she'd been half hoping that Dagur would 'crawl into bed with her', as she'd put it. But he'd just gone straight to sleep and she'd lain there wide awake. Nevertheless, the bond between them was so strong, at least on her side, that she'd initially intended to keep quiet about what had happened.

'Did you murder Klara?'

'I . . . I didn't mean to. I don't think I meant to. I just completely lost it. She came to see me in the night – I was asleep, but she wanted to talk to me; kept insisting she had something important to tell me. Something that needed to come out. So we went for a walk, all the way out to that rock ledge – it was her idea. I've been wondering since if maybe she meant to jump.'

He lapsed into silence. His eyes distant, remembering.

'What did she want to tell you?' Hulda prompted.

'Oh, that she'd killed my sister, of course. I expect you'd already worked that out.'

Hulda nodded.

'Apparently, Katla and Benni had started seeing each other without telling anyone. Benni had dumped Klara – she told me there was a big scene. And she knew why; she'd worked it out. Knew Katla had stolen him – that's how she described it to me. She started spying on them and followed them when they left town – she'd just got a car. After a while she guessed they must be heading up to the summer house because she'd been there several times with Katla and Alexandra. Klara claimed it was an accident. That she'd only meant to shake my sister up a bit and give her a fright. She waited all night, sleeping in her car, for a chance to catch Katla alone. My sister always got everything she wanted, you see? Of course, I loved her very much, she was my big sister, a lovely person, but she knew how to manipulate people. And she was capable of shutting them out in the cold too. She wanted Benni and she got him. Klara's feelings didn't matter. That was Katla all over – she was an incredibly strong character. You could say we've all been living in her shadow for the last ten years, one way or another.'

'What happened at the summer house?'

'A lot of screaming and shouting and threats, apparently. It ended in blows. Klara hit Katla and gave her a shove and my sister banged her head on the corner of a table and . . . just bled to death. I gather it all happened incredibly fast. Klara simply couldn't cope with what she'd done. There was no phone, of course, no way of calling an ambulance. And Klara swore to me that it wouldn't have been possible to save Katla even if there had been. I wouldn't know. You have to understand that I lost it completely. That bloody bitch had destroyed my life, wrecked my family. She was to blame for the deaths of my sister and my dad, and for the state my mum's in. And now she's to blame for the fact I'm going to jail. How ironic.'

'We'd better be going now, Dagur.'

He nodded, adding as an afterthought: 'Then there's that bastard Benni. He's to blame too. He could have saved Dad if he'd had the guts to come forward and risk getting a bit of dirt on his reputation. Fucking spotless Benni. Everything has to be so perfect for him and his parents. Of course, he wouldn't dream of getting involved in a murder inquiry . . . You know, we were on the verge of a punch-up when you barged in on us the other day. Naturally, he denied everything, but after talking to Klara I knew he'd been at the summer house with Katla – though I couldn't admit to him how I knew.'

'It's time to go.'

Dagur closed the door of his childhood home behind him, perhaps for the last time.

He got into the Skoda without putting up the slightest resistance. And grim as Hulda found it to have to arrest this young man for murder, in another part of her consciousness a voice was crying, 'Yes, yes, yes!', and telling her that this was it: the big success she'd been waiting for.

Epilogue

I

Robert, Savannah, USA, 1997

Robert's wife had gone out to see friends and he was sitting alone in the Savannah dusk with a cold bottle of beer at his side. As a strict teetotaller, his wife wasn't too fond of his drinking, but she let him get away with it once in a while. After all, his last physical proved he was in pretty good shape, so she couldn't get on his case too much. In his opinion, nothing beat a cold beer on the porch after a sweltering summer's day.

Robert was thinking back to his time in Iceland. Yesterday's visit had shaken him up. It was years since he'd given any thought to that cold, bleak island, and he found that his memories of his posting there, and the war years in general, were hazy at best. That's to say, he remembered those days as if through a fog, since that period of his life seemed unreal to him now, almost as if it had happened to someone else.

And Anna. Sure, he remembered Anna, brief though their relationship had been. He hadn't made a habit of cheating on his adored wife; in fact, Anna was the only time. There had been something about her that had weakened his resolve, made him give in to temptation. Afterwards, she had vanished and for a while he had missed her, though deep down he knew it was for the best. Yet for reasons known only to himself he had kept a small picture of her, like a passport photo, that she had given him after their first night together. He knew exactly where the picture was and had brought it out this evening and laid it on the table beside his beer in the dim illumination of the porch light.

The photo had yellowed and faded over the years, as you'd expect, but Robert only had to look at it to be instantly transported back half a century in time, to the Reykjavík of 1947, a small town in the process of turning into a city. As an American, he had felt like the representative of a new age. Not all the inhabitants had been equally welcoming to soldiers like him, but he remembered the girls because they were so stunning. And he had never forgotten Anna. It was incredible, really, given the short time they'd known each other, just how well he did remember her. Of course, their relationship had never had any future, and his conscience had plagued him from the very first moment, yet there was a sweet poignancy about his memory of that brief affair. He had been in love with his wife then, as he was now, but his guilt had faded with the passing of time, until now the affair was like a distant memory of an experience that had been as beguiling as it was unexpected. It went without saying that he would never tell his wife. He would take the secret with him to his grave. Under no circumstances could he admit to having an Icelandic daughter.

He'd had his suspicions from the moment Hulda had contacted him to say she was coming over, though she hadn't said anything at first. Perhaps in some mysterious way he had always known that his brief fling had borne fruit. But Anna had never got in touch, which presumably meant she hadn't envisaged him having any part in her child's upbringing. So there had been an element in his decision of wanting to respect her wishes as well.

That's one reason he had lied to Hulda.

But above all he had been motivated by a desire to protect his own interests, to preserve the perfect marriage he had enjoyed for more than half a century. There was no way he was going to jeopardize that in order to be a father to a middle-aged woman. At her age, she didn't need a father any more, and he didn't need a daughter. Not any more. He hadn't been lying when he told her they couldn't have children, though in fact it had been clear that the problem almost certainly lay with his wife, not him – as Hulda's existence now proved. He didn't for a minute doubt the truth of what she'd told him. For one fleeting evening he had shared a table with his daughter. It would never happen again.

He hadn't experienced any particular feelings of regret after she left. You couldn't really miss a stranger. It wasn't as if he'd even known her mother that well. His connection with Hulda was purely biological. Nevertheless, he had unobtrusively studied her as she sat there, wondering if he should sacrifice everything in order to become better acquainted with his daughter. But the need hadn't been there, the bonds weren't strong enough. He had taken the decision for both of them, unfair as it might seem, that the secret should be buried for ever. He knew she wouldn't come back.

But when he looked down now at the old photo, Robert felt a slight pang at the thought that Hulda would never know she had met her father.

He had done one thing for her, though; he'd sent her a copy of an old picture of himself in uniform, taken during the war. His appearance had changed considerably in the intervening years, the gloss of youth long departed – together with his hair – so he had calculated that it was safe to send her the photo. In his letter he had told her, as was correct, that it was a picture of her father. She was unlikely ever to discover the truth.

II

Lýdur, Reykjavík, 1997

Lýdur had never for a moment doubted Veturlidi's guilt –
until now, of course. When the investigation was at its
height he had acted ruthlessly in the belief that Veturlidi
was as guilty as hell, a child abuser and a murderer.

Lýdur had complete faith in his own abilities. All the
evidence had indicated that Veturlidi had murdered his
daughter. Although the man had never been willing to
confess, Lýdur had no problem filling in the gaps. He had
assumed they were almost certainly dealing with a case of
abuse, of chronic violence, that had reached its peak that
weekend at the summer house. It was Veturlidi's summer
house, after all; his refuge. No one else had come forward
to say they'd been there with Katla, and she would hardly
have gone all the way to the West Fjords alone, without a
car, to stay in some bloody hut in the arse-end of nowhere.
No, in his view, the whole thing had been blindingly
obvious.

Lýdur's theory had been as follows: father and daughter

329

had gone up there together and he had started abusing her again. But this time she had turned on him and fought back, resulting in the struggle that had ended in her death. Manslaughter or murder, it didn't matter; that was for others to decide.

Now, though, he knew his theory had been totally wrong: Katla had been killed by her friend Klara, who'd never even been a suspect.

The image had been so clear in Lýdur's mind at the time. All he'd needed was a confession, or some more concrete piece of evidence. The presence of the jumper had been a gift, but perhaps not enough on its own to secure a conviction. Worse, it had only been lying on the floor nearby. How much more incriminating it would be if they could claim that the girl had been holding on to it, perhaps in a deliberate attempt to point the finger of blame at her father. It had been surprisingly easy to convince that local cop Andrés to lie. Too easy, in fact, because of course Andrés had had second thoughts, but then what could you expect from a loser like that? Soon afterwards, he had got in touch with Lýdur, while the investigation was still going on, to say he regretted the whole thing. He was no longer sure that Veturlidi was guilty, especially as they hadn't obtained a confession. Then, as if that wasn't bad enough, Andrés had started saying he needed to come clean, that it was the only way to give the suspect a fair chance of defending himself. The silly old sod had acknowledged that it would be disastrous for him personally; he was bound to lose his job, and the story of his debts and his involvement with the loan shark would be splashed across the headlines. But that wasn't all. He'd gone on to say that Lýdur himself could hardly be kept out of it, as Andrés would have to explain why he had let himself be persuaded to lie and who had put pressure on him to do so. Of course, Lýdur had tried to dissuade him, but he had failed. It was like talking to a brick wall. Andrés had announced that he was coming south to Reykjavík in two days' time to see the police authorities and make amends for his mistake. This had left Lýdur in a hell of a tight spot.

He had had two days, perhaps less, to save his skin. The only way was to force a confession out of Veturlidi, but that was easier said than done. The stupid bastard was a broken man; he seemed to have lost his will to live and his stamina for the fight, saying he fully expected to be sent to prison and for his family to be publicly condemned. But in spite of everything, he couldn't be persuaded to admit to the murder. He refused to 'confess to a crime he hadn't committed', as he put it. Out of sheer bloody pig-headedness.

It had taken Lýdur one night, barely that, to come up with a solution.

He had awoken, while it was still dark, with a brainwave. Stealthily, he had got out of bed and left the house without waking his wife and children. They were used to his blundering about at all hours because of his shifts, so even if they had stirred they were unlikely to have been bothered by his absence.

He had headed for the prison where suspects were held in custody, and, being a regular visitor, was waved straight in. He didn't even need to reveal which prisoner he was going to see. After that it was an easy matter to gain access to Veturlidi's cell and sneak him his belt.

Perhaps Lýdur hadn't properly thought it through, but he had been so sure of Veturlidi's guilt. His insight had never failed him before and he had interpreted Veturlidi's depression and silence merely as further confirmation of his suspicions. Anyway, there had been no other plausible theory. Not really. Not then.

The belt had been a test.

A question of life or death.

If Veturlidi failed the test, his action would be tantamount to a confession. That would be the simplest solution to every aspect of the case. The killer would have confessed, indirectly, and the investigation would end in triumph. More importantly, that old bugger in Ísafjördur would have no reason to upset the applecart and jeopardize Lýdur's career, purely for the sake of appeasing his own conscience. Andrés would see at once that Lýdur's motives had been sound and that there was nothing further to be achieved by stirring things up.

It came as no surprise to Lýdur the morning after to hear that Veturlidi had hanged himself in his cell. It proved to him that he had been right.

He didn't feel remotely responsible for the man's death, either then or later, though, needless to say, he kept it absolutely secret that he had given him a helping hand, so to speak. Naturally, there had been an inquiry into how the prisoner had got hold of the belt, but it had been short-lived and inconclusive.

But now bloody Andrés had popped up again and told the story he had threatened to reveal ten years ago. Lýdur faced losing his job; he had already been suspended. It had been a horrible shock, of course. But when Hulda came to see him, he had for an instant feared that she knew he had slipped the belt to Veturlidi; that his role in Veturlidi's suicide had been exposed. That would have been infinitely worse.

As it was, that detail of the story was unlikely ever to emerge now.

Lýdur had effectively caused Veturlidi's death. This much he realized, this much he knew. But no one else need ever know.

III

Hulda, Reykjavík, 1997

Hulda stood by her mother's grave.

It looked neat and well kept, but she knew she would have to be more conscientious about visiting once autumn set in. Her mother had no one else.

However strained their relationship had been, Hulda had to acknowledge that she missed her. She felt so alone in the world, so lonely.

Everyone around her was dead: Jón and Dimma, her mother, even her father in America.

She was still relatively young – at any rate, not old yet – still healthy and ambitious. She still had so much she wanted to achieve. Fifteen more years in the police: time enough to make her mark there before she had to retire. Then she would be sixty-five, still young. Although she didn't feel ready for a relationship at present, perhaps retirement would be the right time to find herself a good man and start a new life. A chance to get shot of her dreary little flat and move somewhere closer to nature. Yes, there was so much to look forward to; she simply needed to face the future in a positive frame of mind, with happy anticipation.

But the thought of death terrified her.

One day she would be laid in a cold grave. Of course, when the time came she would already have crossed to the other side, yet the thought of being buried in the ground was too much for her.

Prey to a sudden feeling of suffocation, she turned away from her mother's grave and drew a deep breath.

Sigurjón Sigurjónsson

RAGNAR JÓNASSON is the award-winning author of the internationally bestselling Ari Thór thriller series. Before embarking on a writing career, he translated fourteen Agatha Christie novels into Icelandic. He is also the co-founder of the Reykjavík international crime-writing festival Iceland Noir. Ragnar lives in Reykjavík with his wife and two daughters.

Don't miss Ragnar Jónasson's exciting series featuring DETECTIVE INSPECTOR HULDA

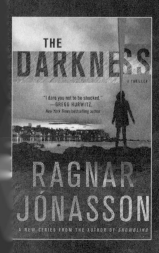

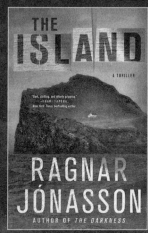

AVAILABLE NOW   AVAILABLE NOW   ON SALE 6/23/20

"*The Darkness* is a bullet train of a novel.....I reached the end with adrenalized anticipation, the final twist hitting me in the face. **I DARE YOU NOT TO BE SHOCKED."**

—GREGG HURWITZ, *New York Times* bestselling author